**NEW HANOVER COUNTY
PUBLIC LIBRARY**

ALL OF THIS IS TRUE

ALL OF
THIS
IS TRUE

A NOVEL

LYGIA DAY PEÑAFLOR

An Imprint of HarperCollinsPublishers

HarperTeen is an imprint of HarperCollins Publishers.

Library of Congress Cataloging-in-Publication Data

Names: Peñaflor, Lygia Day, author.
Title: All of this is true : a novel / Lygia Day Peñaflor.
Description: First Edition. | New York, NY : Harper, an imprint of HarperCollinsPublishers, [2018] | Summary: When Long Island teens Miri, Soleil, Penny, and Jonah befriend a bestselling YA novelist, they find their deepest, darkest secrets in the pages of her next novel, with devastating consequences. Told from different perspectives as interviews, journal entries, and book excerpts.
Identifiers: LCCN 2017034535 | ISBN 9780062673657 (hardcover)
Subjects: | CYAC: Best friends—Fiction. | Friendship—Fiction. | Authors—Fiction. | Secrets—Fiction. | Conduct of life—Fiction. | Long Island (N.Y.)—Fiction.
Classification: LCC PZ7.1.P4454 All 2018 | DDC [Fic]—dc23 LC record available at https://lccn.loc.gov/2017034535

Typography by Erin Fitzsimmons
18 19 20 21 22   PC/LSCH   10 9 8 7 6 5 4 3 2 1

First Edition

For a woman betrayal has no sense—

one cannot betray one's passions.

—COCO CHANEL

MIRI

So, tell me about Fatima Ro. There are a lot of people who are curious about her right now.

All right. But I'm just going to say this outright because it's probably the one thing we still agree on—me, Soleil, and Penny. We were shallow before we met Fatima Ro. We were all about the scene. You know what I mean about the scene: the parties, the trinkets, the lifestyle. We hosted.

Hosted?

House parties at Penny's place. It feels like forever ago. Ugh. [shakes head] All those people, the throbbing music . . . handling all that money.

What money?

We collected a cover charge to fund subsequent parties.

Very industrious.

That's us. [sighs] We met on Orientation Day in seventh grade when we were grouped together for the Graham scavenger hunt. Winners become orientation leaders the following year. We won by splitting up and then finding the last clue together— the school seal on the roof.

You're a good team.

We were, yes . . . before this. Anyway, our parties were epic. The last one we hosted was casino night. We had game tables and chocolate poker chips. It won't be outdone for years.

That's pretty impressive.

[laughs] Oh, please. We thought taking selfies on the roulette table was the stuff of life. The reality was we were bored out of our skulls. You see, the basic human need for emotional intimacy can't be satisfied by a sushi station or a celebrity DJ. Fatima made us realize that. She changed everything for us. Even that phrase, "the stuff of life," that's something I picked up from her.

I wouldn't have said that just now if it weren't for her; I probably would've said something more like "We thought taking selfies was so *Vogue*-worthy." But now, I'm saying "the stuff of life" because Fatima pretty much gave us a whole new language, a new way of thinking, of living. When she took us in, all of a sudden I realized . . . we *all* realized that we were starving to be part of something meaningful. Becoming friends with Fatima Ro—I mean, actually being part of her inner circle—was *it*.

Were you a fan of her novel Undertow?

Definitely. That's how this whole thing started. Absolutely. All of us were fans. Well, we girls were, anyway. Jonah was along for the company. But still, even he was fascinated by her. I read *Undertow* when it first came out. When I found out how young Fatima was—barely out of college—it made sense that I felt close to her writing. She got me. I love *Undertow* as if it's a living being, which is passion in its truest form. That's what separates a casual interest from a passion. I credit Fatima for my understanding of that.

You see, you can be in love with a thing the way you can be in love with a person. A thing can physically trigger the same chemical responses as another human can: oxytocin and vasopressin. Fatima taught me this. Her book proved it. But I just cringe at how the media is comparing it to other novels. Because what you have to understand is that *Undertow* was never a Harry Potter phenomenon. I mean, nobody's wearing *Undertow* Halloween costumes. There's no *Undertow* Disney theme park. But that's what's so authentic about it. If you love *Undertow* it's because you get it, not because there's a Tom Hanks movie and a Happy Meal. This book has a much quieter, more thoughtful following. And to me, it feels more genuine to be part of something personal like that.

Think about it: if you know and love *Undertow* and you meet someone else who truly knows and loves *Undertow*, instantly she's your kind of person. [snaps] You cannot possibly feel that kind of connection with, say, a Hunger Games fan, because that fandom is just too big; it's too *commercial*. It's like, of *course* you like the Hunger Games. Everyone likes it, so big deal, right? But Fatima's following is simply more intimate. Her novel takes a certain, more concerning, er, uh, *dis*cerning reader. So to be a fan of *Undertow* is deeper . . . there's an understanding between people who love it. We share an appreciation for the depths of its messages and for its language. There's a simpatico between *Undertow* fans. It's one beating heart meeting another beating heart. [laughs] There I go, I'm sounding like her again. I know. But I'm grateful for that, for her words—the simpatico and the beating hearts. [laughs] Do you know why I agreed to speak with you, Nelson?

You were impressed that Naked Truth *is number forty-seven in the ratings?*

Hardly. It's because you were the only reporter who actually read both *Undertow* and *The Absolution of Brady Stevenson*. I asked every journalist who contacted me.

Oh, really?

I don't care about ratings or Emmys or how famous a journalist is or isn't.

Thanks.

I wanted to talk to someone who isn't out to persecute Fatima for her art and who would understand how incredibly lucky we were to connect with her. And you do get it, don't you?

Yes. I really do. That's why I want you to tell the side of this story that no one else is telling, about the real Fatima Ro. No one knew her the way you did. This is your forum, Miri.

[smiles] I can't tell you how much I appreciate that, Nelson. I knew I chose the right person. Oh, I'm sorry. I've been so rude. I should've offered you something to drink. May I get you something?

No, thank you.

Water? Iced tea? We have a SodaStream.

I'm good, thanks.

Suit yourself.

Can you talk about how you met Fatima?

Yes. You see, we had a plan when we met her. Soleil will never admit to this now, but we went to Fatima's signing at Book Revue with—I exaggerate you not—a premeditated *plan* to get close to her. It was our *goal* to get noticed by her. That's why I cannot and will not understand their outrage over the new book. Seriously, Soleil and Penny have become so ungrateful when what we wanted from the beginning was to be associated with her. It's sad, really, how bitter Soleil and Penny have grown. I should pity them, honestly. I feel sorry for people who don't believe in loyalty.

They have reason to be upset, though. Fatima did base her new book on you girls and Jonah without even telling you. The book isn't flattering. You're not angry at Fatima at all?

We befriended Fatima *because* she's a writer. You can't hug a lion and then be surprised when he bites you.

But Jonah was beaten into a coma in the Graham School parking lot because of what Fatima wrote.

It wasn't her fault.

The cops found a copy of Absolution *at the crime scene. The perpetrators left it on Jonah's chest while he was fighting for his life.*

Dateline and Mario Lopez just love to play up that detail, don't they? It's sick the way attractive women are portrayed by the media. They're either victims or villains, because those make the sexiest headlines. [sighs] It's easy to win ratings by connecting the crime to a young, pretty writer, isn't it? Think for a second. What do they plaster on the screen every single time they cover this story? Fatima's face.

You're right.

Half the time they don't even show Jonah's. "Beautiful author who seduced teens into revealing their dirty secrets now responsible for boy's coma. Full story at eleven." That's cheap bait. That's not the truth.

Then what is the truth?

That there isn't anyone to blame. You read the book. Art doesn't harm. Art saves. [shakes head] You know, we shared hours upon hours of conversations with Fatima about creative freedom and artistic expression. Soleil documented every word from Fatima's mouth on her phone and her laptop, so I thought she respected all of that. Really, you couldn't stop Soleil from documenting. She was nothing less than obsessed. Her notes were all "Fatima this, Fatima that." Ask her.

I'm not interviewing Soleil. She turned me down. Low ratings. Penny agreed only when I told her that you were in.

Huh. [pauses] Then you should look into getting ahold of Soleil's journal. That would shed light on how desperate she was for Fatima's attention. Seriously, get her journal and her emails with Fatima, too.

I made an offer, but she already sold them to New York City magazine.

You're kidding. [picks up her phone]

No. They're featuring them in a series of online articles starting today, actually. The public's been glued to stories about high school violence for a couple of years now. Fatima, whatever her involvement, has added a whole new element of interest.

[browses on phone] Well. There it is, side by side with an article about Jonah and Fatima Ro. Oh look, a photo of Fatima. What did I tell you? And nice byline, Soleil! [laughs] What a hypocrite!

How do you mean?

Soleil hates Fatima for writing about her, but she's publishing journal entries about Fatima? She can't possibly defend that.

I hear you.

Screw her, right? If Soleil's publishing her side, I'm not holding back.

You shouldn't. Don't let her control public opinion. Don't let her get the last word.

No way in hell.

So, talk to me. Tell me more. What happened at the book signing?

[clears throat] The night of the book signing we took the back of the line on purpose; we strategized that we could talk with Fatima for longer if we were last. We might even get a chance to walk her out; we wanted pictures and to ask her to follow our Instagrams.

The back of the line was all Soleil's idea. She was the writer, as you well know. As the whole free world now knows. She was the one who wanted to wriggle her way into Fatima's life. No. That's not even the extent of it. Soleil didn't just want to be in Fatima's life. She wanted to *be* Fatima. Like I said, people always want to be in the front of the line. But there's a different strategy for everything. Well, I was terrified to meet her, to be honest. I'd built up that moment in my mind; it felt so once-in-a-lifetime. I didn't want to make a fool of myself. Have you ever met someone famous that you loved? Isn't it surreal? To suddenly, after dreaming about it for so long, see that person in front of you? I mean, flesh and blood and breathing and moving and talking and you can reach out and touch them if you wanted to?

I saw Quentin Tarantino once.

So then, you know.

Yeah, I get it.

Well, Fatima was poised and very striking. She's attractive, that's a fact. But in person it's more about her presence than her looks; she's so completely self-possessed that you really can't help but just . . . *stare* at her. Plus, what was so amazing was to look at her and know that *Undertow* came out of her brain. I don't even know how to describe that. I kept thinking about how she had conceptualized this novel that I love; she had crafted it and created it out of her own head. And she was so petite. I don't know why, but that was surprising to me. I just kept marveling at her: How could all these words and thoughts come out of her? Am I sounding like an insane person? [laughs]

Not at all. I couldn't get over how tall Tarantino was.

Really?

Six feet, easily.

See? It's overwhelming when you see these people in a room with you.

Tarantino was on the street. I passed him on my way to the subway.

Great. Well, with Fatima I was so nervous; I had to keep going to the bathroom. We waited in that line for an hour. But when our turn came, Soleil, who'd orchestrated the entire outing, she shook my arm and told me to go up first, so I did. Someone had to take control of the situation. I had my copy of *Undertow* in my arms; I was hugging the thing like a blankie. [laughs] [pause] Excuse me. [blows nose] Allergies. [clears throat] I had the book against my chest like this, and I just talked with her.

What did you talk about?

It's funny because I can hardly remember what I said, but I memorized everything she said to me. I must've introduced myself, and I probably quoted my favorite line from *Undertow* and told her how it affected me. I'm sure I did, since I rehearsed it. I'm not embarrassed to admit that. Each of us rehearsed what we were going to say. We talked about it in the car. If they tell you otherwise, they're lying. Fatima looked straight at me and said, "I'm very pleased to meet you. You have such great energy about you, Miri." That's what she told me. I had great energy. Imagine if Tarantino told you that you had great energy?

That'd be pretty cool.

That's exactly how I felt about Fatima. And she addressed me by name just like that. She was intense. But strangely, at the same time, she *calmed* me. That was her aura. [sighs]

Then I gave her my book to sign, and I introduced Soleil and Penny and Jonah. I was lucky to be first. I think Fatima and I had a special bond because I was first. She considered me a leader, you know.

Do you remember the conversation between Fatima and your friends?

[laughs] Jonah was so funny about the whole thing because he hadn't even read *Undertow*, but you had to buy a copy to be in the line, so he bought one. He didn't have a thing to say to Fatima, so he rambled something utterly ridiculous about novelists being today's most valuable artists. He went on and on about technology—iPads versus television versus books—I don't know what he was babbling about. [laughs] [sighs] [silence]

Is there something you'd like to add?

[checks her phone]

Miri?

Sorry. I'm just anxious about Jonah.

Any news?

No. [sets phone down] Do you think they'll catch the guys that jumped him? They're probably all from his old school. It shouldn't be a huge mystery.

They're working on it.

They'd better. And then everyone can finally lay the blame where it belongs instead of on Fatima Ro.

I'd be down for that. So, after Fatima signed your books . . .

Right. [drinks from a water bottle] It was late. We were the last ones in the bookstore. The staff was stacking chairs, and the lights were off in the back. The register was already closed. Fatima gathered her bags, and the next thing we knew, we were actually, literally walking her out, just like we had fantasized. It was fantastic. I would've said fate, but Fatima doesn't believe in fate, and neither do I now. We carve our own paths.

Does that go for Jonah? Do you believe he's in a coma because he carved his own path?

Maybe I do. You probably think that makes me a terrible person.

Not at all.

I'm just being honest.

I appreciate it.

Anyway, Fatima asked us what school we went to. When we said the Graham School on the North Shore, she was thrilled because she'd just moved into the area—Old Westbury! Are you from around here?

Yes.

So you know it's only two towns from Graham. That's ten minutes from me, five minutes from Penny and Soleil. How did we not know that she'd moved in? We were *neighbors*. [shakes head] We couldn't believe it. We chatted about our school and the shops at Americana. And then, get this—I couldn't even make this up—Fatima said [clears throat], "If you're not busy Thursday night, you should come to the Witches Brew café. I'm giving a book talk at eight."

Awesome.

We were *undone*. I could have died right there on that sidewalk. Cuddling my *Undertow*.

Stranger Than Fiction

The True Story Behind the Controversial Novel

The Absolution of Brady Stevenson

SOLEIL JOHNSTON'S STORY, PART 1

Journal Entry

September 22, 2016

Witches Brew, Hempstead, Long Island

OMGGGG Fatima remembered us when we walked in!!! She waved and said, "Hello, readers from Graham. Glad you could make it." I waved my signed *Undertow* at her. Why? Because I am officially the biggest dork in the universe!

This place is so cool. I love the whole bohemian/mismatched furniture vibe. I'm trying to act like I've been here a million times. As of now, I vow to become a regular. This is it. Our new spot: the Witches Brew. It'll be like our "Central Perk." (I know—must stop watching *Friends* reruns. What have I been doing with my life?)

I'll have a regular order here and the server will know my name. I'll have a favorite table: this one, in the sunroom at the back of the café, this spot against the wall, at this little round table with mosaic tiles in a sunburst design.

Perfect crowd: 12 other people—some our age, others older. Very intimate, like seeing Ed Sheeran at Artists Den. (Gaah! Note to self: Must rewatch the concert video. I've missed you, Ed, my favorite ginger.) Here at the Witches Brew we are the truest of the true Fatima Ro fans. And the four of us have been—wait for it—*invited*!

Fatima: oversized white linen shirt over jean miniskirt, loosely laced Tretorn sneakers, sans socks. Smoky eye makeup. Pale cheeks. Bare lips. Messy hair.

Why can't I look that glam with half my makeup and bedhead? I'd look like an asylum escapee.

Fatima is ordering green tea. I've heard that it has magical properties.

Note: start drinking green tea.

Fatima welcomes the crowd, thanks us for coming. She comments on how cute the café is. She's never been here before either. Hey, maybe she'll become a regular and I'll become a regular and I'll see her here from time to time. We'll be on a

"Hey, how are you?" basis. How cool would that be?

Jonah (rude boy) is playing with his phone. I jab him with my umbrella.

Undertow book talk with Fatima Ro begins NOW:

First draft written over six months at a feverish pace after her mother passed away, very little sleep, very little to eat, limited communication, virtually unreachable other than by landline. The internet did not even exist, as far as she was concerned. Family and friends thought she was grieving, which she was, of course, but she was "not grieving in stillness" but "grieving with ferocity."

"Grieving with ferocity."

Her mother was her grounding force. Her mother was common sense and hard work anchored in reality. Without her, Fatima felt detached from Earth, set in a sudden spiral. As a child, Fatima had too much imagination, was too distractible, too restless. But it was always okay for her to be who she was because her mother kept her tethered to the ground by one toe. When her mother died, *Undertow* was a desperate way to hold on to her mother's love, so that it wouldn't float away forever.

The title, *Undertow,* existed in her consciousness even before she began writing, because she felt as if she were trapped inside one.

UNDERTOW: the underlying emotion
UNDERTOW: rip current, underlying current, force in opposition

Writing *Undertow* was the most difficult thing she has ever experienced because it was her grieving process. By writing the character of "Lara," Fatima was able to drown in loss, feel loss in its deepest depths. She doesn't know how she would've grieved without this place to do it.

Place = the mental state of being "Lara" and writing *Undertow.*

Revision was very much a swimming to the surface—a period of pushing and fighting to propel back into the world—emotionally, physically.

[Fatima is watching me as I'm taking notes. I'm now self-conscious about taking notes. I'm uncomfortably aware of my hands and my fingers and my shoulders and wrinkling my forehead the way bad actors do to fake that they are taking notes about *Undertow* when Fatima is watching.]

Losing her mother was transformative at 20 because it marked an inevitable transformation from child to adult. As a child she was so carefree, but when her mother died, she suddenly felt old. Fatima chose to write Lara as age 17 because that's how old Fatima was when her mother got sick.

Revision of her manuscript was torturous in a different way—it meant revisiting her loss again and again. In shedding the manuscript (from 120k to 80k) there was an emergence of her new self and seeing her own grief from a different perspective each time she reread it. But she fought against the change so furiously at times that revising *Undertow* became so painful she had to put it away for lengths at a time—weeks, and, for a spell or two, months.

In the end, she had this completed manuscript. She had printed it out and couldn't believe the weight of it, literally, the *weight* of its pages. She kept marveling at its weight in actual pounds; she would estimate it, compare it to other objects around the house:

These papers are heavier than this box of tissues.
These papers are lighter than this boot.
< carton of milk
> picture frame
> shampoo bottle
< Bible

Over and over, no matter where she went, she would think about the weight of the manuscript because she was amazed that her grief had literal, physical weight. Grief could be measured in pounds.

"Grief could be MEASURED IN POUNDS!"

She became obsessed with finding out exactly how many pounds.

[Am I really hearing all of this right now? How is this not being filmed and documented for future generations? Even Jonah is listening, balancing a spoon on two fingers. I think he's *weighing*.]

Fatima didn't have a scale at home. But one day she had a gyno appointment, so she brought the pages to the doctor's office, and when she was waiting in her paper robe for the doctor, she pulled the manuscript out of her bag and weighed it on the scale. It was 3.8 lbs.

3.8 lbs.

[Fatima lingers on that thought. We all linger on it.]

[What is Jonah *weighing*?]

Knowing the weight of her grief in pounds, Fatima had a revelation that grief could be contained. It could be purged and then revised to make sense, and it could be *contained*.

[Fatima is looking at me again. Does she want me to stop typing? Is this too personal and I shouldn't be taking notes? Then why is she talking about it to a bunch of strangers?]

[I stopped writing for a few minutes. She stopped watching me. Now I'm writing again.]

She stood in her paper robe at the doctor's office, suddenly very proud of her manuscript. It was the first time she thought of it as a novel—an entity separate from herself—because it was outside of her body and her mind now, contained in this 3.8-lb. package. *Undertow* wasn't a "book" yet in her mind until that moment. Most days it was a beast she was attacking. Other days it was like a wounded animal she was trying to nurse back to health. But there, in the gyno office, it was all of a sudden a *novel*.

She was proud of this *thing* for the first time. But ironically, the person she wanted to call and tell about it?

Her mother.

[My heart is breaking, breaking. It's broken. I'm shattered. I'm sitting in Witches Brew in tiny little shattered mosaic pieces. I never thought I could love *Undertow* more than I already did.]

I. Was. Wrong.

Later . . . 11:53 p.m.
Home

Our plan worked again. We lingered behind. Guy-in-red-baseball-cap did the same, but he only thanked Fatima for the discussion and asked her to sign a book and then went on his merry way. I told Fatima that she made me see *Undertow* in a different light, and that there's so much more to it than I thought. But then she totally blindsided me, practically whacked me in the head with a brick. She said that she saw me taking copious notes during her talk and she ASKED TO READ THEM!

Complete and total panic! I had quoted her. I had mentioned the way she was staring at me. I had injected my thoughts into her book talk about the most difficult period of her life. I'd commented on her makeup. I wrote about her visit to the gyno! What was I thinking taking notes on that? Why would I even think that it was okay to document that? What else had I written? I couldn't even remember.

I asked Fatima if I could clean the notes up first; they were a jumbled mess. If I could just clean them up then I would email them to her later. But as that was coming out of my mouth, I knew she was going to say no. Why would she wait on notes from me? And why would she ever give me her email address?

"I'd really like to see them now," she said. "I'm interested to see what you found most compelling, you were so intense over here, writing everything down. Are you a writer?"

"Not even. But I might want to be," I said.

"Then I'd really like to read them, from a future writer's perspective."

What was I supposed to do? I didn't have any choice but to show her. I felt like she'd caught me cheating on a test and was going to check my answers right in front of me. Miri and Penny were like, *Go ahead. Show her. What's the big deal?* Plus, Fatima called me a *future writer*. So, I sat back down and opened my laptop and I showed her.

I kept thinking *Fatima Ro is sitting with me. Fatima Ro is reading my notes. She's touching my keyboard. She saw my dumbass desktop picture of the movie* The Bling Ring. *I swear, I like the image as an actual photograph—meaning, its composition and color and use of positive and negative space—not because it's from* The Bling Ring. *Okay, I did like the movie on a so-bad-it's-good level, but that doesn't mean I'm a* Bling Ring *person.* I wanted to explain all of this to Fatima, but I was too frazzled.

"Thank you." That was all Fatima said.

Thank you? Was she trying to kill me with awkward? "You're welcome."

She stood and stared at me.

I closed my laptop. Damn *Bling Ring.*

But then she shocked me again. "What are you guys doing right now?"

The only acceptable answer, of course, was "Absolutely nothing."

"Well," she said. "The new book I'm planning is set in a private school. I haven't been to one since I graduated. I would love to see Graham. Will you take me there?"

WHAAAAT????!!!

▶ ▶▶

PENNY

Can you tell me about the night you took Fatima to Graham with Miri and Soleil?

Uh-huh. [laughs] Oh, god. I ruined my lace-up flats that night. Nobody else had them yet! I wanted them to be my new look, like, instead of sneakers or flip-flops. I was trying to up my fashion game. And I thought we were going to sit in a café, not run around Graham at ten o'clock at night. Also, it rained a little that morning, so it was muddy, just my luck. [sigh] It was worth it, though, for Fatima. [pause] Or I thought it was, at the time.

You don't think it was worth it now?

My friend is in the hospital, so no, it wasn't.

I'm very sorry about Jonah.

[checks phone] I keep checking my texts for news, you know? I'm afraid that if I stop thinking about him, something bad will happen and I'll miss it.

If anything happens, I'm sure someone will give you a call. Texting is no way to deliver big news.

[puts phone down] Have you spoken to Miri yet?

Yes.

Does she even care about Jonah?

She's terribly concerned.

I doubt that.

Why's that?

'Cause she doesn't care about anyone but Fatima Ro. She only wants Jonah to get better so that Fatima will be off the hook.

That's a pretty bold statement.

[shrugs]

Miri was that close with Fatima?

For real? She was, like, Fatima's clone.

What about the rest of you? Tell me more about that night.

[deep breath] Yeah, well, the gate to the courtyard was open, so we went in. It was exciting, like we were breaking and entering, but just the entering. I'd never been at school when I wasn't supposed to. And I'd never hung out with anyone famous before. Well, Soleil's older cousin was on *My Super Sweet 16*. But that's not Fatima Ro kind of famous. Anyways, we were sneaking into the courtyard, and Soleil and Jonah were doing the *Mission Impossible* song. [laughs] We felt, like, such a rush, you know? She was Fatima Ro!

Go on.

That night the stars were just, wow, they were so clear. I'll never forget it. We could see the layers, I mean, the stars at different depths. It was like when I went to the planetarium in elementary school, only real. Fatima got up on one of the tables, she lay right on top of it, and she said, "You have to do this! Come on. Do this! Pick a table." So, we each picked a table and lay on our backs. That reminded me of the planetarium, too. Have you been?

No.

The chairs recline all the way back.

Oh.

I picked our regular table where we have lunch on nice days. It was wild lying there at night, and with *her.* I mean, we'd sat at that very table and talked about Fatima Ro almost every day that year, and then all of sudden she was with us, lying on the table and staring at the sky. [pause] It was, like, this crazy-perfect moment. Oh. Except for my shoes. [laughs] Did I tell you they were Stuart Weitzman?

No.

Yeah . . . [sigh] But then Fatima told us the funniest thing. She was at an Amtrak station a few months after she was published, and there was a song playing over the speakers by some old fart—Conway Twitty, she said. An old lady tapped Fatima on the shoulder and whispered that when she was sixteen she fell in love with a boy at the beach club and they made love in her cabana every night while their parents went dancing on the boardwalk, and even all those years later, every time she hears "It's Only Make Believe" she has an orgasm. [laughs]

[laughs] That's a great story.

We were dying laughing. I mean, who says that? And how weird was it that we got to hear it from Fatima Ro? Like, we heard Fatima Ro say *orgasm*.

[laughs] That's funny.

Uh-huh. But that story changed Fatima's life because that's when she developed her theory of human connections.

Human connections?

It's the idea that we should, like, approach each other with open hearts and reveal our authentic selves through precious truths.

What are precious truths?

Um . . . like the old lady's cabana story. That woman was a complete stranger, right? But in a few seconds Fatima knew her better than friends she's had since she was a kid. So, Fatima believes that looking people in the eye and sharing intimate thoughts breaks barriers, makes people fall in love, and can, like, literally end wars.

Huh.

I know it sounds wacky, but it wasn't. It was Fatima Ro, and we were watching the stars, and it made more sense than anything, like, ever. She was talking about how you can know someone for years but never really *know* them.

That's true.

You *see*? Fatima said that it's true of neighbors and people who sit next to you in class because your names are alphabetical, but also your own family members. So, I started thinking about Soleil and Miri and me. I mean, we threw, like, the hottest parties on Long Island, we went to Natsumi, we went to Ed Sheeran, we talked about *Undertow*, but I never felt like part of it, not really. I know what my friends thought of me.

What do you mean?

They thought I was basic, that I was only about clothes and guys and *Pretty Little Liars*. Since they were into their books and were in honors classes and taking AP Psychology, which was, like, the trendy class to take that only accepted a few juniors a semester, they acted all deep and intellectual. It bothered me—a lot, actually—because I had opinions and goals and things like they did.

Sounds frustrating.

[nods] But while I was listening to Fatima and looking at the sky, I realized something sort of big for me.

What was that?

It was *my* fault they thought I was an airhead. Like, how were they supposed to know my thoughts if I didn't tell them? I wasn't transparent the way Fatima said we should be. I wasn't living inside/out or offering precious truths. Like, what did I ever do besides style our party outfits and collect the fifty-dollar cover charge at the door?

Fifty dollars? Holy crap!

Well, they were super-exclusive parties. You wouldn't want just anyone walking into your house, would you?

No, but still. I was thinking more like five bucks.

Do you know how much it costs to rent blackjack tables?

No.

A lot.

Apparently.

[sighs] That night at Graham was the stuff of life. It was the best night since, well, ever. Way better than casino night. But I was complaining about my shoes. Yeah, I was upset about them, but I had revelations and stuff, too. I could've talked about that, but I didn't.

Why didn't you?

I wanted to. But then better things happened.

Better things?

Jonah started singing that old Coldplay song, you know, the one about stars? It was nice. He was happy. [pause]

Jonah wasn't usually happy?

Uh, um . . . I don't really want to talk about him.

That's fine. It's just that you mentioned it.

I just meant that we were all happy.

All right. So what else happened?

We shared being in the universe together.

Hm.

It wasn't weird.

I didn't say it was weird.

Fatima said that human connections don't have to come through precious truths. They can develop through sharing precious experiences, and we were having one by being in the universe together under the stars.

I can see that.

She had shared *Undertow* with us, and we were sharing the stars with her.

I get it.

Most kids start at the Graham School in ninth grade, right? But me and Soleil and Miri, we'd been there since seventh. I was sorta tired of it. I was dreading that junior year would be the same as every other. I don't love Graham the way Miri and Soleil love it. I'm not captain of anything like they are. School's not as easy for me. But that night in the courtyard I knew the year was going to be better; sharing the sky with Fatima Ro was the start of that 'cause I got to do something with my friends that wasn't shopping or Snapchat, you know? It felt, like . . . important.

Cool.

Yeah. And then you won't believe what Fatima said next. She said that she felt positive energy from each of us and that she'd moved to Long Island because she wanted to open her life to new friends and new perspectives. She sat up on her table and looked around at us and said, "I want you to be my people."

Whoa.

For real. [shakes head] Fatima Ro wanted us to be her people.

That was something, huh?

It was everything.

The Absolution of Brady Stevenson

BY FATIMA RO

(excerpt)

When Brady Stevenson moved out of his childhood home, he took his old Coke-bottle glasses but left his wrestling trophies behind. The awards remained as they were for nearly a year—stuffed into the corner of Brady's closet, along with fallen wire hangers, unmatched socks, and an unopened package of Fruit of the Looms that were a size too small, given to him by his nana, who always thought of him as two years younger than whatever age he happened to be.

The day of the move, as Brady lifted his boxes into the U-Haul, he wished for that—to be two years younger. He would do everything over again, both the everyday minutiae and the heartache; he would pick dirt from under his finger-nails, sit through the same class lectures on Poe and the Earth's layers and the divine right to rule, and he would even suffer again through the trauma of losing his neighborhood friend to leukemia. He'd relive it all so that he could un-live one night, the night that led to loading a U-Haul with almost everything he'd ever owned.

But Brady knew better than to wish for impossible things; it made him remember why he was wishing for a do-over in the first place. He swore off remembering as he pulled the rope and slammed the U-Haul shut. This vow lasted as far as the corner of Yardly Drive, when he caught a glimpse of his own reflection in the side mirror.

▶ ▶▶

MIRI

Do you remember when you first learned about Fatima's new book?

Do I remember it? The sound of Soleil screaming over the phone is still ringing in my brain.

She called you about it?

Yes. She was on summer vacation with her cousins in California. Right away I knew it was something serious because it wasn't a text, it was a call, and she was three thousand miles away.

Oh.

So she calls me. I'm in the parking lot of Party City picking up decorations for my aunt's baby shower. I answer. Soleil's in the car with her cousins driving down Pacific Coast Highway, and she's screaming at the top of her voice. I swear to god she nearly shattered my eardrum. She was like, "Oh my god! Oh my god! Fatima stabbed me in the back! She betrayed me! She wrote all about me and Jonah in her new book! Oh my god!"

Wow. How'd she find out?

She and her cousins were listening to the radio in the car, and Fatima came on and gave an interview.

Oh, man.

Fatima said the book was due out next April, and that it was about a prep school kid who keeps a dark secret from his girl-friend.

Soleil must've been out of control.

I stood there holding a dozen pink and blue balloons, and I told her, "Don't lose your shit, Soleil. Fatima wouldn't do anything to hurt you. I'm sure it's fictionalized." But the calmer I was the more hysterical she got. She said, "I'm texting you a link! She screwed us over! That's why she left town. We shouldn't have trusted her. She got her story. Then she didn't need us anymore. And now she's publishing it and it's going to be evvverywhere!"

Stranger Than Fiction

The True Story Behind the Controversial Novel

The Absolution of Brady Stevenson

SOLEIL JOHNSTON'S STORY, PART 1 (continued)

SOLEIL

DOES THIS SOUND FICTIONALIZED

TO YOU, MIRI???!!!

publishersweekly.com/newbookdeals/july/4098899900

Senior Editor Yannik Olstad at HarperCollins has acquired the sophomore YA novel by *Undertow* author Fatima Ro. In *The Absolution of Brady Stevenson*, 17-year-old Brady transfers to an elite private school in order to escape his shameful past. When he unexpectedly falls for Morley Academy honor student Sunny Vaughn, Brady must decide whether or not to reveal his dark history.

▶ ▶▶

PENNY

I was out getting gelato with my friend Natalie Singh. I had hazelnut in a cup, and Natalie got black forest on a cone.

Good memory.

I remember everything from that moment. Soleil's name popped up on my phone. She was calling from vacation, and we basically only ever text, so I picked up. She was freaking out, saying Fatima was on the radio. "Fatima wrote about *us*! Her new book—it's all about *us*!" she was screaming. I was like, "Oh my god, cool! We're gonna be, like, famous!" But then Soleil said, "No, Penny. She wrote about me and Jonah. We were inside/out with her! We told her everything! Everything! Think about what you told her!" That's when I started to cry like a little kid with my ice cream. Natalie kept mouthing to me, "What happened? What happened?" I'll never forget that. And now I can never eat hazelnut gelato again. I really loved hazelnut gelato. [sighs] Fatima ruined everything.

THE ABSOLUTION OF BRADY STEVENSON

BY FATIMA RO

(excerpt)

For my people.

You know who you are.

Soleil kept yelling, calling Fatima a manipulative bitch. "She used me! She deceived all of us!" she said. But I told her, "Fatima's not going to hurt us. Besides, she gave us *Undertow*, so we gave her our stories. It's only fair." That's what set Soleil off. She screamed, "How can you say this is *fair*? She didn't even ask us! I swear, Miri, if you side with Fatima on this, I hate you forever!" I yelled back, "Then hate me. Because she didn't do anything wrong. If you turn your back on Fatima because of this, I never knew you!"

Ugh, that's awful.

She said, "Then we have nothing else to say to each other," and hung up. That was the last time Soleil and I spoke. That's how we got here—on opposite sides of a scandal. [shakes head] We were Fatima's people. Do you know what that means?

Tell me.

Fatima trusted us. Seeing Soleil and Penny speaking against her in public must be devastating. She welcomed us into her home, for god's sake.

She did?

Yes. The first time she had us over was for her housewarming party. We were dying to go, of course. We told everyone at school about it. We planned our outfits. It was an honor to be invited. A person's home is her sanctuary. It's revelatory.

And what did Fatima's house reveal about her?

[laughs] What *didn't* it reveal? We saw her *Undertow* notes and her BCPs.

BCPs?

Birth control pills. She kept them on the kitchen counter so she'd remember to take them with her morning oatmeal.

Stranger Than Fiction

The True Story Behind the Controversial Novel

The Absolution of Brady Stevenson

SOLEIL JOHNSTON'S STORY, PART 1 (continued)

Journal Entry

September 25, 2016

Guess where I am! Fatima Ro's house!

- Ladies and gentlemen, I just took a photo of Fatima Ro's door! A most important new element which I shall add to my art project titled *Doors*. Take note of the original woodwork featuring sixteen hand-carved panels; in need of refinishing yet still rich with charm and character.

- Fatima smells like coconut sunblock and vanilla cookies.

- I must ask her how to do a messy topknot. Hers looks so good with half up, half down! I envy every strand. But my hair is so limp and hers is thick and must have a lot of texture. I hope it will still work on me.

- Approx 20 people (she could've made $1k cover charge!): Fatima's NYC friends; musicians and modely types; a couple of old dudes (old as in elderly)

P.S. I was invited. I am NOT a stalker.

PENNY

September is so confusing, wardrobe-wise. I kept changing my mind about what to wear; I didn't want to look like I was trying too hard, but I also didn't want to look like I didn't care. Fatima was so stylish. I ended up buying something new—an Alice & Olivia minidress with a deep V—and I packed a bathing suit. She said that her pool was still open because of that weird heat wave. We closed our pool right before Labor Day. I was, like, impressed that Fatima's pool was open when it was almost October. She could do anything she wanted living on her own.

Did you make the right wardrobe choice?

I did, thankfully. I got six compliments. Fatima was in a one-piece swimsuit under a really pretty, gauzy cover-up. She was so sophisticated, and not in the way Soleil and Miri tried to be sophisticated. Fatima didn't have to try. She just *was*. I was super nervous to speak to her, but her white cover-up at least gave me something to say. I told her that I liked it and asked where she got it; it was Tommy Bahama. I looked it up later. [pause] All right, I ordered one just like it. But I wouldn't have worn it in front of her. I just wanted it for, like, vacations.

THE ABSOLUTION OF BRADY STEVENSON

BY FATIMA RO

(excerpt)

B rady felt so ashamed of his past that at his new school his goal was to be invisible. He was thankful for the school uniform: khaki pants, white button-down shirt, and a navy tie with yellow stripes. The blue blazer looked custom-tailored on him even though it was straight off the rack; the shoulders were a perfect fit. This new look, with the Morley Academy crest on his breast pocket, was the first step toward invisibility.

The one drawback to the uniform was that Brady couldn't wear his gray hoodie. He missed its warmth around his face and the comforting smell of his own scalp captured inside it. His hoodie enabled him to retreat into his own private space no matter where he was or who was around.

When Sunny Vaughn sat beside him and said hello in studio art class, Brady groaned under his breath. Instinctively, he reached for his hoodie but then realized he wasn't wearing it.

"Sorry," Sunny said, rising from her seat. "I can sit somewhere else."

"No." Brady wanted invisibility, but he didn't want to be rude. Still, he was used to giving monosyllabic responses after nine months of giving monosyllabic responses. "Stay."

"Okaaay." Sunny eyed the boy as she lowered her backpack. "I'm Sunny Vaughn."

Brady sighed. Although he was ready for a change of atmosphere, he wasn't ready for girls. Girls were not part of his renewal plan.

"And you are . . . ?"

He rolled his eyes. "Brady."

"Hi. Are you new?"

Brady nodded. He reached for the back of his head again. Someone should design a blazer with a drawstring hood, he thought. The idea wasn't half bad, but he forgot all about it when he saw the curiosity on Sunny's face. Her expression concerned him. Sunny thought the new boy was awkward and mysterious. She also thought he was good-looking.

Brady didn't know it yet, but being new, awkward, mysterious, and good-looking made him the least invisible guy at Morley Academy.

▶ ▶▶

MIRI

When we arrived at Fatima's house, she hugged each of us, and
then she introduced us to her other guests. She said, "These are
my friends from Graham, my new *people*." I was truly touched.
Obviously, she'd told them about us. There's no denying that
Fatima was a class act. But then Penny turned around with her
silly pastry box and said, "I brought mini cupcakes," as if it were
an eight-year-old's birthday party. Honestly, she could be such
a ditz.

Stranger Than Fiction

The True Story Behind the Controversial Novel

The Absolution of Brady Stevenson

SOLEIL JOHNSTON'S STORY, PART 1 (continued)

Journal Entry

FATIMA RO'S BATHROOM!

Typing this into my phone because I feel the need to document every single detail of this crazy mofo epicness of being in FATIMA RO'S HOUSE.

Toothpaste: Crest Whitening

Floss: Rite Aid brand—Fatima Ro flosses!

Shampoo and conditioner: Pantene

Soap: Dove in the pump

Lotion: Cake Batter Whipped body cream (I have identified the source of her vanilla scent and it is delicious!!! Amazon cart ASAP!)

Unpacked box: Playtex tampons, Always overnights, hair spray, curling iron, headbands, hair ties, claw clips, sunglasses, makeup bags, Velcro rollers of varied sizes, Puffs, cotton balls, Q-tips, Johnson's baby oil, Advil, Tylenol, NyQuil, nail polish

remover, expired antibiotics (?), expired Mylanta, Proactiv, travel-sized Colgates, multi-packs of Secret deodorant, foaming bleach, rubber gloves, sponges, paper towels
Old tub with new shower curtain of NYC skyline in black and white (still smells plasticky and has creases from coming right out of the box)

Uggggh, I think she hated my housewarming gift. I'm a complete loser. Why did I bring her that stupid horseshoe? The internet says it's the traditional present for a new home, but I should know better than to believe everything on the internet. LOSER! LOSER! LOSER!!!

Holy*&@#!!! I am in Fatima Ro's bathroom!
Selfie in Fatima Ro's bathroom mirror is in order:

So cute ☺

It was crazy being in her house—seeing where she lives, seeing her friends, and her boxes everywhere filled with her clothes and stuff—it felt like we were inside a secret or something. I don't know, I can't explain.

That explains it pretty well. Very poetic, actually.

Really? Thanks.

So, what was the house like?

Oh, it was great. Well, no, it wasn't *great*. It was only a little ranch house and was kind of run-down for Old Westbury. It was also a mess because she hadn't unpacked yet. [pause] But it was her *own*, you know? I want to be independent like that when I'm in my twenties. I wouldn't need a huge, fancy house. I'd just want something that's mine, like Fatima's place. Anyways, she had plans to fix it up. It had good bones; that means potential. The house was super retro, like, very deco. Her light fixtures were from the sixties. I told her she should keep those—to just shine them up instead of replace them. She said that she would; she thought that was a great idea.

Nice.

Uh-huh. It felt good that she appreciated my suggestion. She asked me what colors I would choose for the walls and what I thought about the original tile; the bathroom had classic black-and-white hexagons. I started thinking I'd find home decorating ideas for her, like, uh, paint chips and pictures of furniture or whatever that might look nice.

Okay.

I got excited about it because what if she put something in her house that I suggested?

That would be amazing.

I'm really into design, you know. I watch *Mad Men*.

The Absolution of Brady Stevenson

BY FATIMA RO

(excerpt)

Blah, blah, blah, charcoal. Blah, blah, blah, perspective. Blah, warm tones and shading. Blah, blah, Degas, blah. Brady was only half listening to the teacher. He was looking at dusty papier-mâché faces, wooden anatomy figures, and bundles of chicken wire on the far counter, and he wasn't used to the weird odors of the art room—turpentine and wet clay and rusty paint cans—but he was encouraged by their newness. This was the fresh start that he'd prayed for. Over the past year, he often thought about "opposite day"—the game he played in second grade of saying and doing the opposite of everything. That's what he was trying to achieve now—to be the opposite of who he was before.

"So, you like art, huh?" Sunny Vaughn asked, as she flipped to a blank page in her spiral sketchpad.

Nod.

"Do you draw or sculpt, or what?"

Brady did not like art; he didn't do either of the above. He only took the class because his former self never would have chosen it, and neither would any of his former friends. But Brady answered, "Sculpt," under his breath. He'd seen sculptures that were nothing but recycled garbage welded together, so he figured he could fake that and nobody would be able to judge whether or not he had any talent, because let's face it, how the hell could anyone tell?

"Cool." Sunny smiled. Brady avoided looking at her smile on purpose. A nice smile could only complicate his life. "Are you working on anything right now?" she asked.

He shook his head.

"That's mine." Sunny pointed to something leaning against the nearby shelf; a board of some sort covered with a sheet. "It's mixed media on a theme. It's left over from June." She laughed at herself. "I got a little too ambitious and didn't finish. I don't know what else to do with it, but Ms. Vargas wants me to figure it out, so it's kind of turned into an independent project. Are you on Instagram? Because if you are, Ms. Vargas asks us to photograph our progress. Or lack thereof in my case."

Brady shook his head again. This girl could sure talk.

"Oh, well, social media isn't mandatory. Don't you want to know what my project is?" she asked, studying Brady's expressionless face. "When someone tells me one thing I always need to know more."

Shrug. He did want to know about Sunny's project and about her. But what was the point? Friends were not on his agenda at Morley Academy.

"My theme is doors. Well, doors as a metaphor for families and the private lives they live," Sunny said. "When I was little and we were on vacation, my parents and I drove by these little beach cottages, and all the doors were different colors: purple, yellow, bright orange—one was polka-dotted. I've been analyzing doors ever since."

Brady stared at the sheet-covered project. He didn't seem particularly interested, but since he didn't tell her to shut up, Sunny kept talking. "There's something about doors. They can be beautiful and ornate or colorful and friendly or chipped and weathered. But you can never tell what's inside."

Shifting in his seat, Brady looked up at Ms. Vargas. He didn't want to get in trouble for talking on the first day, or on any day for that matter.

"So, that's what *I'm* doing." Sunny meant for this chitchat to serve as an opening. She was usually good at getting a conversation going. For example, next Brady might say, "Well, *I'm* going to do . . ." But he didn't offer anything.

Blahbidy blah shading. Blah, blah, blah, vine charcoal, blah. Blah, blah compressed charcoal. Ms. Vargas swiped slides on the SMART Board. Sunny slid her sketchpad onto her lap and started sketching, so Brady sat back and relaxed a bit. *Blah, blah, blah, contouring . . .*

Ten seconds before the bell, Sunny ripped the sketch from her book and slid it on the table toward Brady. It was a "smiley face" except it was sad. There was charcoal shading smudged all around. Lettering followed along the perimeter of the circle. Brady turned the drawing, following the words as they curved upside down: DON'T BE SO GLUM, BRADY! TURN THAT FROWN UPSIDE DOWN! When turned upside down, the image of the frown turned into a happy face.

"See ya later. Have a good first day!" Sunny said as the bell rang.

Brady grunted in response. The problem with playing "opposite day" was that it was impossible to keep up. The game never lasted for more than a couple hours. Brady remembered this when he accidentally looked up as Sunny swung her book bag over her back. Her smile was as cute as he'd dreaded it would be.

Fatima was twenty-three. Did you find it odd at all that she invited you over and wanted to be friends with you?

What are you trying to say? That I should've known better? That I was some naïve, unsuspecting target who was lured into her den?

I didn't say any of that. It's just that Fatima was very successful and very busy. She must've had places to be and people to see.

Well, I'll have you know that yes, I did wonder why Fatima Ro would want to be friends with us. But the people at her house-warming were all different ages. Some were our age, and others were in their seventies or even eighties—Fatima's former pro-fessors at Columbia. If you had seen her crowd, you would've come to the same conclusion that I did.

Which was?

That Fatima liked to keep interesting company. Simple as that. And for your information, Soleil, Jonah, Penny, and I turned out to be the most mature people at the party. Right after dark, Fatima told half of her guests to leave because they were acting idiotic, as in let's-find-out-if-these-lawn-chairs-will-float-in-the-pool level of idiotic.

Those rowdy retired professors.

The other half.

Just kidding.

[sighs] Listen. The media has manufactured a salacious story. Whatever sells, goes. That's how these things work, I understand. But it's ironic, isn't it, that the news is trying to portray Fatima as unethical while they're spinning their own brand of fiction? It's disgusting what people are saying about her targeting us for her own selfish needs. I want you to know for the record: [leans forward] [looks straight into the camera] Fatima Ro did not *prey* on us. We made an authentic human connection with her. It's called *friendship*. Look it up. She invited us into her world because she had an open heart, an open mind, and an appreciation for multiple perspectives, not because she was bent. She wasn't some fifty-year-old dude in a trench coat circling the playground at recess. [sits back] So, don't even try to twist this into something sick, because it wasn't.

Noted.

Are you patronizing me?

Stranger Than Fiction

The True Story Behind the Controversial Novel

The Absolution of Brady Stevenson

SOLEIL JOHNSTON'S STORY, PART 1 (continued)

Journal Entry

OMGGGGG!!! I cannot believe what I just found right here in the living room under a pile of towels and bed linens!

DRUM ROLLLLL . . . . !

A BOX LABELED: UNDERTOW!!!!!!!

I'm actually dying.

Dying . . .

Dead.

Photo op!

PENNY

It was sorta scary when Fatima kicked those people out of her party.

Why?

Uh, well, she strolled right out to the pool, turned off the music, and said, "You guys need to get the eff out. I'm sorry I invited you. Don't expect to be asked back. Good-bye." She was so calm, and she didn't care at all about losing friends over it. After everybody left, she told us that she was done with those superficial relationships she was trying to hold on to from the city. It was scary to see that Fatima could cut people out of her life like that. I mean, some of those people were her friends from college.

Huh.

She said that kicking those friends out of her new house was symbolic for her. It was, like, the "final transition" to her new life or something. She called it a, um . . . I can't remember the term. Anyways, those people didn't understand honest human connections. She put her soul into *Undertow*, it was her reaching out to them, but her friends barely acknowledged the book. It disappointed her to live inside/out but get nothing back.

That's kind of sad.

I could relate to it, I guess.

How so?

Because. [sighs] Me and my friends held parties at my house, right? The Graham kids loved it, and my parents liked having guests. And they were happy that I was, like, networking and learning planning and organizing skills.

Okay . . .

The thing was, though, that even on regular days, half the school still came over to play basketball or swim or watch TV. But how many of them even knew me? Two? Sometimes I stayed in my room all day and no one even wondered where I was.

Aw . . .

Fatima's friends didn't get the meaning of one beating heart opening up to another beating heart. But she said she could tell from the night in the courtyard that the four of us were open to honesty and to living transparently. She felt it in her bones that we could be open with one another. I wanted all of us to be transparent, too. I wanted my friends to take me seriously. And also, I was afraid to get kicked out of her life, you know?

I understand.

A "tabula rasa"! That's what she called it. Is that right?

Yes. A clean slate.

That was it. Her new beginning. Fatima said she'd been waiting a long time for friends like us. She was an open book with us. [pause] That was stupid. I didn't mean "open book," like, as a pun. Sorry. You can delete that.

[laughs]

Wait. You can delete stuff, can't you? I mean, you'll edit out all the dumb things I say, right? 'Cause I for real say dumb things a lot.

We'll see.

Oh, god. [sighs] [drinks from a water glass]

So, Fatima was an open book?

[laughs] Uh-huh. Soleil found a box labeled *Undertow*.

Whoa. Did she open it?

Fatima did. Soleil and I were whispering about it, and finally, Fatima said, "Just ask me to open the damn thing, why don't you?" [laughs] She sat in the middle of her living room and went through it with us.

What was inside?

Lots of stuff, like her marble notebooks and spiral memo pads and family photos, and there were printed-out copies of *Undertow* at different stages marked up with colored pens and Post-its. Soleil was like, "It's the manuscript she weighed in the doctor's office!" She was really excited. But the biggest deal was Fatima's paper towel roll.

Paper towel roll?

Fatima had this brown paper towel roll. You know, the kind that's from the machine in a public restroom?

Okay . . .

It was one of those. When she unrolled it, it was the timeline of *Undertow* from one end to the other, written in marker. It unraveled all the way to the front door.

Wow.

Uh-huh. But it wasn't a timeline of the plot; she called it an emotional timeline, like what the characters were feeling in their souls through the entire book, along with what she was feeling while she was writing it.

Oh, that's fascinating.

Everyone went crazy over it. For me, though, I thought the photos were more interesting. Fatima's mom was really young, or she looked really young. But for some reason, the timeline was, like, major, so I didn't say anything. I didn't want to insult anyone. You know, Fatima stole the paper towel roll from an Olive Garden.

Really?

Yeah. She literally unscrewed the machine thingy with her bare hands and pulled the roll out.

Ha! How funny.

Isn't it crazy? I mean, I never thought that Fatima Ro would eat at an Olive Garden.

THE ABSOLUTION OF BRADY STEVENSON

BY FATIMA RO

(excerpt)

That night, Sunny Vaughn pulled out her laptop and searched the name "Brady Stevenson" online. He hadn't told her his last name, but she caught a glimpse of it on his class schedule, which he had placed upside down on their table.

Her Brady wasn't on Facebook or Instagram or Twitter. The only Brady Stevensons Sunny found were either out of state or in-region but seventy-one years old. Seventy-one-year-old Brady Stevenson was on Facebook. His page was dedicated to classic cars, two of which appeared to be stored in his own garage—a red Jaguar and a little black MG. But this was the wrong Brady Stevenson, so Sunny wasn't interested in investigating further into the old man's car collection.

▶ ▶▶

MIRI

Even Jonah was impressed by the timeline, and that's the truth. He took a picture of it like the rest of us did. That timeline alone is proof of how sensitive Fatima is as a person and as a novelist. She lives and writes from an emotional place. When emotions are released in a creative way, you can't harness it, and you certainly can't censor it.

Are you referring to The Absolution of Brady Stevenson?

Yes, I am. She had every right to write it. This is the United States of America. You can't dictate the subjects for an artist. Inspiration can come from anywhere. And just because Fatima was inspired by us doesn't mean our relationship wasn't genuine. People write songs about their girlfriends and husbands and mistresses all the time. How is that any different?

Good point.

Tell me. Where's the *New York City* magazine exposé calling Taylor Swift a predator?

Stranger Than Fiction

The True Story Behind the Controversial Novel

The Absolution of Brady Stevenson

SOLEIL JOHNSTON'S STORY, PART 1 (continued)

Journal Entry

Pics of Fatima's emotional timeline—she's teary-eyed as we unravel it. "If I'd had the theory of human connections before my mom died, things would have been different."

> ME: Still have not showered. Still do not care. Unwashed, uncombed. Unfed. I can't be filled. I'll never be filled, never, ever be filled.
>
> Chapter 15
> LARA: If she leaves, the emptiness will be too wide and too deep to fill. I will not know how to fill it. I will never be able to fill it. It will never be filled, never be filled, never be filled, never, ever be filled.

ME: Panicked in the middle of the night. No one to call. Who can I call? Staring at my phone. I want to call, call, call, call her. I didn't do it when I could have. I. DID. NOT. CALL. HER. Why didn't I call her? What am I left with now? A voicemail I am too afraid to dial because I will hear her voice and then not hear her voice. This phone—it laughs at me, Hello hello hello hello hello hello . . .

Chapter 17
LARA: I'm clutching on to him, digging my fingers into his back, pressing myself closer to the edge. I need him, I need anything to fill me, to make me feel reckless and young. In darkness, I will sneak back home where she will yell and yell because I am a careless, careless child. She will sound strong in voice and stand tall in body, and she will know better than to die, for I am only a careless, careless child who needs her. Here. Now. This is how to stop time. Here is where to touch me. Here and here and here.

How perfectly heartbreaking.

▶ ▶▶

PENNY

I overheard Fatima and Soleil talking in the bedroom while she was teaching Soleil how to do a topknot.

What were they talking about?

Um . . . [pause] They were talking about Jonah. [silence]

Go on.

[nods] Fatima was curious about him because he was so quiet and standoffish: Was he okay? Was he upset? Was it something she'd said? That sort of thing. Soleil explained that that was just Jonah being Jonah. But Fatima wouldn't let it go. [shakes head] She should've just let it go.

What do you mean?

Uh . . . I don't really want to talk about this.

I think you know that it's important, Penny. Otherwise you wouldn't have brought it up.

Okay, okay. Um . . . [pauses] Fatima thought he was, like, obviously troubled. She said that since Jonah was having difficulty making an honest human connection, we should all make an extra effort to find out about him. That way we could help him with whatever he was going through. Soleil said that she didn't want to pry; she was afraid that might push him away. I heard her say that she'd tried to search him online when they first met, but nothing came up. Fatima asked Soleil to find a way to get close to him. Transparency would be for Jonah's own good. And then . . . [pauses]

Tell me.

Fatima said, "You read *Undertow*. You've seen my notes. I've shared everything with you. This is what it means to be transparent. I'm sure you can get him to open up to you. It's the only way we can truly be authentic friends." Soleil idolized Fatima, you know? She would've done anything she asked, so of course she did.

She was Fatima Ro.

She was.

THE ABSOLUTION
OF BRADY STEVENSON

BY FATIMA RO

(excerpt)

Three towns away, at the exact same moment that Sunny closed out of her search bar and clicked over to watch *Arrow*, Brady Stevenson searched online for "Sunny Vaughn."

There she was on Facebook, for all to see. Brady poked around, hoping to gain some insight:

Sunny Vaughn

CURRENT CITY AND HOMETOWN: Long Island, NY

MUSIC: Imagine Dragons, Ariana Grande, Charlie Puth, Bruno Mars

TELEVISION: Freeform, Bravo, Stranger Things, The CW

BOOKS: The Drowning

OTHER: Dylan O'Brien, Kate Winslet, Marc Jacobs, Sephora, Sugar Factory

FAVORITE QUOTES: "You have every right to a beautiful life."
—Selena Gomez

ABOUT SUNNY: former hula-hoop champ, current procrastinator, future something to do with words or art or film or food or all of these at once

RELATIONSHP STATUS: single

Sunny's Instagram featured a series of photos documenting the progress of a #MixedMedia #VargasStudioArt project on a theme: doors. The first few photos were of Sunny's materials, including a large piece of plywood, dollhouse doors, photographs of doors, illustrations of doors, paintings of doors, magazine cutouts of doors. In the next few photos, Sunny had painted the plywood black and mounted the mismatched doors onto it. The effect was that of an eerie apartment building with mysterious residents. Sunny meant what she said. The girl was really down with #DoorsAsAMetaphor.

Brady opened up a new tab. He Googled "The Drowning" and found a book by Thora Temple. "Thank you, Amazon books," he said aloud.

After an abortion and expulsion from her Catholic school for cutting classes, seventeen-year-old Jules Grady is forced to accompany her mother on a tour of the castles of Ireland. Convinced that the tour is nothing but a ploy to keep her from her boyfriend and set her on a straight and narrow path, Jules packs little more than a bad attitude. But when Jules learns that her mother is ill and this trip is likely her last, Jules tries to reconnect with her before it's too late.

Brady liked to read, but he was more of a nonfiction guy. He liked stories about the Vietnam War and obscure medical history in particular. When Brady allowed himself to aim high, he thought he might want to be a surgeon. He used to put model jet fighters and battleships together without looking at the instructions, so he felt that focus and precision were his strong points. He also liked the idea of concentrating so hard on a task that all other thoughts and cares would fall away. Saving lives would also be nice. He wanted to contribute something positive to society. He wanted that more than anything.

Although *The Drowning* was nothing Brady would normally read, he dropped the book into his Amazon cart just in case. In case of what? Brady didn't have a clue.

▶ ▶▶
MIRI

You should ask Penny about Fatima's key to her sliding door.

Fatima gave her a key?

You're surprised? Ask her. In fact, while you're at it, ask Penny if she ever gave it back. Fatima may not live there anymore, but I will bet you my sweet sixteen money and my car that Penny still has that key on her little Kate Spade ice-cream-cone key ring.

How are you so sure of that?

Because no matter what weepy-eyed story Penny may tell you about Fatima manipulating her, don't buy into it. It was special to be a part of Fatima's life, and Penny knows it.

Stranger Than Fiction

The True Story Behind the Controversial Novel

The Absolution of Brady Stevenson

SOLEIL JOHNSTON'S STORY, PART 1 (continued)

Journal Entry

Fatima gave me her email address after all: fatima.ro.author@ gmail.com!!! Thus doing a silent happy dance inside my soul! What does this mean? It means we're BFF and we're going to do each other's nails while we sing the *Frozen* soundtrack! No. Not quite. But it does mean that she wants to get to know more about me and the girls and Jonah (if I ever get him to talk to me, that is). I'll keep trying.

PENNY

Fatima had the cutest cat, little Mulder. He looked like a kitten, but Fatima said he was full grown. He was gray with little white feet. So sweet. He had this fuzzy toy on a stick that was really gross. It was like a chunk of chewed-up rat fur. He loved it, though. I was playing with him for a while, but when the party got loud, he hid in the bedroom. Fatima saw how much I liked him, so she asked me if I wouldn't mind coming by to feed him once in a while, like, if she was out late or whatever.

Great.

It was flattering to be asked. It was nice to know that she trusted me. She gave me the key to the sliding door.

Did you end up doing that? Going over to feed the cat?

A ton of times. She texted me when she needed me. I started to bring her some design stuff, too.

Like what?

At first, I brought a bunch of paint chips with yellows and oranges. She circled two colors that she liked, so the next time I came I brought her the two samples and those mini sponge brushes. I was like, Fatima Ro's totally gonna paint her house a color that I brought! I couldn't believe I had her phone number and her key. I still can't believe any of this happened, to be honest.

THE ABSOLUTION
OF BRADY STEVENSON

BY FATIMA RO

(excerpt)

B rady's eyes widened at the sight of the indoor basketball court with crisp blue and white lines. Sunlight filtered through skylights onto the yellow letters *TRP*, which were probably Paloma's father's initials. Brady knew Paloma had money. Her Range Rover gave that away. He just didn't know she had indoor-basketball-court money. This is what he'd come to see: the way the Morley kids lived. There were stories of over-the-top parties at this house. Brady thought he'd come by, check out the luxe life, and then leave. No need to get attached.

The hardwood court was so shiny Brady could've eaten off of it. It'd be incredible to play on it. He could almost hear his sneakers squeaking and the ball swishing through the basket. He missed the pure rough-and-tumble physicality of sports—not only of his sport, but all of them. At Morley, he held back in PE by pretending to be uninterested. Consequently, when captains chose teams, Brady got picked maybe ninth or tenth or twelfth: after guys who played a junior varsity sport but before the skinny kid with a peanut allergy bracelet. At his old school he was always chosen first. None of that mattered anymore, though—that's what Brady told himself. He was done with that nonsense of being first, of winning and losing.

"Do you want to shoot?" Sunny asked, seeing how impressed Brady was. "People come over to play all the time. Paloma won't mind. If her dad's home he'll come down and join you."

"Nah." It would feel too good to let loose on a court like that. Brady didn't want to be reminded of life as an athlete.

"It's a nice court, isn't it?" Sunny asked.

"Nice?" Brady laughed. Sunny obviously had money, too. Most of the kids at Morley Academy did. The degree of difference could only be measured by the size of their toys. Brady wasn't rich. His Morley tuition came from his grandparents, who insisted that their only grandson get another chance at success.

"Do you play any sports?" Sunny asked as she continued the house tour through a wine cellar with a hidden door to the game room.

"I wrestle," Brady blurted out of habit. He caught himself and shook his head. *Stupid, stupid, stupid.*

"You *do*?" Surprised, Sunny turned and placed her hand on the billiard table. "Wait. You're on the *team*?" She hadn't seen him with any of the wrestlers at school. He hadn't made any friends at school yet, as far as she could tell, which was one reason she had invited him tonight.

"No. I meant I *used* to wrestle," Brady stammered. "I don't now."

"Oh . . . why not?"

"Uh . . ." He pulled the strings of his sweatshirt. "I just don't."

"I'm sorry. You don't have to tell me." Sunny spun carefully on her heel. This wasn't going well. "You're better off anyway. Our wrestling team sucks. Not kidding. Lacrosse, that's our big thing. And girls' soccer. And boys' soccer. And swimming. Oh, and girls' fencing. Basically anything but wrestling." How could she get Brady to open up if he got defensive so easily? No more questions, she decided. She'd stick to on-the-surface topics and hope to get to know him better from there, let him sit back and get comfortable first.

MIRI

My phone just buzzed. Excuse me. [checks phone]

No problem.

Phew. It's nothing. [sighs] It's my mom from upstairs. She wants to know how much longer we'll be.

Just a few more minutes for today.

Okay. [texts back] I'm sure that if something happens, I'd get a call, but still. I can't stop checking my texts.

That's all right. Miri, how did your parents feel about your friendship with Fatima?

They were ecstatic.

Were they? Why was that?

[laughs] Are you kidding? My parents adored her. They're divorced; they argue about the weather, but they agreed about Fatima. I'll ask my mom for you. [texts] "Mom, what did you think of Fatima?" [looks up] They watched her interviews online and thought she was such a doll. They were dying to meet her but never had the chance. Mom kept telling me, "That

girl is so well-spoken! It's good to associate with quality people, Miri. You should write that you're friends with her in your college applications!" [laughs] Which I did. And it worked, mind you. I'm going to Brown.

Congratulations.

Thank you. [phone buzzes] [reads text] She wrote, "Good kid. Very smart. Media is bloodthirsty." Well, there you have it. Before Fatima came around, my parents hated the direction my social life was taking.

I guess they weren't big on the scene.

They thought the parties were a gateway to becoming a coke-head. "We built our businesses with sweat, not parties with pigs in a blanket!" [laughs] That's Mr. Tan. The only reason they tolerated the hosting was because I arranged to donate ten percent of the money to charity. I picked Dress for Success, which provides women in need with professional wardrobes for job interviews and such.

Nice.

I know. Fund-raising looked great on my transcript. That's why my folks eased up about the hosting. But when I took up with a successful author who stayed in on Saturday nights to watch

Willy Wonka and the Chocolate Factory? My parents were beyond relieved. By the way, we *never* served pigs in a blanket—just for the record. We would rather have starved. [phone buzzes] [texts back] "Okay, Mom! Stop texting now. It freaks me out because of Jonah! I'll tell you when we're done." [looks up] Sorry, Nelson. She wants to come down for a snack, but she's afraid of the camera.

She can come down. I can put this on hold for a few minutes.

No, no. Her hair's in rollers. She's not coming down.

I don't mind.

She minds. [sighs] [drinks from a water bottle] Anyway, I know that this is going to sound terrible, but the truth is that Jonah was a tragic YA character the second he walked through the Graham gate. Of course Fatima wrote about him! He had that brooding, mysterious thing happening. It begged for—no—it *screamed* for attention. That's why we were all so hung up on WWJ in the first place.

WWJ?

"What's with Jonah?" It was a thing between Soleil, Penny, and me because Jonah was so private. Before Fatima came into the picture we already had this little game going on to figure him out. We'd text each other "WWJ" sometimes a dozen times a day and hypothesize about his secret life.

What were some of the hypotheses?

Oh, we took it to a stupid level most of the time. I'm thoroughly embarrassed by it. I admit it. For example, one time at Fatima's house, Soleil was in Fatima's closet, looking through her dresses. Jonah sort of flipped out and went on this tirade about it being an invasion of privacy. It was the most random reaction, especially since Fatima was fine with it. She was fully transparent with us by that time. We didn't know what to think of Jonah's fit. So the girls and I texted each other, "WWJ?" And I joked, "He's into women's clothes, and the sight of the black-and-white DVF wrap dress pushed him over the top." [shakes head] I told you, it was stupidity. I shouldn't have said that. But in all honesty, our curiosity about Jonah came from a place of concern. Like Fatima, we cared about him. We wanted to know what was going on in his head so that we could support him in whatever way we could.

Stranger Than Fiction

The True Story Behind the Controversial Novel

The Absolution of Brady Stevenson

SOLEIL JOHNSTON'S STORY, PART 1 (continued)

DATE: September 26, 2016

TO: fatima.ro.author@gmail.com

FROM: soleil410@gmail.com

SUBJECT: Dear Fatima

Dear Fatima,

Thank you for having all of us at your housewarming. We had such a great time, and I was really inspired by your notes on *Undertow*. I hope you like the horseshoe gift. You're right—it's supposed to go over the door. But I still can't figure out if it should point up or down for good luck. I've seen myths for both ways, so I guess whichever way you prefer is fine.

I know what you mean about Jonah. He's sweet but so distant, with "a lot of blanks to fill in," as you said. You asked me to start writing to you with what I already know, so I'll start with studio art class, since that's where we met. For his "Social Commentary" project he made a sculpture out of all his old computer and phone chargers. Ms. Largos, our art teacher, said it spoke volumes about the wastefulness of modern society and the American family's monstrous hamster wheel of consumerism. It was the first time I saw Jonah smile, so I asked him to hang out with us. That night he came over to Penny's house. I let him in and gave him the grand tour while Penny and Miri were downstairs in Penny's home theater.

I'll write more soon.

Soleil

P.S. I'm working on a mixed-media art piece called *Doors*, it's a metaphor for the secrets people keep. Is it okay if I use a photo of your front door? No name or address or anything. If you're interested you can see the project on my Instagram #LargosStudioArt. It'd be awesome if you want to follow me. If not, that's okay. Just thought I'd share.

▶ ▶▶
PENNY

The news keeps using the word "sensational" to describe everything that's happened. I always thought that sensational meant something positive, like the same thing as "fantastic." But I guess it means more like entertaining?

Yes. Something that stirs up interest, causes a sensation. Does this surprise you?

Everything surprises me. I've been surprised for over a year.

That's understandable.

Can I ask you something?

All right.

Do you know where Fatima is now?

No.

Would you tell me if you did?

I don't see why not.

Okay. Well, I hope little Mulder's all right. He had the sweetest little face.

The Absolution of Brady Stevenson

BY FATIMA RO

(excerpt)

Sunny led Brady to the back staircase and talked about a safer subject than Brady's athletic history—the fact that there was a screening room downstairs with surround sound, a stocked concession stand, and an enormous U-shaped sofa.

In the basement, Paloma and Marni turned but did not get up from the ridiculously large couch that made them look like toddlers.

"Hi! Welcome to marathon night!" Paloma lifted her soda.

Brady pulled his tattered gray hoodie off his head.

"Check you out in civilian clothing," Marni said. "Loving this whole Morley Academy fugitive look you have going on."

"Hi." He waved awkwardly and then stuffed his hands in his pockets. "Thanks for, uh, inviting me."

"He speaks." Marni hit Sunny on the arm playfully.

Sunny was pleased that her friends seemed to like Brady, because she was hoping he would come around more often from now on. Good-looking guys were usually so loud, always horsing around in order to make their presence known. Their company was overbearing after the first twenty minutes. Brady's shyness made him so much more appealing than the tiresome hot guys of Morley.

The girls bickered rhythmically, as if their conversations were rehearsed. They quipped about which episode to start from, how long to microwave chocolate syrup, and whether Stainmaster carpeting was a brand of carpet or a special coating that could be added to any carpet. Amused by the girls' banter, Brady laughed quietly to himself. He was surprised at how relaxing it was to hang out with girls. The energy was higher but also gentler than palling around with his former guy friends, who, now that he thought about it, were constantly competing: with video games, with who should get the last slice of pizza, with whose sneakers were cleaner, whose car was the shittiest, nearly everything. It was also a relief to discover that while he was in the girls' company, he wasn't alone, but yet, he wasn't the center of attention.

Brady's parents wanted him to focus on schoolwork at Morley. But grades weren't going to be a problem now that he wasn't wrestling; there was more time than ever to study. He was eating better, too—he couldn't stop eating—since he didn't have to worry about making weight for tournaments. Food, so much more of it, helped him to concentrate better in class. As long as he was doing well in school, his parents would be happy. It couldn't hurt to spend a little bit of time with these girls.

As it turned out, Brady liked the home theater even better than the basketball court. The snacks were top quality, it was dark, and when Paloma pressed Play on the girls' favorite show, Brady didn't have to say a word.

[laughs] We forced Jonah to watch a *Pretty Little Liars* marathon. He was totally fine with it, so right then and there, I figured that settled Jonah's big secret. Obviously, Jonah was *gay*! Straight guys can't watch *PLL* without commenting on a girl-on-girl kiss. No way!

Sounds like a reasonable litmus test to me.

Right? He was so totally gay! Once in a while Jonah asked who was who and who did what, but basically that was all he said—no typical guy remarks about boobs, asses, or the girls' tiny little skirts. He mostly just listened to our commentary. Oh, and he ate all the Red Vines.

Did you share your assessment with Soleil and Penny?

Of course. I texted them. I felt like I won the whole game.

You texted them while you were with Jonah on the sofa?

It's a huge sofa.

Okay. So what did they have to say about Jonah being gay?

Penny texted back, "Ohhhhhhhh!" with a dozen *H*s. Soleil said she didn't believe it. She didn't get the gay vibe from him, as if she was some kind of expert. Clearly, she didn't want to believe it because she wanted to jump him. I called her on it, but she texted, "Just friends, I swear." But I knew that she had a thing for him. Jonah was definitely her type with his pale skin and the messy hair and his square shoulders. [laughs] Soleil has this thing for square shoulders and good posture. She says it emits confidence. To each her own. I texted her, "You're wearing your water bra." How obvious could she get? It's not like she was wearing that contraption for *us*. But she texted back, "No!!! It's laundry day—no other bras left!" Soleil is the world's worst liar. But whatever. They're her boobs. [glances off to the side] Excuse me, Nelson? Do you mind if we pull the shades down a bit? I just caught my reflection in that mirror over there, and this lighting is not flattering at all.

Stranger Than Fiction

The True Story Behind the Controversial Novel

The Absolution of Brady Stevenson

SOLEIL JOHNSTON'S STORY, PART 1 (continued)

FROM: fatima.ro.author@gmail.com

TO: soleil410@gmail.com

SUBJECT: RE: Dear Fatima

Genuine human connections require sharing something of substance. When I wrote *Undertow* I bled on those pages—and this is what I get in return??? Don't ever send me a "Dear Fatima" letter again.

FROM: soleil410@gmail.com

TO: fatima.ro.author@gmail.com

SUBJECT: RE: Dear Fatima

I'm sorry. I didn't mean to insult you. What should I send you?

FROM: fatima.ro.author@gmail.com

TO: soleil410@gmail.com

SUBJECT: RE: Dear Fatima

Figure it out.

Tell me about WWJ.

What?

WWJ.

How do you know about that?

[no response]

Did Miri tell you about it? She's saying that Jonah getting hurt is my fault, isn't she? She's throwing me under the bus!

I didn't say that.

I didn't mean anything by WWJ, I cross my heart. [crosses her heart] It was nothing serious.

What was it, then?

It started when Soleil first invited Jonah to my house. I didn't know him, but it was okay, a lot of kids come by, like I said, no big deal. But he was new, and I thought we would get to know him a little, but we were all on my sofa watching TV and trying to joke around with him, and he barely said a word. It was, like, way awkward.

So I texted, "What's with Jonah?" to Soleil and Miri. Miri texted back that he was gay, and that made sense, you know?

Okay.

That's how the whole WWJ thing started. But it was never supposed to turn into anything. I didn't mean for it to get out of hand. I never expected to find out about—

[silence]

Penny?

It's late. You should probably go.

Just a few more—

I can't. I have final exams soon. I'm not a brain like everyone else. I have to study. My parents already planned my graduation party.

The Absolution of Brady Stevenson

BY FATIMA RO

(excerpt)

The lunch tables in the courtyard were prime real estate at Morley Academy. Brady simply had to accept an invitation to sit there with the girls. The perfect early-autumn weather elevated his mood. He felt more social than usual. No one was paying any attention to him as he took a seat. It was as if he actually belonged. Sitting tall in his uniform, he liked being accepted in this school, with this group. He would just keep his mouth shut, that's all, and everything would be fine.

Marni and Sunny came straight from fifth-period AP English. They had veered Ms. Krauss away from her lesson on J. D. Salinger and initiated a lively class discussion on Thora Temple's *The Drowning*. "Ms. Krauss went on a tangent about the love story. I didn't get to finish my point about the extended metaphors," Marni said, continuing the conversation as the lunch period began. "I was going to say that the castles are supposed to be a reference to heaven."

"Yes, I read into that, too, especially in the last few chapters." Sunny nodded.

Brady listened. The girls' enthusiasm for a book and their ability to engage their English class on the topic impressed him.

Marni unfolded a paper napkin across her lap. "There's a line in the Bible about rooms in a mansion or something."

Sunny gestured with her fork as she spoke. "It's like Jules's mother is near death and about to enter the kingdom of heaven."

"Right." Marni took her phone out and started Googling. "Ugh, what is that line?" she mumbled. "It's going to annoy me all day if I don't find it."

In my Father's house are many mansions, Brady thought as he unwrapped his roast beef sandwich. He was Irish-Catholic and attended the five o'clock mass every Saturday night with his parents. Recently, he even went to chapel without them. This had surprised him. He had always thought that if given the freedom to choose, he would pass on church. It was comforting, though, so he couldn't stay away.

"Here it is," Marni said, chewing on a stalk of celery dipped in peanut butter. "'In my Father's house are many mansions; if it were not so, I would have told you. I go to prepare a place for you.'"

There's a Psalm of David that's similar, which Brady knew, too. *Thou preparest a table before me in the presence of mine enemies: thou anointest my head with oil; my cup runneth over. Surely goodness and mercy shall follow me all the days of my life: and I will dwell in the house of the Lord forever.*

"So, the castle represents God's house." Paloma looked from Marni to Sunny and waited for their approval.

Marni glanced dismissively over her shoulder. "Obviously."

Deflated, Paloma sat back in her chair.

"Sunny, did you notice that half the class has read *The Drowning* since we brought it up last time?" Marni asked.

"Trendsetters!" Sunny and Marni said in unison as they snapped a selfie. The routine started last year when all three girls started wearing scarves with brooches and nearly the whole student body copied.

Paloma sighed. "Have you read *The Drowning*?" she asked Brady. She didn't know any boys who'd read it, but since Brady was gay, she figured that he might have.

The book cover he'd seen online popped clearly into Brady's mind. It was a photograph of the bottom of a concrete pool and bubbles rising to the top, the title handwritten in slick, black ink. "No," he answered, keeping his knowledge of *The Drowning* to himself.

"Oh, it's brilliant. Really, truly." Paloma smiled weakly. "We're, like, uber fans."

Brady's heart softened a bit toward Paloma for trying to include him in the conversation. At the same time, Paloma's fondness for Brady grew an inch or two. She was relieved that he'd joined their group; she liked the calm, quiet way he balanced out the scale.

UNEDITED VIDEO FOOTAGE

NAKED TRUTH TV

Nelson Anthony interviews Miri Tan and Penny Panzarella

May 3–17, 2018 (cont'd)

© Push Channel 21, Bellmore, NY, 2018

▶ ▶▶I 0:44:20 / 3:04:23   ◀)) ━━ ⌐ ˥
                                                      ∟ ⌡

MIRI

[scrolling through phone] I was just reading a bit of *New York City* mag while you were setting up. Soleil was *so* dramatic.

Do you want to tell me more about her, since we're on the topic? The camera's on. I fixed the shades this time, the lighting looks great today.

Thanks. [applies lip gloss] Well, there's a lot I can say about Soleil. For one, that email from Fatima sent her into a spiral. I'd never seen Soleil that worked up before. Seriously, she showed up to school late, near tears. She wanted to please Fatima so badly. Looking back at it now, I think Soleil was developing a bit of an unhealthy obsession with her, honestly. She wouldn't show me the email at the time, but it's here now. [holds up phone] She asked Fatima to follow her overdue art project on Instagram. Who does that but the sad and the desperado? What an embarrassment. Anyway, Fatima requested that Soleil be more genuine. It all makes sense now. Soleil told me that she wanted to be more candid and share something of substance with Fatima.

So, what did Soleil do about it?

I *told* her what to do.

Which was . . .

To follow the most fundamental concept of human connections—show Fatima the precious truth. Soleil kept a journal practically every day, so I told her that she didn't necessarily have to write anything new for Fatima. The most inside/out writing would be diary entries that she never thought anyone would ever read, right? Remember how Fatima asked to see Soleil's notes at the Witches Brew?

Yes.

Fatima insisted that it not be edited in any way, so I knew that *that's* what she wanted to see—Soleil's authentic self, commenting on Jonah's uncensored Jonah-ness. So, I don't know what Penny has been telling you, but Soleil's emails to Fatima were *my* idea, not Fatima's. She never forced Soleil to write her anything.

Aha.

Soleil got a lot closer with Jonah and with Fatima after that, which was all she wanted. But ask me if I ever got a thank-you from Soleil out of it.

Did you?

[snorts]

Stranger Than Fiction

The True Story Behind the Controversial Novel

The Absolution of Brady Stevenson

SOLEIL JOHNSTON'S STORY, PART 2

DATE: September 29, 2016

TO: fatima.ro.author@gmail.com

FROM: soleil410@gmail.com

SUBJECT: stuff from my journal

I thought you'd be interested in stuff from my journal instead? It's unedited. I know that's important to you.

SEARCH: Jonah Nicholls wrestling team

→ Nicholls State University Athletics: NOT A MATCH

→ St. Bonaparte's School, Camden, New Jersey

→ Photo: NOT A MATCH

→ Burbank High School, Burbank, California

→ Photo: NOT A MATCH

SEARCH: Jonah Nicholls wrestler

→ Do you mean Jonah McNicholl?

NO. I DO NOT.

SEARCH VIDEOS: Jonah Nicholls

→ Jonah Hill Plays "Loser" High School Wrestler in SNL

Video: NOT A MATCH

→ Ultimate Barbecue Tips with Jonah and Nick:

NOT A MATCH

→ Nicholls Guitar Chords for cheaters: NOT A MATCH

(but bookmark this page for the guitar chords)

Damn it. WWJ????

TO: soleil410@gmail.com

FROM: fatima.ro.author@gmail.com

SUBJECT: RE: stuff from my journal

Better. More like this. Let's keep trying to reach out
to him. By the way, I looked at your *Doors* project on
Instagram. Followed you. It's a decent start, but if there's
a way to add even more depth to the concept, it could be
much stronger. Think about *Undertow*; there's a mother/
daughter story, there's a layer of romance, a layer of
religious symbolism. Any time you can create depth in a
piece of art, the better. Interested in seeing your progress.

[walks through the kitchen to the backyard] I thought we could talk out here today. It's so nice out.

This is perfect. What a great backyard. This is a ridiculously amazing pool.

Thanks. We just opened it. It's almost warm enough to go in. [sits at outdoor table]

Thank you for sitting with me again, Penny.

You're welcome. Our housekeeper made us a fruit platter. Help yourself.

It's beautiful. Thanks.

Things have gotten a lot worse for me, like, in the media and everything. [shakes head] That headline yesterday . . .

"Penny: Privileged Provocateur"?

Yeah. [sighs] And that picture of me is everywhere. It's from my cousin's wedding! I was junior bridesmaid. That's why I was wearing that jewelry. I changed out of my dress into sweats so that I could run around and do errands and decorate her wedding-night cabin before the reception. I don't wear Cartier with sweats. That picture made me look like an Orange County Housewife! [cries]

I'm sorry it's been so difficult for you. It's an awful headline. Terrible alliteration. How are you holding up?

I don't know. [composes herself] I guess I'm just avoiding the internet and TV and stuff. I'm trying to, anyway.

That's probably for the best.

[places a spiral notebook on the table] My father said it's important for me to share my side of things even if I don't want to. He thinks that all the negativity toward me has been caused by lack of information and misunderstanding. That's why we called you back.

Your father's a smart man.

He said if I tell my side maybe I won't get blamed as much. My parents hate that people are blaming me.

Of course they do.

Dad was the only one who didn't like her, you know.

Fatima?

Yeah.

Why was that?

Um, well, it wasn't so much *her* but the fact that me and my friends didn't spend as much time here anymore. Dad didn't grow up with money. He was basically a huge dork when he was my age, so he built this house to finally have, like, the cool place to hang out. He was proud to have lots of people around to enjoy it and keep him company. He works from home a lot. He books talent for concerts and TV specials.

I see.

But I was the first one to get a driver's license, and my friends didn't want to be here anymore. They wanted to go to Fatima's house, so that's where we went. It was also kinda nice to have, like, freedom. [pulls grapes from the platter]

Sure it was.

But when Mom told Dad that Fatima was, like, a legit author, he thought she'd be a good influence on me. He always wanted me to read more. [eats a grape] He hates her now, though.

I understand.

[looks toward the window] *Dad!* [leans forward] Don't watch! Just go inside. God! I can do it. It's *fine*. I got it. Go inside. [sits back] Sorry.

That's okay. He's just concerned. It's nice that he's so supportive.

I know. It's not, like, a normal thing that happened. [glances at the window again] Plus, I think he's mad at himself for not, like, following his instincts about her or something. I heard him talking to Mom about it.

So now he wants to clear your side of the story.

Uh-huh. [eats]

You said over the phone that you wanted to talk about the Undertow meetings in particular?

Yeah, um, Miri's meetings?

Right.

Well, Miri wanted to start a group for *Undertow* fans at school to read aloud and analyze stuff. And she also wanted to teach about the theory of human connections. She thought it'd bring the student body closer, 'cause we have cliques and that kinda thing. [sighs] It's hard being in my group. People think that because of money we get favoritism when we don't. I know *I* don't. I have a C average, and I got, like, three detentions for my skirt being two inches too short. Anyways, Miri wanted to break down social misconceptions at school or something like that. She gets crazy passionate.

[opens her notebook] So, one night we were at the Witches Brew, and Fatima told us that there are actual steps you could follow in order to make authentic human connections. I took these notes. [flips through the pages] We all took notes; I kept a notebook, Miri kept a notebook, Soleil was on her laptop. Jonah didn't take notes, but he listened and ate pork sliders.

When Fatima spoke she was just, like, heartfelt. You paid attention to her. You know what I mean? You *listened*. [pause] She started out talking to the four of us about the steps and how they worked for her with strangers. And then in, like, fifteen minutes, the whole café started listening. People turned their chairs, and it became this *thing*.

That's amazing.

For real. She was super charming, you know?

It's obvious.

Here's the stuff I wrote down. It's weird to think about this, but there are random people from the café that night who wrote the same notes. Uh . . . [reading from a page] "Look each other in the eyes. This is the most basic principle of making an authentic connection, but it's surprising how rarely people do this." [flips pages] "Use the person's name. This instantly makes your subject feel valued and seen." Sometimes Fatima would pause after an important sentence and look at you and force you to think about it. Like, she said, "That's all any of us wants, isn't it? To be seen and valued." And then she stopped right there and looked at everyone until that sentence sunk in. [shakes head]

She was very charismatic.

Uh-huh. [sighs] It's kinda not fair.

What do you mean?

Well, most people are lucky if they're talented at one thing. Like, you'd think it'd be enough for her to be a writer, but Fatima was good at speaking and theories, plus her style was *Vogue*-worthy. The rest of us are just, like, trying not to fail physics class, you know?

I understand.

But anyways, there's more. [reads from notebook] "Be observant of your subject and make an observant statement. Mirror their body language. This makes people feel comfortable. Ask open-ended questions." And then I took down a list of open-ended questions . . . [takes deep breath]

You know, I realize Fatima's delivery was intense, but the steps seem like sound advice to me, as far as techniques for effective communication are concerned.

That's what I thought, too, at first. But somewhere . . . somewhere it went wrong. I think it was the open-ended questions. [pauses] If she didn't have so many of those maybe I wouldn't have tried so hard to find answers.

[Penny's father calls from the window] Tell him about the cult meeting, Penny! Tell him that!

[Penny looks to window] Dad! Stop! I'm fine! Just stay inside. And don't call it that! [shoos him away] . . . Sorry.

It's okay.

I was just going to tell you about the meeting.

Go ahead.

Well, Miri posted an announcement:

UNDERTOW *DISCUSSION and FATIMA RO'S*
THEORY REVEALED
GRAHAM COURTYARD
Saturday 9 p.m.

Ahh, the courtyard at night . . .

Yup.

I see where this is going.

Miri knew what she was doing.

And the stars?

They were perfect.

The Absolution of Brady Stevenson

BY FATIMA RO

(excerpt)

After a long day at school, Brady was happy to come home to Cletus, his eleven-year-old boxer mix. He rubbed his dog's wrinkly face with both hands and greeted him. "Hey, Clee! Hey, my main man!" He secured Cletus's leash and led him outside.

When Brady was in middle school, he had too often been lazy about walking his dog. He'd come home tired and hungry from practice. All he wanted was a video game break or a nap. Sometimes he'd connect two leashes so he could stand in the doorway while the dog walked over the patio and peed on the grass. Brady had recently spent time apart from Cletus. He missed the simple presence of his dog breathing and existing beside him. When they reunited, Cletus's muzzle was whiter than Brady remembered. It had been turning whiter and whiter since, a reminder of the preciousness of their time together. These days, Brady walked Cletus twice around the block every single afternoon, rain or shine, with a lump in his throat full of gratitude.

The duo returned from their walk to a package from Amazon on the front stoop. "We got a package! See that?" Brady lifted the box and let Cletus sniff.

Cletus wagged his tail and darted his head from side to side.

"Does it smell good?" Brady asked in a high-pitched voice. "Does it smell like Axe and Bluetooth headphones?"

Inside the house, Brady let the dog off the chain. He took the package up to his bedroom with a seltzer and a plate of leftover chicken drumsticks. A voicemail played in the kitchen. BEEP! "This is Michelle at Dr. Nihati's office. Dr. Nihati needs to make a change in schedule and would like to move Brady's session from five p.m. to four p.m. this Monday, if that's okay. Please give us a call back to confirm. We apologize for any inconvenience. Thank you." BEEP!

Brady closed his bedroom door behind Cletus, who was licking his chops. "This chicken is not for you. Bones are bad news, bud. Bad, bad news." Brady put his food on the desk and sliced the package open with a pair of scissors. Taking inventory of his Amazon order gave Brady a thrill. He could understand how easy it would be to form an addiction to online shopping, or anything, really—gambling or gaming or internet porn or whatever.

iPhone water resistant case with built-in screen protector
Anker wireless Bluetooth headphones with 8-hr. playtime
Trashed: Famous Art Created from Garbage by Felix Woo
AXE body spray, Excite, 4 oz. (pack of 3)
Car console organizer with 6 large pockets + adjustable

dividers for keeping miscellaneous items

PUMA front-zip jacket with sherpa-lined hood

2 packs of Calvin Klein men's 3-pack cotton stretch boxer
briefs in black

*Boys of '67: From Vietnam to Iraq, The Extraordinary Story of a
Few Good Men* by Charles Jones

The Drowning by Thora Temple

Brady and Cletus lay on the bed surrounded by Brady's new things. He unwrapped the body spray and placed each can in the compartments of the car caddy. He imagined the stock guy in the Amazon warehouse who had pulled his orders from the shelves. Brady could appreciate a quiet job like that. At Amazon, he could drive around in a little cart from aisle to aisle. He'd probably be allowed to listen to his music all day, too; that'd be a really nice perk. The best thing about it was that filling orders probably didn't require much human interaction, yet the work would ultimately make people happy by fulfilling their wishes.

With a chicken drumstick in one hand and *The Drowning* in the other, Brady read about Jules and her boyfriend, Sam. The book detailed their rushed, heated car sex in the parking lot of their Catholic school and Sam's jealousy over text messages that were, strangely, from Jules's biological father. The beautiful, very graphic language in a book that was supposedly for teens shocked Brady. *The Drowning* was juicy. *The Drowning* was hot.

This is what girls read?

Brady kept on reading long after he'd finished his after-school snack. He was breathing heavier now, rapt as Sam's hand slid up Jules's shirt and Jules's skirt inched high up over her thighs.

So, this is what the hype is all about.

Several chapters later, Margaret was taking Jules to the doctor to take a "proper" pregnancy test instead of a drugstore stick. The anxious mother prayed the rosary while her daughter's fate was decided.

No wonder . . .

Brady picked up a pencil and scratched a note in the margin next to the words "drugstore stick": *Pregnancy tests. How do these things work?* He'd always wanted to know. He planned to look it up later and then fill in the answer. He had a habit of marking up his books with notes like these—questions, opinions, sometimes memories that the story brought to mind.

Brady turned page after page. Cletus snored and drooled. By chapter sixteen, Margaret and Jules were on a flight, traveling over the Atlantic Ocean toward Dublin. Jules was shushing her mother, who was reading from the Bible, *"If we confess our sins, He is faithful and just to forgive us our sins, and to cleanse us from all unrighteousness."* Brady underlined the passage. His cell phone buzzed. When he looked up to reach for it, he was surprised at how dark his room had become.

> SUNNY
>
> Heeeey! Thora Temple signing
> Sunday night at Book Revue. Dreams
> do come true! COME WITH US!!!

Brady couldn't believe Sunny's timing. Of course he should meet Thora Temple. He sat with his phone for a few minutes to avoid seeming overeager. He scratched Cletus's neck while he contemplated how to sound casual, like a guy who hadn't been reading *The Drowning* all afternoon.

> BRADY
>
> I dunno.

> Come on! We need someone to
> stop us from embarrassing ourselves
> with our fangirling!

> OK, I guess.

> Yaaaas!!!☺!!!

Brady turned on his reading lamp. He studied the photo of Thora Temple on the back flap. She was in her twenties? She looked more like eighteen or nineteen. He wondered whether some people were destined to be so accomplished at a young age or whether anybody could do it given the right set of circumstances and a sufficient collection of inspirational don't-give-up/puppies-climbing-up-a-staircase memes. Brady knew what it meant to do something memorable at a young age. But memorable isn't the same as admirable. He should hold on to his dream of becoming a surgeon. No offense to Amazon stock boys, but medicine would be a better way to live up to his potential and give back to the society that had afforded him countless privileges, as many people had reminded him.

So, Brady would be seeing Thora Temple in person. Just like that. Or maybe it wasn't "just like that." Maybe months or years had been leading up to this meeting.

Thora Temple's half smile in her author photo was full of knowing. She looked as if she had answers to the questions Brady had been thinking about for a very long time. If he were to ask her something this Sunday, it would be: *Do you believe in absolution, the cleansing of the body, mind, and soul? Is that why you wrote* The Drowning? He wrote these questions on the inside cover, knowing that in person, he'd never be able to put those words together without sounding like the biggest fangirl of the group. He might be able to answer these questions himself by the time he finished the book. That's what he hoped for. If *The Drowning* was half as good as the girls claimed it to be, the odds were with him. Brady rested his head against his dog's thick, warm neck and breathed in the earthy, oily scent. For now, this smelled like absolution to him.

Penny's father is going to tell you that Fatima Ro brainwashed us into holding a meeting and recruiting new members into her "cult" [uses air quotes]. But I am stating for the record: [looks straight into the camera] Undertow Society was a *club*, like Students Against Driving Drunk, Young Entrepreneurs, and Speech and Debate. I should know, I'm Debate captain. I repeat: Undertow Society was a club. Not a cult. And it wasn't Fatima's concept in the first place. She would've been perfectly content with the four of us and a pot of green tea at the café. I deserve all the credit for Undertow Society since it was my idea and my idea alone to bring readers together in appreciation of literature and to celebrate its positive impact on our lives.

Stranger Than Fiction

The True Story Behind the Controversial Novel

The Absolution of Brady Stevenson

SOLEIL JOHNSTON'S STORY, PART 2 (continued)

MEETING NOTES

October 15, 2016

Undertow Society Meeting #1

Meeting objectives: Establish a safe, open forum for fans of *Undertow* and Fatima Ro where we can get to know one another in the spirit of the Theory of Human Connections and practice the steps of developing human connections.

I. Roll Call

II. Exercise A: switch tables and lie beside someone you're not friends with; share the sky

III. Reading from *Undertow* by Miri, excerpt from Chapter 14

IV. Discussion/analysis of excerpt

V. Introduce the concepts of the Theory of Human Connections: Miri will give a practical example of making a human connection; steps to making a human connection

VI. Connect the excerpt and *Undertow* as a whole to Fatima's development of the Theory of Human Connections

VII. Exercise B: apply the Theory of Human Connections! Look each other in the eyes; acknowledge each other's presence; make and express an observation; answer an open-ended question—What do you want from this life?

VIII. Discussion: effects of Exercise A; how to apply the theory to our daily lives; how the theory can change society

IX. Closing: read favorite *Undertow* lines—open to all attendees

▶ ▶▶

PENNY

So. Like. Miri sat on the same table Fatima picked the night we brought her to the courtyard, and when Soleil and I tried to sit up there with her at the start of the meeting, she told us we should all get our own tables so that we could spread ourselves among the group. I was like, "What do you mean *spread* ourselves?" And she goes, "If people have questions or anything." But what questions would people have? I mean, come on. I saw what she was doing, trying to be the center of the meeting— trying to literally *be* Fatima Ro. She sat up and crossed her legs like Fatima and even spoke like her, talking about how we should strive to share our "precious truths." [pauses] I believed in the theory too, you know? For real. I thought we were going to run the society together the way we planned at the Witches Brew. Fatima even helped us come up with what to do—the agenda and all. It was interesting talking about human connections and thinking of who we should recruit. It was like a fun kind of homework, and I hate homework.

So how did the rest of the meeting go?

[groans] It was pretty much, like, *The Miri Show.* She talked about herself and how the theory has helped her and Fatima become close friends. She didn't really care about analyzing the book or spreading the theory. She wanted an audience to listen

to how she was besties with the famous author. I didn't even want to listen anymore.

But how did the group respond to her?

They were so into it; it was gross how into it they were.

And what about Soleil? What was she doing during that time?

Soleil? Oh, she wasn't even paying attention, 'cause she was on a table whispering with Jonah. I'm not sure how he ended up over there with her; he was supposed to make an authentic connection with a new member. [pauses] So, maybe it wasn't so awful that Miri wanted to be the leader or whatever. But I thought that knowing Fatima and learning about making deeper connections was supposed to help us break the cliques and grow closer as friends, but we weren't using the theory as a group. People were just using it for, like, their own individual reasons.

Huh.

Miri was using it to get closer to Fatima, and Soleil was getting closer to Jonah.

You're right.

And I wasn't using it at all. I was just . . . [pause]

You were what?

I don't know . . . the *cat sitter.*

That sucks. What a crappy feeling.

Uh-huh. And another thing? One night there wasn't any cat food left. I told Fatima she was running out, but did she listen? No!

Oh, no.

Yeah. So, what did I do because I'm, like, a good person and I didn't want the cat to starve? I went and I bought it myself. It's, like, this special diet stuff for a sensitive digestive tract. It was expensive. It doesn't come in small packages, either. It was the big bag or nothing. It was heavier than the cat. I left the receipt on the table, but Fatima never offered to pay me back.

Wow. I would've been pissed.

I *was* pissed! I just didn't have the nerve to say so. She bought a whole house but wouldn't give me $79.88.

[Penny's father calls from the back door] Penny! Show him the book excerpt!

[Penny turns to face her father] I'm going to! Go away, Dad! [sighs] Ugh. I'm sorry.

No problem. Do you have an excerpt for me?

It's the *Undertow* passage Miri read that night. [unfolds a few sheets of paper from inside her notebook] My dad made a copy of it. He thought you might want it.

Yes, I do. Thank you. This is great. [holds the excerpt to the camera]

Sloan Kettering calls it a chemotherapy suite, as if it's desirable, as if it's the VIP lounge of cancer. At Sloan, the word "suite" really means, "Hey, sucks to be you in this shithole, but here's a pleather recliner and a flat-screen TV."

Mom likes to binge-watch her favorite comedies while she gets her cocktail of anti-nausea meds. She says that the only way to get through something like this is with familiar plotlines with familiar punch lines delivered by familiar faces. Sitcoms are Mom's emotional comfort food, especially now, when she's not particularly interested in actual food. I'm not a sitcom fan. The acting's corny. The laughter's forced. Parents are overinvolved in their kids' lives—always sitting on the edge of the bed for a heart-to-heart, always yelling at coaches on the soccer field or making their kids' egg-parachute projects. Mom asks me to choose the show this time, so I say *Frasier*, the one show of hers I can tolerate because at least it's smart and there's no cookie-cutter suburban family of four.

Today, Frasier is pretending to be Jewish in order to date a Jewish woman he met at the mall. When she shows up at his apartment, Frasier's father stuffs the Christmas tree in the bathroom, and brother Niles, dressed as Jesus for a Christmas pageant, hides in the kitchen. Mom and I laugh at the appropriate places. Laughter is, as they say, the best medicine.

Without warning, my mind wanders to a morbid place: by Christmastime Mom won't be here anymore. I try to shake the thought, but each time the *Frasier* audience laughs, the thought rushes back. The next time I see this *Frasier* episode will probably be by chance. I'll be flipping through channels one day and come across it, and instantly I'll remember that the last time I watched it was with Mom in the chemo "suite" before she died. This episode, this show, is now ruined for me forever. Or maybe it has become more precious? I won't know how I feel about it until it happens—the inevitable channel surfing and *Frasier* sighting. When will it happen? This is one more thing to fear. The audience will still be laughing, but my mother will be dead.

I miss a joke (something between Frasier and Niles), so Mom slaps me on the arm. I chuckle and adjust my face. The nurse comes in to attach Mom's tubes and start the chemo drip. As we watch the TV, I suddenly wish that we were laughing at our own stories instead—we haven't told our own stories all year. I want to turn the TV off and ask Mom to tell me about the time she went on a date to the beach and the pads popped out of her bikini top. I want to hear her describe the way they "floated on top of the water like soggy dinner rolls." I want to tell her again about my first date in seventh grade with Trevor Logan and how his mom came, sat beside him in the movie theater, and fed Trevor snacks from her purse.

I'm panicking inside at the thought of losing our moments and stories, our words, our laughs. I want to hear them and tell them now. There's no time left. I won't be able to rewind us or find us on television when I'm flipping through channels late at night. Tell me, tell me, tell me, and I'll tell you. We had all this time, but it's over now. Between counting medications and arguing and avoiding each other, we squandered it.

I turn the volume down on Frasier and Niles and Martin and Eddie the dog, and I turn to Mom.

"What happened to the sound?" she asks.

"Hey, Mom, tell me about that time on your date. Remember? That date to the beach . . ."

Mom laughs even before she starts the story. Her laughter cracks my heart wide open. I listen to her voice, and I bleed and bleed.

I remember this part. Fatima's really, really good. This is some emotional stuff.

Right? It got to me, even though I was mad at Miri. It got to everybody—the whole atmosphere, I guess—the stars, the reading. I also had Fatima's voice in my head about sharing our truths. I paired up with Natalie Singh. She was, like, the top of our class, as in a 4.2 GPA. It was my idea to invite her, because she's a good role model and everything. I didn't think I'd end up on a table with her. She seemed nice enough, but I'd maybe said two sentences to her before in my whole life. It was way awkward lying there with her. When we sat up, we were supposed to make eye contact, acknowledge each other's presence in the here and now, and exist together in that moment. That was all stuff Fatima talked about, but it was a different thing to try it with someone, like, in real life. It's sorta like the person in front of you changes from a being into a someone. Oh, I don't know how to put it, but it worked. I felt like I *saw* Natalie during that.

It sounds like it was incredibly impactful. You know, I'll be speaking with Natalie and a few other students who were there that night.

You will?

Yes.

Oh, good, cool. Tell Natalie I said hi.

I will. I'm interested to hear Natalie's take on the theory exercise.

Me too, for real.

Tell me about the open-ended question. Hey, do you like what I did there? That was an open-ended question about an open-ended question.

[laughs]

Sorry. I couldn't resist. Go ahead.

[laughs] Well, um, the question was, "What do you want from this life?" [pause] I told Natalie that she was noticeable because she was the top of the class. Miri was so driven, obviously. [rolls eyes] Soleil was pretty, and Jonah was the new guy. They were all noticeable for something. Then I said that I wanted to be noticed, too. [pauses]

What is it?

I don't know why, but I felt like crying when I told Natalie that. It's stupid. Whatever.

Not "whatever." It was your precious truth. It was important to you. There's nothing stupid about that.

I guess, thanks. I thought about the question for a long time. I kept trying to come up with a different answer, but I couldn't. "You can't hide your true self." That's what Fatima said.

She was right about that, wasn't she?

[silence]

Wasn't she?

[nods]

Any thoughts on that?

[shakes head]

All right. Well, your father called Undertow Society a cult. Do you think Fatima's following was a cult?

What? [looks up] Ew, no. It wasn't a cult. We just liked the book and the theory. And we liked Fatima, that's all. We didn't light candles or anything, and we weren't chanting. Those were only rumors.

What is a cult, in your opinion?

Uh, well, it's when there's a guru guy who's, like, super weird, and people go along with his kooky ideas even if they don't make sense. He has, like, a bunch of followers who are never allowed to leave. I would never join anything like that.

NATALIE SINGH

The theory exercise felt like we were becoming friends in fast-forward. I don't want that to sound superficial because I don't think it was. I think that if both parties are sincere, it really is possible to get to accelerate friendship. With Penny, I'd seen her around school and always thought of her as quite confident because of her influential circle of friends. They're part of the Graham Sevens—students who started at Graham in seventh grade.

What makes that so special?

There's the money, for one thing. Most families wait to send their kids to Graham in high school because why waste the money on seventh and eighth grade? For their families, it's not a big deal. And then there are the relationships. Those who enroll as freshmen all begin as strangers, while the Graham Sevens have already been friends for two years. Those circumstances make the Sevens more powerful, in a sense. Teachers and faculty don't admit to favoritism, but they definitely choose Sevens over others for leadership roles, because they know them better. You have to work harder to get ahead if you're not one of them.

I see.

I went to one of Penny's parties. I could only afford one; I'm here on scholarship. It was pretty lavish. I assumed Penny was just as bold as the whole production. But after speaking with her, I saw how insecure she really was. It was surprising, but it helps me to understand how she would be influenced by someone like Fatima Ro. [pauses] In terms of Fatima's theory and the exercise? I learned that both parties of a conversation have to respect the other person's thoughts and feelings in order to achieve an authentic human connection. Penny and I were receptive to the exercise. It's why we're friends today. Tell her I said hi back.

I will. Natalie, may I ask what your answer was to the open-ended question, "What do you want from this life?"

Sure. I said that I wanted a fair chance. That was my answer: a fair chance in life. I think that's all we can ask for, don't you?

EMMA IRVING

Miri asked us what we wanted out of life and I said, "*This!
This* is what I want—to live and breathe the theory of human
connections—to be open and honest, to know people on a spiri-
tual level and be a positive force in society." At the first meeting,
I made an authentic connection with a complete stranger within
the span of five minutes. And I wasn't even drunk! [laughs] I have
to tell you with sincerity that I was inspired. I couldn't wait to do
more and to pay it forward. My head was spinning about young
people squandering time and words and opportunities. I didn't
want to squander. I wanted to live inside/out and start a whole
movement. I thought, how rich would our lives be if we related
more deeply with the people we loved and spoke to strangers to
feel that Fatima Ro *simpatico*? What could we achieve if we got to
know our classmates, our neighbors, if we worked together and
helped each other? [laughs] [shakes head] I can't believe what a
sucker I was for the whole scheme. I never would've guessed that
Fatima was such a whack job. But isn't that the way with a lot of
these people? There's that fine line between genius and batshit
crazy. God. [shakes head] I was such a *fan.*

QUINN DONNER

Undertow was my favorite book. Hands down. Miri and Soleil
turned me on to it. I'd never heard of Fatima Ro until the two
of them started talking about her in AP English. They basically

made Fatima famous at Graham with their class discussions and then the secret society. Our teacher, Ms. Grauss, was Fatima Ro–obsessed, too. Obsessed. And Ms. Grauss is très cool; she's that teacher who lets us read on the lawn when it's warm out. So, I was down for the whole *Undertow* thing. The meetings. The readings. All. Of. It. I even went to the book signing at Book Revue. I was third in line. Ms. Grauss gave me extra credit, not that I did it for that reason. Soleil and Miri wouldn't take extra points; they said meeting Fatima was a reward in and of itself. I needed the boost, though. Sometimes you have to take advantage. Graham is crazy competitive. It's like that survivor show *Naked and Afraid* except in uniforms. Look. I got a picture with her. [shows a selfie with Fatima Ro] She was so warm toward me. It's lame that people are blaming Fatima for what happened to Jonah. No way was it her fault. I feel terrible for the guy and all, but not too terrible, if you know what I'm saying. And can you really fault Fatima for writing about him? Jonah came to her like a novel on a platter, practically. Fatima Ro is pretty much my idol. Her and Hillary Clinton. [pauses] Wait. Was the *Naked and Afraid* comment too much? Can you scratch that? I don't want to disrespect my school.

MARCUS DEAN

Shit. That meeting? That was just a lot of hippie psychobabble mumbo jumbo. But Quinn was into it, so I went. I go where Quinn goes. I'm pussy-whipped.

THE ABSOLUTION
OF BRADY STEVENSON

BY FATIMA RO

(excerpt)

"I see her!" Sunny bounced on her heels and slapped Brady on the arm.

"Oh my god, she is so cute," Marni whispered.

Paloma lifted her phone above her head. "I think I can get a shot from here."

Brady peeked through the crowd. Secretly, he was just as excited as the girls were to catch a glimpse of Thora Temple. He had finished reading *The Drowning* and couldn't stop thinking about Jules, Sam, Margaret, Irish castles, and forgiveness as a gift to others and to oneself. Like the character Jules, Brady knew firsthand what it felt like to be an embarrassment to his parents. Through *The Drowning*, Thora Temple seemed to read his mind like no one else had, including his therapist, Dr. Nihati.

Brady spotted the author through the spinning rack of literary postcards and past a tall blonde in spiked boots. He immediately felt that Thora's wisdom was too large for her body, and so it had no recourse but to spill out of her as words upon words upon words. He stared as Thora tossed her wild hair behind her shoulders and posed for a selfie with a fan. Her half smile matched her author photo—she was exactly who Brady had envisioned she'd be. "It is, of course!" he heard her say playfully, but didn't catch the context.

The line bunched up toward the front, blocking the author's table and Brady's view. He shuffled his feet. He'd have to wait his turn to see her again.

"Oh, buck up. This isn't so bad, is it?" Marni asked.

"No. It's fine. I like bookstores," Brady said.

"I'll be right back. I have to pee." Marni patted Brady on the back. "Save my spot."

"I'll hold your book," Sunny said.

Brady looked down at *The Drowning* in his hands and laughed at himself—he now owned two copies. As he waited, he contemplated what to say to Thora. The novel hit so close to home that Brady couldn't even admit that he'd read it. It's funny, he thought, the reasons we don't talk about something are because it's either not important or because it's too important. There was no way he could ask her the questions he'd written in his copy at home.

He decided instead to tell Thora that writers are our most valuable artists. In these modern technological times, a book is the simplest, easiest, cheapest form of entertainment. Even with iPads and smartphones, the book is still indispensible. This would be Brady's way of thanking Thora simply for being a writer. During a time when Brady couldn't watch television or use the internet, books had kept him company. Words whiled away hours that he might've otherwise spent feeling down, feeling ashamed, feeling . . . just *feeling*.

As he moved up the line, Brady's affection for Thora deepened. He suddenly wanted her to know him inside and out, the way she knew her characters: Sam, an emotionally abusive older boyfriend; Jules, a selfish, unappreciative daughter; and Margaret, a rigid, controlling mother. All these people were hurt and flawed. They were ugly inside. But Thora gave them resilience and hope. Brady wanted Thora to know him as deeply as she knew them, because even in her least lovable characters, Thora found goodness.

"I'm back." Marni strained her neck to peek over the line. "Did I miss anything?"

"No, nothing," Brady said, but it felt like a lie.

MIRI

My Undertow meeting was a major turning point in people's lives. Quinn Donner, Emma Irving, they already loved the book. But after my meeting, they were fully committed to the theory of human connections. They made friends with Greg Tivoli and Minka Neeves that night, maybe lifelong soul mates, because of the theory.

That's great.

No no no. You don't understand. Greg Tivoli collects back-scratchers from amusement parks, and Minka Neeves gave a school presentation on taxidermy.

[laughs] Not the most popular kids at Graham?

They had *no* friends before this meeting. They weren't even friends with each other! [laughs] That is the power of the theory of human connections. And that is why Emma and Quinn and I decided to start a movement.

Stranger Than Fiction

The True Story Behind the Controversial Novel

The Absolution of Brady Stevenson

SOLEIL JOHNSTON'S STORY, PART 2 (continued)

In attendance:

Miri, me (Soleil), Jonah, Penny, Marissa June Weaver, Gaby Simpson, Miles Kelly, Elena Westcott, Yasmin Contreras, Yael Levy, Toby Levy, Ursula Houston, Mackenzie Ryan, Marcus Dean, Inés Rodriguez, Victoria Unger, Ava Balasteras, Greg Tivoli, Quinn Donner, Alexa Nagatsu, Emma Irving, Minka Neeves, Natalie Singh

PENNY

Even though I was tired of Miri, I stayed the whole time because I was a loyal friend. I was trying to be a bigger person and not let my feelings about Miri spoil Fatima's message. But do you know what happened then?

No. What?

I was telling Miri how good everything went. I was being *nice*, when Emma Irving and Quinn Donner swooped right in and pushed me aside. They were like, "Oh, Miri, that was the greatest passage ever in the history of all passages!" and "I never thought I could connect with someone as instantly as this. We're, like, soul mates with Greg and Minka for life now." They were being completely fake. As if they'd ever hang out with Greg or Minka. Taxidermy is so nasty. For real! Like, get a better hobby, Minka, maybe with *alive* animals.

[laughs]

But anyways, they were all, "Let's start a *movement*. We can change the world through human connections, with Fatima's guidance." Ugh. It was so *obvious*; all they wanted was to meet Fatima, who was Miri's BFF in the whole world. And I saw this look in Miri's eyes that really creeped me out.

What look?

Like she was on a power trip or something. Emma and Quinn were kissing up to her so bad. And who was I? Nobody, as far as they were all concerned. God. *I* was the one with Fatima's house key. *I* was the one who refilled Fatima's refrigerator when she got low on milk and juice.

You did?

Yeah.

Huh.

Only a few times.

Did she ask you to do that?

The first time. After that I just did it to be nice.

That was *nice.*

Thank you. I thought so. [sighs] Oh, and *I* was the one who brought her fabric swatches for window treatments. They were really high quality, too. One was blue with a white geometric pattern. Another one was white with a blue geometric pattern.

[sighs] After the meeting I was standing around the courtyard like an idiot. Miri had her new Undertow squad or whatever, and where were Soleil and Jonah? Nowhere. They left together. I guess something happened underneath that blanket. I wasn't jealous. I just, like, never felt so alone before, not even the time I snuck upstairs during one of my own parties to take a nap.

The Absolution of Brady Stevenson

BY FATIMA RO

(excerpt)

M arni was reading a passage from *The Drowning*.

> *Jules didn't test the temperature with her toes or take time*
> *to warm her skin under the sun. She didn't deserve a*
> *gradual, measured cooling. She ran head-on toward the*
> *water and dove straight into the ocean. It's the only way*
> *to sneak up on the body: take it from dry brittle hair and*
> *cracked elbows and knees to wet at the roots and bone-*
> *chilled in an instant. Trick the body into believing it's pure*
> *again, as clean as the day it was born. Submerge. Shock.*
> *Trick. It's possible to deceive it, but only for as long as you*
> *can hold that one bitter-cold breath.*

Marni sat cross-legged on the table. Her intonations, the way she breathed and paused as she read, were familiar to her friends because she borrowed them from Thora Temple.

When Brady read that same passage at home, he curled into the fetal position under his covers and held his breath to see if he could feel pure for that long. Tonight, Brady couldn't connect with Thora's words at all, not with these poseurs around him quoting passages from *The Drowning* as if they were Demi Lovato lyrics. They ruined the excerpt and the theory. Brady's appreciation for *The Drowning* was quiet and internal, as it should be. Marni and her crew were turning this into a rock concert. What did anybody here have to feel impure about anyway—ruining expensive shoes on a muddy night? Thora's words belonged to him alone, not to this goody-goody bunch of faux fans.

The last thing Brady wanted was to connect with Talia Cohen, a girl wearing a headband with cat ears and carrying a purse she made from a cereal box; he most certainly didn't want to lie on a lunch table with her under the stars. At the risk of being rude, Brady left his assigned place. He went over to Sunny's table, tapped Gary Hodges on the shoulder, and, as politely as possible, asked Gary to get lost.

Sunny turned her head. "What's up?"

"Hi." Brady settled beside her.

Sunny had a blanket over her legs. She spread it out to cover them both. At that moment, Marni's reading faded into the background. As the space under the blanket warmed and Sunny's knee fell against Brady's leg, all Brady could think about was chapter twelve—the chapter that led up to Jules's and her mother's confrontation: Jules gets caught in her bedroom with her boyfriend, Sam. She's half naked in his lap with her legs wrapped around his back.

Marni continued, *"Jules felt that childhood had slipped away so far and so fast that she could hardly recognize herself, and she didn't like the person she had become . . .'"* Instead of reflecting on his own fallen childhood, all the arousing scenes of *The Drowning* replayed in Brady's mind—those passages Marni and Sunny referred to as the "sexy times."

Sunny had let Brady into her life without hesitation, and Brady had been lonely and reserved all these weeks, so he said, "Oh, screw it," to himself and reached his hand out toward her. Sunny caught her breath as Brady's hand slid inside her jacket and grazed her stomach. It took a moment for her to register that his touch wasn't accidental; Brady wasn't just stretching or joking around; he meant to touch her, he wanted to touch her, and so he was. It took another moment for Sunny to realize that he was touching her exactly the way Sam had touched Jules in *The Drowning.*

Sunny and Brady locked eyes. Beneath the stars and the blanket, he trailed his fingers lightly in a circle around her belly button. Sunny wondered whether or not he knew that this move was how and why Jules became so physically attached to Sam to begin with.

"Do you . . . *know*?" Sunny whispered.

Brady wrinkled his brow.

She shook her head. Brady hadn't read *The Drowning.* He would've said so if he had. Maybe this was a regular move that all guys did? "Never mind." Sunny closed her eyes and concentrated on Brady's fingers. He traced back and forth, just inside the top of her jeans. And then he stopped. Sunny opened her eyes, wanting more. Brady's face was inches from hers. He reached behind her neck and kissed her with his lips already parted because he'd held back his own needs for a long time. He felt far, far behind.

"'Jules could not understand why she wasn't allowed to have this person without everything else falling apart.'" Marni's impassioned voice floated in their direction. *"'Was this the only way the universe could find a balance? By taking so much away in order to grant her this one pleasure?'"*

Brady broke away. "I'm sorry. I shouldn't have done that." He rose and hurried toward the gate. "Dumb fuck," he muttered to himself as he pounded the gate open.

Sunny rushed after him, clutching her blanket. "Brady?" she called. The gate clanked behind her. Brady got into his car and slammed the door. Sunny followed after him. She opened the passenger door and got in. "What's wrong?" She searched his face for a clue.

"Nothing!" Brady yelled. He was angry at himself, not her, but it was hard to tell the difference. "Nothing," he said, softer.

Sunny's phone buzzed.

PALOMA

WWB???

SUNNY

He's not gay.

"Brady, whatever was happening between us—it's okay. I mean, I wanted to . . . I *want* to."

Brady stared out the window and weighed: *my past weighs more than that rock; it's heavier than that boulder; it's heavier than this car . . .*

"What is it? I know you've been keeping something from me. I didn't want to push, but it's affecting you, so I really wish you'd tell me what it is." Sunny felt she could deal with anything; she liked Brady enough to handle it if there was another girl or if he was transferring schools and didn't want to get too close or if his family was having problems. "You know what Thora says. It'll be good for you to be inside/out. When we're honest with each other we feel less alone. That's what tonight is for, isn't it? To be transparent? You can tell me, no matter what it is."

Brady gripped the steering wheel. He wasn't going to tell anybody. Ever. The whole point of moving was to keep the past in the past. His parents and grandparents told him to start all over again. But they never told him *how.* Could he be a new person and keep a secret at the same time? Or did he have to reveal who he once was in order to become someone else? He didn't know.

You can't hide who you really are. Look into her eyes and share your authentic self. Your true self always surfaces eventually. Every day Thora's words needled him from the moment he woke in the morning until he closed his eyes at night. "I . . ." He pressed his

forehead against his knuckles. "I don't know how to start over."
He forced the words out.

"I don't know what you mean, Brady," Sunny said gently.
"Tell me what you mean."

"I used to wrestle . . ."

"I remember. You mentioned it once."

Brady took a deep breath so that he could get through the
rest. "I used to wrestle . . . for South Carlisle."

South Carlisle.

Sunny knew the school for the same reason everyone on
Long Island knew South Carlisle. The headlines were all over
the news a year ago: WRESTLING TEAM ACCUSED
OF ATTACKING SOPHOMORE IN HIS SLEEP; HIGH
SCHOOL TEAM ACCUSED OF SEX CRIMES AT WRES-
TLING CAMP; HAZING SCANDAL DEVASTATES LONG
ISLAND COMMUNITY.

Sunny had thought she was prepared to hear anything. She
wasn't. Brady pulled his hood over his head and sniffled against
the steering wheel.

A security guard tapped at Brady's window. Brady looked up
at the man's name tag: T-Bone. "Hey, hey! What's all this? No
one's allowed here after hours." T-Bone swirled his flashlight
into the car. Brady turned his key in the ignition and drove
away as Sunny placed her hand on Brady's arm.

▶ ▶▶

MIRI

At the time, I had no idea what happened with Jonah and Soleil at that meeting. I thought they ditched me to get tacos or something. Jonah has this thing for tacos. When he gets a craving he legit *has* to have 'em. Seriously, they're like crack to him. When he wakes up in the hospital he'll probably ask the nurse for Chipotle in his IV. [laughs]

Okay, now I'm getting hungry.

What is it with guys and food? You're like bottomless pits. And you never gain any weight. How infuriating. [drinks from a water bottle] Anyway, it was pretty rude of them to leave my meeting like that, if you ask me. I looked up and saw them rushing out at the climax of my reading. I think I got a taste of how Fatima felt when her friends didn't appreciate her book. But I wasn't about to stop what I was doing to ask Soleil where they were going. I'd planned that reading for days. I was not pleased. I know *now* why they left, of course, I read the book— it was the night of a thousand fuckups—none of which were Fatima's, mind you.

Stranger Than Fiction

The True Story Behind the Controversial Novel

The Absolution of Brady Stevenson

SOLEIL JOHNSTON'S STORY, PART 2 (continued)

PENNY

Hey Soleil! Security busted us.

Sitting in my car at Warwick &

Flower Field. Where are you guys?

Are u making out? I'm so excited for u!

Heard from Miri? She left with Quinn

and Emma but don't know where.

OK. Driving now. Where to? Soleil?

Meet at Fatima's?

Hello . . . . . ?!!!!?

SOLEIL

No. Tired. I went home.

PENNY

Soleil texted that she was home, but that was a lie.

How did you know?

I know because it took her so long to text me back that by the
time she finally did, I was already getting to Fatima's house, and
I saw Jonah's car out front.

Oh.

[shakes head] Soleil and Jonah were sitting in the car. I could
see them through the back window.

They didn't notice you?

No. I had my mom's Mercedes. She wanted my Range Rover
for her weekend with her girlfriends at the Cape. Why would
Soleil lie to me? I mean, we're best friends. I would've understood if she wanted to be alone to fool around with Jonah. I
would've wanted that if I liked someone. So, why wouldn't she
just tell me?

That's a good question.

I didn't want to be, like, the crazy overreacting friend, though. So, I texted Soleil again to make sure I wasn't jumping to conclusions. Like, maybe she changed her mind last minute and didn't have the chance to tell me yet that they went to Fatima's.

That was a rational move.

I thought so. I texted, "Are you home for the night?"

And what did she answer?

She said, "Yes."

Bummer.

THE ABSOLUTION
OF BRADY STEVENSON

BY FATIMA RO

(excerpt)

SUNNY

Thora? Are you home?

Brady & I need somewhere to go.

THORA

Come over. What's wrong?

I know WWB.

What?

South Carlisle

???

Google.

Jesus.

Brady and Sunny sped wordlessly down Northern Boulevard. Brady couldn't figure out how to defog the windows. He'd meant to study the manual to memorize the dashboard controls but hadn't gotten around to it yet. Sunny looked on as Brady cracked the window open, ran the wipers, turned some dials. Still foggy. He leaned forward to wipe the windshield with his sleeve. He worked at it, wiping a wider and wider circle to clean a spot.

They drove on with the words "South Carlisle" suspended in the air around them and between them. Brady turned the radio on to defuse tension. Bad decision. The song "Cake by the Ocean" was playing—a peppy, celebratory song that made the moment even more uncomfortable than before. Sunny had listened to it a hundred times and even danced to it. She'd never realized until now how stupid the lyrics were. Brady let the song play in an attempt to act normal, as though there was no one in the car whose life had been ruined by the most sickening high school scandal in recent Long Island history.

In Thora Temple's driveway, Brady cut the engine and then the music. He turned his lights off and watched the fog disappear from the windshield. The house looked dark and lifeless even though Thora was inside. Sunny imagined Thora in her bedroom searching articles about the South Carlisle wrestling team: eight boys against one; coaches asleep down the hall; three ringleaders shouting orders for the others to carry out as the victim cried and pleaded.

Brady couldn't bring himself to look at Sunny. Instead, he stared at the house and weighed. He'd once been obsessed with his wrestling weight; he was now obsessed with the weight of his pain. *My past is heavier than this house; it's heavier than that tree with its roots that crawl and reach and stretch and tangle into the earth.*

"I keep weighing," Brady whispered, finally breaking the silence. "The way Thora said about her grief."

Sunny understood. She remembered everything Thora said.

"But there's nothing heavier," Brady said, choking up. "No matter what I weigh, nothing's heavier than . . ."

Afraid to move, almost afraid to breathe, Sunny peered at him from the corner of her eye. Whatever Brady said next could never be taken back. Sunny would have to know it and deal with it. It would become her weight to carry, too. *What's more powerful than words?* Thora had asked the four of them once. They couldn't come up with an answer.

"I came to Morley Academy for a fresh start," Brady said. "I was afraid that if anybody knew, if *you* knew . . ." He hesitated. If he revealed his precious truth, Sunny would be disgusted.

Sunny twisted and twisted the blanket that lay in her lap. "You don't have to explain anything to me, Brady. You don't owe me a thing." She turned to him. "I'm so sorry that happened to you." Sunny's voice shook. "I don't know what else to say, except I know that you didn't deserve any of it. I'm sorry you had to go through that."

Brady froze. Then he looked Sunny in the eyes, just as Thora had taught him. "No, Sunny, that's not . . . I have to tell you . . . I used to be different . . . at South Carlisle I wasn't the way I am here. I wasn't in art. I didn't join book clubs. I didn't even have girls as friends . . . I was a wrestler, and won trophies. But I stuffed them in the back of my closet and left them because they didn't matter anymore, I couldn't even look at . . ."

Sunny couldn't bear to hear him relive the torture and humiliation. She knew now where his darkness came from; there was no reason for him to recount the details for her sake. "Don't. It's okay." She squeezed Brady's forearm. "You don't have to tell me anything, because I can already *see* your truth, okay? I *know* now. And I'm still here," Sunny said. "Thora says that's all a person really needs—to be seen and acknowledged and to know they're not alone. That's all that matters, right? I'm here. You're not alone."

Brady couldn't believe God's mercy. Sunny didn't want to hear any more. He didn't have to tell her. Brady closed his eyes and prayed silently. *Thank you, Lord Jesus Christ. Thank you for this tabula rasa.*

THORA
Are you guys coming in?

SUNNY
I think so. It's up to Brady.

OK. Whenever you're ready.

Let me know if you need

me to come out.

Thanks.

Sunny peered up from her phone. "Thora wants to know if we're coming inside. Do you want to talk to her? Because you can. Or not. She'll just want to share being in the world with you."

"Does she know?" Brady asked.

"Yes." Sunny was sorry for breaking Brady's confidence but was sure it was all right with him. "We can tell Thora anything, can't we? We can be inside/out with her."

"I know. It's okay." Brady saw a curtain move in Thora's bedroom window. He wanted to go inside, where the low ceilings and thick walls seemed to hug him every time he walked through the door. But he was afraid of how Thora might feel about him now. He wanted so badly for her to like him. "I don't want to bother her," Brady said.

"It's not a bother. We can just have someplace to hang out if you don't feel like going home," Sunny said. She looked at the houses across the street, one with a wrought-iron door, another with a glossy black door. There was no possible way to know people's troubles.

The light turned on inside Thora's front hall. She was

expecting them. Brady fiddled with his phone. A new photo popped up on Marni's Instagram; it was of Thora sitting on her living room floor with her emotional timeline. The caption read:

Change your life.
FOLLOW THE PRINCIPLES OF THE THEORY
OF HUMAN CONNECTIONS
#TheTheory #TheDrowningInterrupted

The photo convinced Brady that Thora could help him. She had learned to control her grief. She had left New York City in order to start anew. Finally she was living the life she wanted to live with the people she chose to share it with. She knew how to start over.

"I kind of have to pee," Sunny said, bouncing her knee.

Brady looked up at the front door and saw movement behind the frosted glass. "Let's go in, then."

"Good. Okay." Sunny really did have to go to the bathroom. And she couldn't handle Brady's secret by herself. She wasn't a psychologist. She wasn't even Brady's girlfriend. She needed Thora almost as much as Brady did.

Thora opened the door to find Sunny clutching her yellow blanket and a shaken, stone-faced Brady.

"We didn't know where else to go," Sunny said, teary-eyed.

Thora couldn't help but throw her arms around them both. "Hey, it's okay. You're okay, you guys," she whispered. "Everything's cool. You can always come here."

The security guard came, and that's when we all scattered. I get goose bumps just talking about it; it was invigorating, so . . . *clandestine.* I knew that by Monday morning everybody would be talking about our meeting. As they say, any publicity is good publicity. But you know that, being a journalist.

Yes. What did you do after the meeting?

We went straight to the Witches Brew.

Wait. Who was "we"?

Oh, sorry. Me, Quinn, and Emma Irving. Our server was beautiful—Delia, no, Dahlia, I think. Her eyes! Whoa. She looked like . . . a beautiful alien.

Okay. What then?

Quinn and Emma had never been there before, can you believe? By that time, I had an internal compass pointing straight there, so I navigated while Emma drove. She'd had her license for three days, so I wasn't completely confident with her behind the wheel. We made it in one piece, though. And her convertible is the cutest. What is it . . . an Audi, maybe? It's probably a nightmare in the snow and ice, but it's chic. [sighs] Anyway, the café seats until midnight, which was perfect because we were still wired from the meeting and getting kicked out and everything. There was no way we were going home; we were just getting started dissecting *Undertow*, and we never got to do the flash readings of our favorite lines. Not to mention that we were *starving*, so thank god for that place! We had the vegetable dumplings, spring rolls, macaroni and cheese. Don't judge. Like I said, we were *starving*; the macaroni and cheese absolutely could not be helped.

Hey, I love macaroni and cheese.

But again, you're a bottomless pit.

[laughs]

Oh, and we ordered green tea. They bring you a teapot for the table.

How very Fatima Ro.

I know. [laughs] Being in that space that I associate so closely with Fatima fueled me even more somehow. I felt purposeful; I can't explain it. And it wasn't only the café that made me feel that way. After practicing the theory of human connections and speeding out of Graham the way we did, the three of us were on a high, hyperfocused on spreading the theory.

We still had our copies of *Undertow* with us, and I had my notes and the agenda from the meeting. So, for the flash readings, instead of reading aloud, we started posting and texting quotes on our social media: #TheTheory, #UndertowUninterrupted. We added pictures of paragraphs and page numbers and spouted out *Undertow* phrases. And then I was posting my pictures with Fatima along with steps of the theory. [drinks from a water bottle] There's no telling who we influenced with our messages that night. That's what Fatima said about her novel: you hope that you can reach a few readers here and there, that your message will speak personally to somebody. But you can never know the true impact.

Stranger Than Fiction

The True Story Behind the Controversial Novel

The Absolution of Brady Stevenson

SOLEIL JOHNSTON'S STORY, PART 2 (continued)

Journal Entry

October 15, 2016

10:16 p.m.

Fatima's bathroom

In. In. In. In. In. That's all I wanted—for Jonah to let me IN.

I just wanted to know: *What are you thinking? What are you hiding? What are you weighing?* But now that he's told me, I can't *un*know it. What do I do with this now?

My brain can't register. Overwhelmed. Unprepared. I remember: we were at Penny's house. I asked Jonah if he played sports. He said, "I wrestle," as if he'd been saying it for years. Then he said, "I *used* to. Not anymore." But he wouldn't tell me why. I kept thinking about it while we were watching TV. *Why?* And then Miri texted that he was probably gay, so I thought maybe quitting wrestling had something to do with that? Maybe his teammates found out he was gay, and they couldn't handle it or acted like jerkoffs about it, so he quit. Or maybe it was something much simpler—an injury that ended his career or a lost championship that he couldn't get over. Each of those reasons made sense. Normal problems for a normal teenage boy. But the real reason is so far from normal, I don't even know what to say to him. Why does the reason have to be THIS???

All the jokes that went back and forth between me and Miri and Penny! We're morons.

Here we've been, talking about precious truths and transparency while he's been holding this secret the whole time. *Poor Jonah, poor Jonah, poor Jonah.* Thank god for Fatima. We're with her now, so Jonah will be okay. I don't have to deal with this by myself.

Standing here, leaning against Fatima's sink. I don't want to open the door. Wish I could hide in this bathroom forever. Imagine how Jonah feels about facing the world.

I'd better get to the living room. I don't want him to think I can't handle this.

PENNY

What'd you do while Soleil and Jonah were in Fatima's house?

I sat in my car, like, forever, and just played on my phone, what else? Everyone abandoned me. [sighs] I was nothing but a good friend to them.

I'm sure you were.

Did I tell you we won the scavenger hunt on Orientation Day?

Miri mentioned that.

It's prestigious to win it. All the winners since the school opened have their pictures on the wall. The dean announced our names and gave us medals in front of everyone. He made us, like, the instant A-crowd.

Huh. Nice.

Yeah. We wore our medals the first day of school. [pauses] [turns around] There's a hidden hot tub over there, behind the waterfall.

I never would've noticed that.

Soleil and Miri used to love it here. And Dad got us concert tickets all the time. We went to Rihanna, Ariana Grande, Ed Sheeran, Bruno Mars, even Jingle Ball.

How awesome.

He was about to get everybody passes to see Meghan Trainor, but then I got ditched, so I told him I didn't want them anymore.

The show at Radio City?

Uh-huh.

Oh, that's too bad. I heard it was excellent. I like Meghan Trainor. She has a terrific voice.

[sighs] Thanks for reminding me.

I'm sorry. Okay, so, you were sitting in the car . . .

I was sitting in the car, and then all of a sudden Miri started posting pictures on her Instagram—pictures of *Undertow*, pages from it, and also pictures of her and Fatima and quotes, like motivational sayings about the theory of human connections. And then Quinn and Emma were doing the same thing. I could've posted quotes. Fatima said deep stuff to me too, you know.

I'm sure.

She told me that a person's greatest success or downfall can be traced back to one pivotal human connection, one moment in time that created ripple effects toward either achievement or destruction.

So, why didn't you post quotes from the car?

Nobody asked me to. You know Miri. If I posted on my own she would've found something wrong with it, like, "What are you doing? You don't even understand the standards for each post. You didn't even get the hashtag right," or whatever she'd say to make me feel stupid.

You're probably right. I can see her saying something exactly like that.

And *then*. [slaps table]

What.

I looked closer at the pictures.

And?

I noticed that the books were lying on top of these huge black-and-white menus and next to a bowl of macaroni and cheese.

Nooo.

Yes. They were at the Witches Brew. I wanted to scream! Miri went without me and took those kiss-ass girls to our secret place with Fatima. That was *our* café. *Our* spot. How *dare* she! Anyone else could see the menus and figure out where they were.

Pretty thoughtless.

And they were sitting there with pasta and dumplings. I was sooo hungry!

THE ABSOLUTION
OF BRADY STEVENSON

BY FATIMA RO

(excerpt)

Thora sat so close to Brady that their legs touched. "Everything's all right," she said. Brady felt the author's hand on his back as she leaned closer, smelling of vanilla and ChapStick. "There are no secrets here. We're inside/out in my house, remember? In my house we can be who we are with all our bruises, and we're good enough," Thora said. "I promise you that we are."

In my Father's house are many mansions: if it were not so, I would have told you. I go to prepare a place for you.

"I'm good inside. I'm good. I'm not a bad person . . ." Brady said, because he believed it was his precious truth.

Thora grasped the boy's hand. "Of course you're good inside. Of course."

Brady thought about Sunny and how it felt to kiss her under the sky. "I still deserve stuff," he said, to convince himself as well as Thora.

"You deserve everything you want, Brady. No one thinks you're bad."

Thora was the most brilliant person Brady knew. If he were rotten inside she'd be able to see it. Brady pressed Sunny's blanket to his forehead, aching to ask two questions: *Do you believe in absolution, the cleansing of the body, mind, and soul? Is that why you wrote* The Drowning? He just couldn't bring himself to say them.

"No one's judging you. We all care about you so much. What happened to you doesn't change that."

Brady began to cry, overwhelmed by her belief in him.

Thora leaned forward. "I can help you, Brady. I can lift this weight for you."

Brady sat completely still.

"I was selfish and horrible to my mother before she died. I wasn't there for her when she needed me the most because I was too afraid to watch her slip away," Thora said. "I couldn't accept that she could actually leave me. I thought, as long as I was the same bitchy, ungrateful brat, she'd have to stick around to set me straight the same as she always did. I said and did unforgivable things. I didn't make up with her when she was alive." Thora twirled the charm on her necklace—the letter *T* set in diamonds and white gold. "I thought I'd never survive the regret. Some days I thought I'd die from shame. But it's possible to get past that."

Brady clung to her every word. How? How could he get past his shame? He could never hold his breath long enough.

"In *The Drowning*," Thora continued, "Jules reconciled with her mother before she died. I fixed my mistakes through her. Don't you see, Brady? I've done it before—I rewrote myself out of pain," she insisted. "Now that I know your precious truth, I can do it again; I can lift your weight, too."

Brady could hardly believe what Thora was saying: she would rewrite him.

"And then your pain will take on another form. It'll be outside of your body. It'll scatter and be absorbed into the universe."

Grief can be contained and revised and measured in pounds! Brady squeezed his eyes tightly, imagining his anguish severing and dividing and then vanishing into thin air.

"You saw the timeline I made. You read it, didn't you?"

Brady wiped his tears. "Yeah. I read it."

Thora squeezed the boy's arm as she whispered, "What did I feel by the end—me and Jules? What did we both feel?"

Thora's sure, steady eyes told Brady that everything she was saying was possible. She could give him a revision, a do-over. Today was opposite day. She could make it so that wrestling camp never happened. Or she could give him a decent life with a future to look forward to. Thora Temple could write anything.

"Tell me. When I finally reached the end of the timeline, how did I feel?" Thora asked one last time.

Brady collapsed on the author's shoulder and cried. "Free."

"That's right." Thora hugged him. She was going to make Brady one of her characters, and she would love him like one.

MIRI

We took flyers from the entryway—ads for bands and craft fairs, notices, things like that—and we wrote notes on the back. We came up with this whole plan for how the theory of human connections could reach more people. It was a three-point strategy to spread the theory from different angles. I delegated each of us to be in charge of a specific branch: social media for me, school outreach for Emma, and recruitment for Quinn.

Very thorough.

Believe it. We laid out three sheets of paper, one for each branch, and we brainstormed ideas. I don't know what the hell they put in that green tea, but our ideas just kept flowing and flowing. We were on fire. Fire.

Stranger Than Fiction

The True Story Behind the Controversial Novel

The Absolution of Brady Stevenson

SOLEIL JOHNSTON'S STORY, PART 2 (continued)

Journal Entry

10:25 p.m.

Fatima's kitchen

Can't go in yet. Jonah is in the living room with her. Trying to make out what they're saying but can't hear it all.

J: I'm good inside. I'm good . . . (blubbering) I'm not a bad person . . . (blubbering)

F: Of course you're good inside. Of course. You deserve everything you want, Jonah . . . No one's judging you. We all care about you so much. What happened to you doesn't change that. And I can help you, Jonah. I can lift this weight for you. I was selfish and horrible to my mother before she died. I couldn't accept that she could actually leave me. I thought, as long as I was the same . . . be the same . . . (whispering) . . . the same as she always did . . . I didn't make up with her when she was alive. I thought I'd never survive . . . (whispering) . . . it'll scatter and

be absorbed into the universe . . . (whispering) . . . You read it,
didn't you?

J: (blubbering)

F: (whispering) . . . I feel by the end? . . . Jonah? . . . Tell me . . .
(whispering) . . . how did I feel?

Jonah's crying now on her shoulder. He's relieved.

Thank you, Fatima. I owe you my life.

The next thing I knew, there were pictures from the café of, like, a dozen people.

Oh, jeez.

Didn't I tell you that would happen?

You knew it would.

It was a mob of Undertow people from the courtyard: Natalie Singh, Elena Westcott, Yasmin Contreras, the Levys, Ava, Inés. Even Greg Tivoli and stuffed-dead-animal girl. Everyone! They were in *our* café, acting like they'd been hanging out there for years. Such wannabes. Miri was only being selfish, trying to be the center of attention. There went the Witches Brew. Miri spoiled it for all of us. Fatima couldn't hang out there after that, not with those random kids hounding her.

Of course she couldn't.

Where would she get her green tea?

THE ABSOLUTION
OF BRADY STEVENSON

BY FATIMA RO

(excerpt)

The temperature had dropped since Brady and Sunny left the courtyard. On the author's front stoop, Sunny hugged her blanket tightly around her body. Brady, eyes closed, filled his lungs with the crisp air.

"Are you glad we went in?" Sunny asked after a beat.

"Yeah. Thanks for coming with me." For the first time since wrestling camp, Brady felt that better times were coming his way.

"You don't have to thank me," Sunny said. She thought Brady was so brave to talk to Thora and to stand here with his head held high.

The two weren't quite sure what to say. They heard the lock turn on the other side of the door. The front hallway went dark, leaving the couple in a shadow. Brady's eyes adjusted to the dimness. He smiled a little at Sunny. "You remind me of Linus from Charlie Brown."

"That's just what a girl likes to hear." Sunny laughed, and he did, too. Brady rarely laughed that way. They stood for a moment, shuffling their feet. "So, you had a good talk with Thora?" Sunny asked.

Brady nodded. Thora's words were floating around in his head. He deserved everything. "I can't believe I'm friends with her, you know?" He was Thora Temple's fan, and by some magical stroke of luck, she was his friend, maybe the best friend he'd ever had.

"I know. Neither can I." Sunny's eyes widened. "I still look over at her sometimes, and I'm like, what is my life right now?"

Brady turned his phone over in his pocket. Thora had given him her number and told him to call anytime. Day or night. He would call her, too. She never said anything she didn't mean. His relationship with her wasn't a romance but "one beating heart meeting another beating heart." She was going to make everything better.

"Brady, I just . . ." Sunny didn't know where to begin, but Thora had told her to be honest about her feelings. "I know that you've been through a lot. But no matter what happened in the past, I'm here. I'll always be here for you as a friend. Or even . . . as more, if you want that. But if you don't, I understand. It's a lot. I know." Brady must not be ready to get close to anyone. That's probably why he'd broken their kiss in the courtyard. Even so, Sunny wanted to keep the option open.

"I'm happy about that," Brady said.

"So . . . friends? Or . . . ?" she asked. "Not that you have to know now, because you don't. I'm just saying that either one is okay with—"

Brady pulled at Sunny's blanket. "I'm freezing."

She raised her arms over Brady's shoulders and pulled herself toward him. "Is this all I am to you? A warm blanket?"

No, you're my second chance. You're my reclaimed innocence. You're my hope beyond hope, Brady thought.

Brady didn't break in her arms. He didn't shatter or pull away. Sunny hugged him closer. Brady's body drew warmth from hers. They held each other until they were both warm.

Brady only wanted to express his gratitude to Sunny for being such a loyal friend. But Sunny squeezed the back of his head in a way that begged, *Kiss me, Brady, please kiss me.* So, he kissed her. But as he did, he promised to earn this kiss by becoming the boy she believed in. He cupped Sunny's face in his hands as they parted. "Be my girlfriend," he whispered. If Sunny—Morley honor student and favorite of Thora Temple— were his girl, he must be good inside. It had to be the precious truth.

There I was with the three-part plan spread out on the table and my book open, right? So I start talking about Fatima, about the grueling emotional process she went through to write *Undertow*. And then all of a sudden, we understood Fatima and the whole book. Over brownies and tri-flavored gelato, something clicked for us in that café. [snaps]

Something?

[looks through her phone] We were talking about the book and its parallels to Fatima's real life, how chapter after chapter, the character Lara follows Fatima's emotions almost exactly.

Okay.

She was writing autobiographically, not in terms of plot, but in terms of her human connection with her mother and in terms of Fatima's emotions and the consequences of her actions.

Yes, I noticed that.

But then! The parallel ends. [slaps table] Just like that. There's a distinct point of separation between Fatima and Lara. They're not in tandem anymore. Right here. Look. [shows timeline photo on her phone]

CHAPTER 23

ME: I used to feel everything, emotions aflame. Joy, fear, adoration, frustration. But now, nothing but regret—while awake, while asleep, while waking and falling asleep—regret has replaced everything and all, completely. I've forgotten anything but.

LARA: Finally, we are us again. I am me and she is Mom. And that is that. "Tell me about the date you had, remember, the one at the beach" is all I had to say. She laughed. I laughed. And we are back. So is the light. A ray of light. Lighthearted. We are feather-light. You are the light of my life.

Do you see what I see?

[pauses] Fatima didn't reconnect with her mother, but Lara did.

Yes! That's exactly what happened. In reality, Fatima pushed away from her mother when she was ill. But the moment Lara asks her mother about the beach date, Fatima changed the course of Lara's ending. And by doing this . . .

Fatima and Lara were able to reach the same emotional conclusion.

That's right. Fatima lived through Lara. She made different choices and got a different ending.

She got a do-over.

Stranger Than Fiction

The True Story Behind the Controversial Novel

The Absolution of Brady Stevenson

SOLEIL JOHNSTON'S STORY, PART 2 (continued)

DATE: October 15, 2016

TO: fatima.ro.author@gmail.com

FROM: soleil410@gmail.com

Subject: !!!!

Home now. 11:49 p.m. Under the covers. Typing so fast
and trembling. Too much to process. Can't wrap my brain
around it.

I'm so confused. Please don't judge me. When he told
me about South Carmine, I was wondering—*Does this
mean we aren't going to kiss again?* I don't know what's
wrong with me. I'm supposed to be horrified about what
he told us. I am. I really am. BUT . . . I made out with
him on your front stoop. And I can't help that I'm soooo
excited and happy that it happened. I know this makes me
a selfish person. He was crying not five minutes earlier
on your living room sofa. He was a mess, face smudged,
voice raspy, and his lips were salty from tears, which is

something I shouldn't even know because I shouldn't have kissed him in the first place. I should've offered to listen and comforted him with supportive words, not jumped his bones when he was so obviously not emotionally healthy enough to have his bones jumped. What the hell is wrong with me??? I'm a selfish, selfish, lustful person. They say you never know your true character until tragedy strikes. Well, I've just discovered the real me: I'm the passenger on the *Titanic* who shoves children and elderly out of the way so that I can get into a lifeboat.

I'm small and weak.

Weak.

Weak.

Weak.

And then (yes, it gets worse or better) he asked me to be his girlfriend, and I said yes. What was I thinking?

Now I'm Googling, and I can't stop. These articles are horrendous. *Poor Jonah, poor Jonah, poor Jonah.* Nothing about these articles tells me that it's okay to go out with a guy who's been through this. I'm only going to screw him up even more. I don't know what I'm doing.

liherald.com/stories/South-Carmine-High-School-students-assault-program

At South Carmine High School, Students Call Sex Assault "Part of the Program"

From August 27–September 1, 2015, 18 students ages 14 to 17 from South Carmine High School attended wrestling training camp. On the first day of classes in September, only 17 of those students returned to school. By third period, rumors were circulating throughout campus that the absent tenth grader was sexually assaulted at camp. Details of the assault spread as the day went on: the boys had been drinking beer in their room past curfew; three ringleaders ordered five other teammates to wake a sleeping sophomore team member; they stripped his clothes off and dragged him to the floor. The attack, which lasted 13 minutes, according to a blurry video clip of the event, involved forcing the sophomore to perform various sex acts with a wrestling dummy (a stuffed, life-sized body-shaped training device). When they returned to South Carmine High School, some members of the wrestling team were overheard boasting about the incident. Others denied that any wrongdoing had occurred. When questioned in the hallway by friends about what happened at training, one wrestling camp attendee winked and answered, "Nothing that wasn't part of the program."

PENNY

I was about to leave, really, I was just about to turn the key, but then Fatima's door opened. So then I couldn't go. They would've heard me and seen my headlights.

Right.

I should've left two minutes earlier. Then I wouldn't have had to see their whole make-out session.

They were making out?

Yes. Right in front of Fatima's *door*—Soleil must've loved that. She should've added a picture of that to her art project. But it gave me a second to text Fatima and ask her if she'd heard from Soleil and Jonah.

What'd she say?

She said no.

Oh.

Why'd they all have to lie to me?

I don't know.

Eventually Soleil and Jonah stopped sucking each other's faces and left. I went straight home after that.

It was some night.

Maybe for other people. It wasn't so much for me. [sighs]

Sorry about that.

It doesn't matter.

Still, it sucks to be left out.

[shrugs]

The Absolution of Brady Stevenson

BY FATIMA RO

(excerpt)

BRADY

Hey.

THORA

Hi. Got home ok?

> Yup. Just checking if this
> is really your number.

It is. You're looking for Tony's
Pizzeria, right?

> Uh . . .

I'm kidding! It's Thora!

> Haha funny. So thanks for the
> talk and for letting us come over.

You're welcome. I meant everything
I said. You'll be fine, Brady. How are
things with you and Sunny?

We're good.

Happy to hear it. She's such a great
girl. I think you're good for each other.

Me too. I asked her to be
my girlfriend. I'm ready to
take that step, move on with
my life, thanks to you.

Aww, that's great.

You think so?

Yes. I'm happy for you. Let's talk
again—same time tomorrow, ok?

Ok. Sweet.
Should I text you or . . .

Just call me. I'll be around.

Ok bye.

Good night. Everything's
going to be all right. Bye.

MIRI

Quinn came up with a plan to have tank tops made to help us with recruitment.

Tank tops?

Her mom owns a print shop that makes promotional items. She handles practically every bar and bat mitzvah and event on Long Island. For Quinn's sweet sixteen pool party, Quinn gave all the girls booty shorts that said SWEET across the ass. They were vulgar and adorable. We adored them, naturally. So for Undertow Society, she got us these teeny little tank tops with the words LOOK INTO MY EYES NOT AT MY CHEST across the boobs and #TheTheory on the back. Whenever we wore the tanks, people would ask, "What's #TheTheory?" And so we'd explain it and invite them to a meeting.

Clever.

Quinn Donner is a marketing phenom. Then I came up with a Twitter account to work with the T-shirts; anyone could share a precious truth with #TheTheory. [searches through her phone] Look. People posted things like, "My precious truth is that I'm afraid of red foods. #TheTheory," "I still cry every night about my dead cat. #TheTheory." See? There must be hundreds of them. "Me and my girl made an authentic human connection with our pants down. #TheTheory." Okay, well, that one's probably a joke, but most of them are serious. And here's a picture of us in the tank tops. [shows photo of several girls pouting, wearing white tank tops with red lettering]

Vulgar and adorable.

[sits tall] Thank you so much.

Stranger Than Fiction

The True Story Behind the Controversial Novel

The Absolution of Brady Stevenson

SOLEIL JOHNSTON'S STORY, PART 2 (continued)

DATE: October 15, 2016

TO: soleil410@gmail.com

FROM: fatima.ro.author@gmail.com

SUBJECT: RE: !!!!

Soleil, you poor thing. Don't be so hard on yourself. You haven't done a thing wrong. You've been the best friend to him that anyone could possibly expect. Jonah felt comfortable enough with you to kiss you; he even trusts you enough to want you as his girlfriend. Those are good things.

We're both doing the same thing—reading these awful articles. It's frightening to learn that someone you care about has been hurt. But you can't ignore his past. He's been through unimaginable pain that will probably always be a part of who he is. Reading about South Carmine is a way to achieve an authentic human connection, especially if he doesn't want to talk about it.

Get one thing straight. You're not screwing him up! You're making that sad, troubled boy happy. What a beautiful thing. I've seen him moping around. You've given him so much to feel optimistic about. You're not weak— you're compassionate and affectionate. Don't feel guilty for a second.

You can also be sure of this: he and I talked until he was spent. Believe me, he had nothing left to say by the time you two left. And if it didn't feel natural for him to get physical with you, he wouldn't have. Do what feels right for you. You and Jonah are adorable together. It was apparent from the start that you two had something special. Nothing heals wounds better than love. If you make each other happy, that's all that matters.

I hope you know that I'll never judge you. I thank you for being transparent with me. You and I are the only ones who know Jonah's secret. We have to keep it for him and tell each other everything, and I mean everything, or else it'll be too much for us to shoulder alone. Jonah needs us both, and you and I need each other.

▶ ▶▶

PENNY

The worst thing was that when I got home I still kept seeing
food pictures from Miri, Natalie and the Levys, and the rest of
them. I was so mad. They were having mac and cheese and sliders and brownies . . . ugh. So I was going to make macaroni and
cheese for myself, but we didn't have any left. We have a smart
pantry—when we're low on something the computer puts it on
our grocery list. Then a service delivers it. It was on the list, I
checked, but it was Friday, and our delivery doesn't come until
Saturday. [sighs] Sometimes life is so unfair.

THE ABSOLUTION
OF BRADY STEVENSON

BY FATIMA RO

(excerpt)

B rady opened his laptop to visit Sunny's Facebook page.

RELATIONSHIP STATUS: single

He wasn't expecting to see anything different. He'd only dropped her off at home thirty minutes earlier. He couldn't believe such a disastrous conversation ended up so, so, so . . . *hot*. He and Sunny were so freakin' hot together on Fatima's front stoop.

Sunny hadn't posted anything for three days, not since an announcement for the Undertow meeting. Was that meeting only hours earlier? It felt so long ago. Sunny's profile photo, of her leaning against a railing on a boat, was gorgeous. Her hair was windblown. She was looking up at the camera so that you could somewhat see down her top, and her expression was sexy and cute combined. He'd always wanted a girlfriend who was sexy and cute combined. But the picture might've been too perfect. While he appreciated the cleavage and the hair, the photo made Sunny look one-dimensional, which she most certainly wasn't. She was kind and compassionate. The photo zapped those qualities away. Kindness and compassion are a lot to ask of a photo, so while Brady looked at it, he also thought of her saying, ". . . no matter what happened in the past, I'm here. I'll always be here for you as a friend. Or even . . . as more, if you want that." Man, she was such a sweet girl.

Sunny was one of the only people he knew who was on Facebook. She said she did it for her grandmother in Florida, who liked to keep up with Sunny's life. Among many admirable qualities, Sunny was also a good granddaughter.

Brady opened a second tab to play an Ed Sheeran video, a song that Sunny liked when it came on in the car. Suddenly it was Brady's favorite. He was more into alternative rock at the moment, but this is how wrapped up he was in Sunny Vaughn.

He opened a third tab and visited the Morley school website. The students on the site were perfect and perfect together: the black guy, the white guy, the Asian girl, the white girl, the Latino guy. They stood in Morley blazers and science lab goggles behind beakers and vials of bubbling liquid. Their ethnically ambiguous teacher wearing a lab coat looked on proudly. *One Heart and One Mind.* There were dozens of events listed on the calendar that Brady didn't know about. There was the Snow Ball, Student Art Exhibit, Charity Banquet Night, Junior Ring Ceremony, and a Junior Class College Fair.

He usually didn't pay much attention to the goings-on at school. He attended Morley in body, but emotionally he was empty. He went through the motions, collected high enough grades, kept a low profile, and left all forms of school spirit to the girls. If he and Sunny were a couple, he'd have to become a more active participant in order to keep up with her. The thought of joining and belonging to something again and having someone special depend on him was exciting. He could take Sunny to the Snow Ball in January. She'd like that. Dances were a very TV teen drama thing to do. He could ask the DJ to play the Ed Sheeran song. He was thinking like a good boyfriend already.

Brady traced his cursor over the words "Junior Class College Fair." At one time he thought he might like to go to Cornell, Northeastern, MIT, or Harvard. After wrestling camp, he'd dismissed the thought. But now? Thora made him think that it might still be possible. Sunny had been talking about Vassar or Sarah Lawrence, BU, maybe Columbia (like Thora). He wanted to be in her league, at the very least. The worst boyfriend is the kind who holds a smart girl back. He didn't want to be that guy. This relationship was going in a very positive direction, and they hadn't even been official for an hour yet.

Brady opened a fourth tab. He skimmed quickly through Marni's Instagram photos from the Witches Brew. She was still at it, posting *The Drowning* quotes up to the minute.

"This escape was only temporary, Jules knew. But it was good enough for now. Who was ready to face forever anyway?"
#TheDrowningUninterrupted #CantStopTheDrowning

You had to hand it to Marni. She definitely knew how to commit. That's what Thora expected from true friends. That's what Thora would get from Brady, too: devotion.

Brady checked on Sunny's *Doors* project at #VargasStudio-Art. Sunny was making progress. One illustration was replaced by a photo of Thora Temple's front door. Brady recognized its dry wooden paneling and the glass on both sides. He had stared at it from the car and also kissed Sunny in front of it. He thought about his mouth on hers and clicked back to Sunny's Facebook photo.

RELATIONSHIP STATUS: in a relationship

Brady laughed. He was the luckiest guy. And wouldn't Sunny's grandmother be thrilled? He shut his laptop and yawned. The events of the evening fell over his eyelids. Unlike every other night that year, he fell asleep immediately after the Lord's Prayer.

MIRI

How are you doing today, Miri? That top is a great color for the camera.

Thanks. [clears throat] My allergies are kicking in. I'm good, though. [coughs] I want to talk about Monday morning at Graham Assembly. Everyone was talking about my meeting the way they used to talk about the parties.

Graham Assembly?

Faculty and students meet in the auditorium every first and third Monday for goal-setting and unification. *"Unius animi, unius mentis."* One heart and one mind.

Must be a private school thing.

Graham is steeped in tradition. But like I said, getting chased out by security was the best thing that could've happened to us. Picture it. Suddenly Undertow Society was this dangerous, forbidden meet-up. Everyone wanted in on it. Do you know what Fatima once said about hosting?

No. What?

She said, "There's one thing cooler than owning the scene, and that's *dis*owning the scene."

[laughs]

She was right. Quitting parties earned us a certain mystique. The whole school wanted to know what we were into if not the parties. Fatima Ro became the next big thing.

You seem to have a lot of influence on your classmates.

Trendsetters! Click! [pretends to take a selfie] [laughs] Yeah. Everyone was talking about the secret society that got chased off campus. Once the story built some momentum, people were saying that the cops came. There was even talk of us smoking pot and burning candles while chanting passages from *Undertow*. The stories took on this very dark element. And dozens of kids claimed to have been there who weren't. We took attendance, remember. But just so you know, there were no drugs.

That wasn't Fatima's thing. She actually has a whole philosophy about alcohol and drugs in life and in novels—that they're a cop-out excuse for poor behavior and a weak device for advancing plot. There's always a deeper reason, a psychological motivation for our actions, and it's an author's job to figure that out. But that's beside the point. There were no drugs. *Ever.*

But you didn't correct any of the inaccuracies about the Undertow meeting as you heard them.

What are you, crazy? [laughs]

Publicity.

That's right. At assembly, kids were asking if we really knew Fatima personally, so we rapid-fire posted pictures on Instagram. Now, you have to remember that our pictures were not the kinds that any fan could've taken with Fatima at, say, a signing or even bumping into her on the street. They were clearly taken over time, very intimate in nature. We were wearing different clothes in each one; we were lying on the woman's living room floor; Fatima and Soleil were modeling their topknots in the bathroom mirror. Some of the *Undertow* fans commented, "Photoshopped!" and were being catty. Jealousy is an ugly troll. Fatima used to say, "There will always be negative bitches." [laughs] [coughs] Becoming a successful writer at twenty-two made her no stranger to that.

I'm sure.

That topknot, by the way, became an absolute *thing* at Graham after Soleil posted that photo, and Soleil couldn't get enough of showing everyone how to do it the Fatima Ro way. Teachers were wearing that rat's nest of a hairdo, I'm not even exaggerating.

I can imagine.

Fatima joked that I made her famous at Graham.

Now she's just famous. Period.

Right. The famous "seductress." [uses air quotes] [sighs] You know, I would've wanted Soleil to be more involved in the movement. Normally it would've been exactly the thing she'd jump on. But after she and Jonah got together, I just didn't see her devotion to it anymore. Obviously they left the meeting to feel each other up, since that was just so much more pressing an issue. [pauses] Isn't it funny? How we could pick apart and analyze *Undertow* for months and months, oh, with its themes of the temptations of the flesh and the sins of the daughter, but the second a cute guy shows a glimmer of not being gay, all logic and any previous loyalties just fly out the window.

Stranger Than Fiction

The True Story Behind the Controversial Novel

The Absolution of Brady Stevenson

SOLEIL JOHNSTON'S STORY, PART 3

DATE: October 16, 2016

TO: fatima.ro.author@gmail.com

FROM: soleil410@gmail.com

SUBJECT: Articles

Have you seen these???

longislanddaily.com/metro/news/features/293849/

South Carmine: A District Steeped in Hazing Culture

Prior to last month's alleged hazing incident involving high school wrestling champions, there were dozens of complaints to the South Carmine School District regarding hazing, as indicated in records going back several years. South Carmine is known among its students, as well as those in neighboring towns and rival sports districts, as a school with a hazing culture that runs deep. Complaints have ranged from name-calling and "checking" in the hallways (where a student bumps another in order to knock the books out of his arms) to "pantsing" (pulling someone's pants down), and dousing students with urine, and escalate to the most recent case of sexual simulation and assault. School administrators failed to pursue the majority of complaints from years past, while other incidences were barely investigated past the questioning stage. In some cases, students were advised to drop their complaints or run the risk of jeopardizing their place on a sports team.

Hazing practices were also reported in South Carmine Middle School. Complaints date back six years, which is as long as the district holds disciplinary records. These include reports of a student's clothing getting stolen from a locker room, a student being held down while being smothered with soiled underwear, and food tampering.

When asked about the frequency of hazing in their school district, South Carmine student athletes said they are well aware of the school's history of hazing. In fact, they expect some degree of initiation upon joining a team. "Everyone knows it goes on," said Henry Lafferty, 18, a South Carmine senior. "When you go out for a sport, you brace yourself because you know that something's coming." Jeff Bukowski, 17, a South Carmine senior, said, "Some people get it worse than others, but it's meant to toughen you up. If you're respected, if you're good enough, you don't have anything to worry about." Michael Yang, 18, basketball team cocaptain, said, "I don't know that everything that's been said about the wrestlers is true. If a guy's got something against another guy, you never know what he'll make up about you." Bryant Hersey, 17, a South Carmine honor student, said, "When it comes to the hazing in general, it's just part of being in the group. A lot of kids would trade places with you if they could be part of something important."

nychronicle.com/articles/news/headlines/920392221/

Long Island Community in Uproar

Parents and community members in the South Carmine School District have expressed outrage today at Judge Perry Larsing's swift decision to sentence the three ringleaders, ages 16, 17, and 17 of the high school wrestling team hazing incident to 9 to 12 months in a juvenile detention facility. Judge Perry Larsing had already been criticized for trying the boys as minors; many South Carmine residents expected the boys to be tried as adults due to the nature and severity of the crimes. Psychologist Rosemary Vince of Stony Brook University stated, "The brain isn't fully developed until around the age of 25. It is unreasonable to expect adult behavior from an underdeveloped brain." However, many Long Island parents disagree. "These kids are old enough to know right from wrong. If they're old enough to win a tournament and get on honor roll, they're old enough to take responsibility for assaulting a teammate. They should've been tried and sentenced as adults," said Thomas Lerner, South Carmine resident. In response to the public criticism of his leniency, Judge Perry Larsing responded that sentencing the young boys as adults would likely "cause more harm than good" and that he wanted to spare the former championship high school wrestlers from "undue trauma."

SOLEIL
Are you still up? Did you see my email?

FATIMA
I just finished reading.
Heinous.

I can't believe those guys only got 9-12 months. That means they're already out by now?!!

Unfuckingbelievable.

They're probably laughing their asses off at this very moment.

Fuckers.

And it was a juvenile facility. It probably wasn't even that bad. They get school

and recreation in there. Education and
ping pong! I looked it up. It was
probably nicer than some people's
homes.

Fucking paradise.

That asshole Judge Larsing didn't want
to "cause more harm than good."

Fuck him.

How can I have normal conversations
with Jonah tomorrow after reading this
stuff?

You'll figure it out. Not to criticize,
but you never had normal conversations
with him. Seriously, what has he ever
talked about? Why change now?

Haha. You're right. It's always me
babbling about stupid stuff and him
agreeing with me.

Actually sounds like the ideal relationship.

There would probably be zero divorces if
marriages were like that. Look, knowing
his precious truth and reading these
articles about him should bring you closer
not further apart.

You're right. It should.

Get some sleep.

I'll try.

▶ ▶▶

PENNY

How did you feel about Soleil and Jonah?

Like, as a couple?

Yes.

I liked them together, plus I wanted Soleil to be happy. Back then I thought it was what Soleil wanted, but I don't know anymore. I think Fatima pushed her into being with him.

Is that what she's been telling you?

No, she doesn't really like talking about it. It's hard for her; she's really upset. [sighs] Soleil asked Fatima for advice. I remember it clear as anything. The Monday after the Undertow meeting, I was standing with Soleil at her locker before first period. She kept fixing her hair, and she redid her lip gloss three times. I'd never seen her that nervous before. It wasn't an excited type of nervous. It was more like she was second-guessing about being with him. I asked her if she was happy, and she said, "I don't know yet." She texted Fatima for advice. I saw Fatima's answer.

What did she say?

"Get him, girl! Keep calm and girlfriend on." [shakes head] Fatima pressured Soleil into going out with him.

You don't think Soleil would have been in that relationship if Fatima wasn't involved?

No. And now she's a mess. Fatima just wanted to see what would happen. She played with them as characters for her novel because she wasn't talented enough to think of her own story.

Whoa. That's a pointed statement.

I'm getting angrier about it every day.

I can see that.

I heard it on *Extra*. Mario Lopez said Fatima was like the chess player Bobby Fischer and that she set us all up like pawns for a fall.

Penny, I thought you were staying away from television and the internet.

I was. I mean, I am. But I can't help it if it's on at Soleil's house. She watches everything.

Soleil saw that?

Yes.

What'd she say about it?

She didn't say anything. She cried.

The Absolution of Brady Stevenson

BY FATIMA RO

(excerpt)

Sunny looked so pretty that morning, even prettier than her profile picture. She looked up from her phone as Brady walked toward her.

She'd been texting with Thora all morning, asking, "Is this the worst idea or not? Am I ready for this? Is he? Should we kiss or not? Should I bring up South Carlisle or avoid it?" Thora told her to do whatever felt right and to "Keep calm and girlfriend on." So that's what Sunny intended to do.

Brady quickened his pace. He looked better than ever; his eyes were clearer, brighter. It must've done him good to unload his past and let Sunny in. He smiled for her, at her, about her. That could only be a positive thing.

"Hey."

"Hey."

For all their pent-up emotion, "hey" was the only syllable they could manage. There had been too many words exchanged at Thora Temple's house; they were fresh out of words at the moment. Paloma, who was standing beside her best friend, cleared her throat. "Hi, Brady. How was the rest of your weekend?"

"Fine. How was yours?" Brady asked, to be polite.

"Okay." Paloma checked the time. "Well, uh, I should go to class early. Maybe it'll show initiative." She slipped away just as Brady leaned forward to kiss Sunny on the cheek.

"Hey."

"Hey."

This relationship was going to take time. That was okay. Brady had lots of time to spend with Sunny and make himself recognized as her boyfriend, which was a pure, hopeful person to be.

Brady had spent his first two months at Morley trying to blend into the crowd. This morning he draped his arm over Sunny's shoulders and walked with a slight sway as if to say, *Check me out. I'm Sunny Vaughn's boyfriend. She chose me. I must be a regular guy with nothing but regular-guy problems. Here's my regular-guy swagger.*

"Hey, someone scored a little bit of sunshine," Brady heard someone say in the crowded hallway.

Sunny and her new boyfriend turned into the art room and took their usual seats. It felt different and exciting, sitting together as a couple, rather than as just friends. "So, do you want to hang out after school?"

"I do. I can't today, though." Brady ran a hand down Sunny's arm. "I have, uh . . . a thing." He wasn't prepared with an excuse. Sunny knew he didn't have sports or clubs.

"A thing?" Sunny searched his face.

Brady didn't want her to think he was having second thoughts about dating her. "I see a psychologist on Mondays," he confessed. At least she'd know the reason was important.

"Oh." Sunny pulled the wire of her spiral notebook. One thought clouded over her: *My boyfriend was the South Carlisle sophomore.* She hadn't slept much the night before—too many articles about the hazing scandal. Details of wrestling camp cluttered Sunny's mind, reminding her of how emotionally fragile Brady must be.

Brady hung his head. "We don't have to talk about it."

"All right." She was afraid the topic would come up. She was also afraid that it wouldn't. Sunny didn't want him to think she didn't care. She looked around. Their classmates were settling into the classroom. "But we can, if you want to," she said softly. "We should be inside/out. It's healthy for us."

"I know. I know that we can talk about anything, but . . ." Brady wanted to put an end to this. He could be one of those perfect Morley website guys with a pressed shirt and a science experiment with just the right amount of bubbles in the beaker. "I don't want to. I've been working really hard to move on with my life. And I want us to be a normal couple."

"Okay." Sunny was so relieved, she actually sighed aloud. She didn't want to dwell on South Carlisle any more than he did. She wanted them to be a normal couple, too. Anyway, Brady had a psychologist. Thora was right. Brady didn't need his girlfriend to counsel him. "So then, we won't talk about it.

Unless you change your mind, and that'll be fine, too."

"I won't," Brady said, louder, his final words on the matter. He was so courageous moving forward this way.

"I do have one question for you, though." Brady wrinkled his brow. "Is your real name Sunshine Vaughn?"

Sunny laughed. "Yes."

"How did I not know this?" Brady touched Sunny's hair in a very comforting, normal-boyfriend-like gesture.

"I don't know." She pulled on his lapel. *Just do what feels right,* Sunny thought. "You never asked."

"It's perfect." He squeezed Sunny's leg under the table. "Perfect."

▶ ▶▶

MIRI

Penny absolutely reamed me out about taking Quinn and Emma to the Witches Brew. [laughs]

Why is that funny?

Because that's when I got the idea for my Instagram series for Undertow Society. I called it #FatimaWasHere, which was pictures of places around town that Fatima had been. I literally went back to the Witches Brew and posted a photo of her favorite table with the caption "#FatimaWasHere. Where? Your guess is as good as their hot cup of Yemen Mocca Sanani." If you think that Penny was angry enough already, you should've heard her then. "It's a violation of her privacy!" These were photographs of public places, and Fatima gave me permission to post the series, so there was no reason for Penny to get bent out of shape over it.

First of all, Fatima said that if she'd had the theory of human connections years ago, things would've been different for her and her mother. It was important to spread her message. That was the purpose of the movement! We were already helping people. Even Penny made a friend out of it. She and Natalie Singh made an authentic connection. And secondly, let's get real about privacy. Penny spent god knows how many hours alone in Fatima's house. We can't pretend that she didn't snoop around and poke her nose in every last drawer and cabinet and closet. I'm not judging, mind you. Anyone would've done the same. Curiosity is human nature. Hell, Soleil listed everything in Fatima's medicine cabinet.

I read about that.

Penny used to take Fatima's magazines and read them in school.

Really?

Us Weekly and *Cosmo*, *Teen Vogue*, the occasional *Allure*. She would leave these god-awful paint samples and sad little fabric swatches all over the house for Fatima, too. No one had the heart to tell Penny they were hideous. As if Fatima Ro, the most effortlessly stylish woman I've ever met, would have Penny decorate her house. What fantasy was Penny seriously living in?

Did Fatima say the samples were hideous?

She didn't have to. It was plain to see. Fatima humored her, but she was only being kind. She didn't want to crush the girl. [laughs] Do you want to hear the funniest thing?

Always.

You know the street photos of people's houses on Google Maps?

Yes.

Soleil and I typed in Fatima's address once because she wanted another image of Fatima's door for her art project. So we zoomed into the picture, and guess whose car was in the driveway of Fatima's Google Maps photo.

Penny's.

Penny's! How hysterical is that? It just shows that she practically spent more time in that house than Fatima herself.

That's pretty funny.

I'm convinced that Penny wanted to *be* Fatima. She no doubt fantasized about living in her house and hanging some tacky curtains. Fatima gave me permission for the Instagram series. She was all for me expressing myself. She accepted that her book took on a life of its own, meaning whatever happened after *Undertow* was published was out of her control. That goes back to the original issue at hand, doesn't it?

Which is?

Whatever happened after *The Absolution of Brady Stevenson* was published is also out of her control.

Stranger Than Fiction

The True Story Behind the Controversial Novel

The Absolution of Brady Stevenson

SOLEIL JOHNSTON'S STORY, PART 3 (continued)

SOLEIL

WTF am I reading right now in my
psychology class?????

FATIMA

What?!!!

Strategies for overcoming
trauma. Denial: acting as if an event
never happened. Compartmentalization:
keeping different parts of your life
separate. Traumatic dissociation: zoning
out, going through the motions of life on
autopilot.

My boyfriend is a textbook case study
for my 4th period AP Psych class.

PENNY

Is it fair to say that you spent more time at Fatima's house without her than with her?

Uh, yeah, I guess so.

Did you ever go over there without her knowing?

I was welcome to. Any of us could go. She was transparent with us. Her house was inside/out. I went there, but I respected her space, I swear. All I did was play with the cat and read her magazines. I never did anything that I wouldn't want her to do at my house. [pauses] Except . . .

What?

I looked through her DVR list once.

Why?

To see what shows she liked; I just wanted to have something to talk to her about.

Well, I don't think that's so bad.

But then I tried to watch one of her shows, and I accidentally deleted it!

Oh no.

Her DVR didn't have the same drop-down menu as mine. The Erase bar was in the same place as my Play bar, so I hit the wrong thing, and her remote was overly sensitive. I barely even pressed it!

That's the worst.

I freaked out.

Did you tell her?

No. I was scared for weeks that Fatima would know I watched her DVR and that she was missing an episode of *Chicago Med.*

Did she ever mention it?

I don't think she ever noticed. Oh, god, what if she did notice but she just didn't say anything?

Would that still matter to you at this point?

Yes. No. Oh, I don't know. [phone buzzes] Excuse me.

No problem.

[reads text] No change in Jonah's condition.

I'm sorry to hear that.

Me too. [texts back] [sets phone aside] Soleil's mom, Dr. Cora Johnston, is a doctor at the hospital where Jonah is. Did you know that?

No, I was wondering how you were keeping such close tabs on him.

That's how. She checks in on him when she can.

That's nice.

[pauses] How long can someone stay in a coma before they start to . . . not do so well anymore?

I don't know too much about it. That'd be a good question for Soleil's mom. But I have heard that the younger and healthier a person is going into it, the better they do. And you can't get much younger or healthier than Jonah.

[silence]

What's on your mind?

That girl, uh, Bobbi Kristina Brown.

Whitney Houston's daughter?

Yeah. There was something on TV about her last night. She was young, but she didn't do well in a coma.

That wasn't the same situation. Her coma was drug related, so I'm sure she wasn't in prime condition. Jonah was an athlete.

[silence]

What is it, Penny?

I didn't know he was an athlete at first.

No, I suppose you didn't.

I wish I never found out.

THE ABSOLUTION OF BRADY STEVENSON

BY FATIMA RO

(excerpt)

Out of the Legos, Spirograph, Rubik's Cube, My Little Pony, SpongeBob figures, and origami paper on Dr. Nihati's table, Brady picked up pieces of K'NEX that had been formed into a crane contraption with a pulley and bucket at one end.

"Who made this?" Brady asked. "I mean, not his name or anything, but, did a kid make it or did an adult?"

"A kid made it. A little girl."

"Oh." Brady tilted the crane forward, scooping up an imaginary mound of earth with the bucket. "Sweet." He put the toy down and settled into the firm leather chair.

"Something about you is different today." Dr. Nihati pursed her lips into a suspicious smile.

Brady felt transparent. Thora would be proud of him for being authentic. "Like what?"

"Your mood has changed. Something happened, and you want to tell me about it. Am I right?" Dr. Nihati's sort-of-British-sort-of-Indian accent was soothing. Her voice had a way of unfolding Brady. She must've known this. She was too smart not to. It was as if she'd worked on her inflections and her intonations in school along with the theories of Freud and Carl Jung and those other dead textbook guys.

"You're right. Something sorta did happen. A good thing."

"That's great."

"Dr. Nihati, do you believe in signs?" Brady asked.

"Signs?"

"Yeah, like, signs from God or the universe or some higher power giving us messages that can change the trajectory of our lives?"

Dr. Nihati crossed her legs. Her tights made a faint zip sound beneath her skirt. Brady stopped himself from glancing at her legs. Hopefully Dr. Nihati knew that he had a lot of respect for her and for women in general, for that matter. "I believe that if we are looking for signs, we often find them. If we are not looking for them, we do not."

"Oh." Brady could accept a little bit of that explanation. Coach used to say that if you believe you're a winner, then it's more likely to happen. That doesn't replace training or conditioning or the circumstances of a particular match, though. All of those things factor in, too, so mind over matter can't possibly account for everything.

"Is there a particular sign you believe you have received that you would like to tell me about?"

Brady remembered Sunny in his car that night. *I'm sorry you had to go through that . . . You don't have to tell me anything.*

"Brady?"

"Well, I thought . . . I thought that maybe I had to tell some-one—Sunny, the girl I told you about—I felt like I needed to tell her details about what happened last year. But then I got a sign that I shouldn't."

"Then you weren't ready to tell Sunny at that moment. Per-haps you will be ready another time. It is up to you. Friendships take time. That is understandable. But they do also take hon-esty."

This is where Brady had to disagree with Dr. Nihati com-pletely. Sunny didn't want to hear more, so that was a *sign*. It wasn't up to him to tell her. It was up to Sunny and God. Sunny was responsible for stopping him from speaking, just like she was responsible for squeezing the back of his head the way she did. That was another sign—one of affection and desire. Dr. Nihati was wrong.

"Brady, have you ever heard of confirmation bias?"

"No," Brady said, and he was certain he didn't want to hear about it now.

"Confirmation bias means that we make note of those images and instances that confirm our current beliefs more than we make note of those things that do not."

Brady inspected the K'NEX crane more carefully. It was pretty complicated. He felt sad now for the girl who made it. What brought her to Dr. Nihati? Probably nothing good. Brady was sure of that. Maybe she wasn't as far along in her therapy as he was. She might've lost a parent. Or maybe her folks were in the middle of a nasty divorce.

"For example," Dr. Nihati continued, "let's say your best friend moved away to Florida, and lately you've been feeling a bit guilty about not making an effort to visit him. And suddenly it seems like there are commercials every two minutes for Disney World, and every time you open your computer there are internet ads for airline tickets to Florida. And when you go to the store there are sales for oranges and orange juice and orange soda . . ."

Brady balanced the K'NEX crane with his left hand and pulled the bucket down with his right hand. *The girl who made it was pretty clever to be able to make this thing in a forty-five-minute session. She probably wants to be an architect or an engineer. This girl has mad skills. She deserves to go to MIT and be a fucking engineer no matter what brought her to this room in the first place,* Brady thought.

Dr. Nihati leaned forward. "You see, those ads and sales have always been present. Only now you're noticing them because they confirm your current belief that you should visit your friend. You may interpret these images as signs, but this is actually confirmation bias. Do you understand?"

Brady looked up from the K'NEX crane. Dr. Nihati meant well; sure she did. Brady had to respect her with that diploma on the wall and her tortoiseshell glasses and her long gold chain with a little magnifying glass hanging on the end and all those mandatory, very shrink-like things about her. She was doing a fantastic job. But Brady knew that Dr. Nihati was a woman of science, not of religion. That was fine. He couldn't blame her for not believing in signs. Dr. Nihati was great. But a priest would probably say something totally different. Everyone has their own expertise. No big deal. "Oh, sure, sure." Brady nodded. "Confirmation bias. That makes a lot of sense. Thanks." None of it mattered anyway. Thora was going to help him to move on even if Dr. Nihati couldn't.

"Do you want to talk about the signs you've been seeing?"

"No. Nah." He shook his head. "They're not signs anyway, right? No. I think I just want to talk about, uh, some methods to fall asleep better, because I'm still not doing so well with that," Brady said, even though he'd been sleeping more soundly than ever. "Even when I think I've slept enough, I'm still tired, so I doubt I'm getting a real, deep sleep. Like, I'm probably not hitting that REM level of rest, you know?"

"I see . . . okay." Dr. Nihati raised her eyeglasses and rested them on top of her head. She was very professional, really. "Well, are you avoiding video screens at least an hour before bed? No cell phone, no laptop or TV, no iPad?"

"Yes. I'm doing that. No screens."

"That's good. What do you do instead?"

"Read, mostly. I've been reading a lot."

What were Soleil and Jonah like as a couple?

They were perfection. Relationship goals.

Really?

Like a Season One couple on a CW show.

Season One?

Gorgeous. Also sweet and happy and always on the verge of tearing each other's clothes off.

Ah. [phone buzzes] Excuse me. I've gotta take this.

No worries.

Hello? You're kidding . . . When? . . . Who are they? . . . Wow. Okay. Is this public knowledge? . . . All right. Yup. Will do. Right. Thanks for the call. Bye.

They caught the guys?

Just arrested five kids for assault.

Finally! Thank the lord.

The cops have been closing in on these arrests for a couple of days now.
I'm glad they finally did it.

So, who are these assholes?

Three guys from South Carmine. Two others. They're all between six-
teen and eighteen.

I *knew* it! Didn't I tell you?

You called it.

[picks up phone] I'm texting Fatima.

Do you think she'll answer?

It doesn't matter. I just want her to know, and I want it to come
from me.

___

Stranger Than Fiction

The True Story Behind the Controversial Novel

The Absolution of Brady Stevenson

SOLEIL JOHNSTON'S STORY, PART 3 (continued)

___

DATE: October 18, 2016

TO: soleil410@gmail.com

FROM: fatima.ro.author@gmail.com

SUBJECT: AP Psych

Got your text. You're right. Trauma = 100% Jonah. This psychology stuff is fascinating and also incredibly helpful and insightful. Necessary in order to learn more about him. Very sorry—I don't mean to trivialize. I should've paid attention when I took AP Psych my senior year, but I didn't (too busy, I guess, sneaking out of my bedroom to meet a bad boy).

I see why it's a shock to see your new boyfriend reflected in a PowerPoint lesson. Don't freak. This is a good thing: learning about Jonah from a psychological standpoint will help us to better understand him even if he's struggling with being inside/out. So, Jonah fits the descriptions in your psych curriculum. This only means he's going through normal coping strategies. It's probably better to be definable than not.

Don't overanalyze. I had friends in college who were premed. They thought they had every single illness they studied. They didn't, obviously. It's called confirmation bias—once you have an idea in your head, you start to see confirmation of it everywhere. For example, if you need to buy an obscure item like a pet stroller, you start seeing pet stroller ads and articles and people with pet strollers. It seems like they've exploded everywhere, but in actuality, it's because you're only noticing them now. That's an asinine example—I don't know what I'm getting at here. I'm just trying to explain that you have Jonah on the brain, which is expected, and that everything's completely okay. You think about him whenever you hear an Adele song, I'm sure. Seeing Jonah reflected in your AP Psychology homework is no different than that.

Jonah is so much happier now that he's with you. He smiles, for god's sake! Do you remember him at my book signing with his sad gray hoodie, mumbling to me about TV and art and whatever the hell else? He's practically a different person now. You're helping him along, so he's going to be fine. So are you.

▶ ▶▶
PENNY

How are you feeling about the arrests?

I'm glad they got caught. I hope they get put away for a long time.

Any other thoughts?

[covers face]

Penny?

[shakes head]

Are you okay?

[no response]

Why is this making you so emotional?

[shrugs]

You didn't cause this, Penny. It's not your fault.

[no response]

Do you want to talk about this?

No.

The Absolution of Brady Stevenson

BY FATIMA RO

(excerpt)

Brady sat up in his bed. His right earlobe was going numb against his cell phone. "I used to have this recurring nightmare . . ." he said, switching to his left ear.

"What was it?" Thora's voice was so reassuring; she could get almost anything out of him.

"I dreamed that I was locked away someplace terrible. Cletus was getting older and older back home, but I couldn't get to him."

"Oh! How sad."

"In the dream, I needed a key to unlock my door from the inside, but I could never find it. Every night I'd look in the same exact places, like under the mattress, under the plant, in my sock drawer, but I'd know from having the dream before that it wasn't in any of those places. I was afraid that Cletus was dying and that I couldn't see him to pet him or talk to him or anything. I'd wake up sweating and crying. I had that dream basically every night."

"That's awful," Thora said. "Where were you?"

"What do you mean?" Brady tensed.

"Where were you locked away in the dream?"

"I don't know. An institution of some kind. I wasn't allowed out—in the dream."

"That's terrible."

"Yeah. It stopped, though. I don't have that nightmare anymore."

"That's good. It must be a healthy sign."

"Must be." Brady sank deeper into his pillow, grateful to be in his own bed.

"It really means a lot that you're transparent with me this way, Brady."

"It means a lot to me, too. I didn't think I'd make any new friends after . . . what happened."

"I didn't think I'd make new friends after I got published. I spilled my soul in *The Drowning*, and so I expected people to be real with me in return. Instead, my friends resented me for being successful when they were getting rejected to grad schools and turned down for internships. When I did meet new people, they couldn't see past the author. It's been hard to find authentic human connections until now."

"That's the scary thing for me. I'm always afraid that if people find out that one thing about me, they won't be able to see anything else," Brady said, feeling very understood.

"Sunny still sees you for you."

"I hope so."

"I know she does, because she's been candid with me, too. You should take her out on a proper date. Better still, you should introduce her to Cletus. Share your universe with her, let her into your life a little bit. Make her feel like she's part of it."

"You think so?"

"She would love it." Thora sounded excited, which made Brady excited. "Where do you like to walk Cletus? Is there a park you go to?"

"I actually found this one beach spot that allows dogs, Sands Point. I've been taking him there. It's nice and quiet most days." Sands Point had a few regulars. There was actually an old guy with a pug, a couple with a scrappy mutt, and a single woman with a golden retriever. It had become Brady's favorite place on the North Shore. "I just wish I could let Cletus off his leash, but you're not allowed to do that. I'd really love to see how fast he would be if he could run free."

"Hang on," Thora said. Brady could hear her typing. She always seemed to be typing when they were on the phone. "Are you talking about the beach at Sands Point Preserve? The place with a stone castle?"

"Yeah. Why?"

"There's a Fall Medieval Festival coming up."

"I don't know. It sounds a little geeky," Brady said. His old self probably would've laughed at kids at a medieval festival.

"No, no. It looks fun. Knights, horses, jousting. They put up tents, and people wear costumes."

Brady's old self definitely would've laughed at kids in costumes. "Costumes?"

"You don't have to wear a costume. But you should take Sunny and Cletus. It'll be the cutest date. Sunny will love the castles. There are Irish castles in *The Drowning*. She'll be so into it."

Brady could picture it already—him and Sunny holding hands along the beach while Cletus played chest-deep in the water. The three of them could hike up the hill to the castle and stroll around the festival. "Are you sure?"

"Yes. Ask her to go. But ask her in person. No texting!"

"Okay. I'm just out of it. I feel like I'm a year behind when it comes to girls. I really want things to work out with her."

"Then take her on a proper date, and it will. I promise you."

"Thanks. I hope so." Brady checked his phone; his battery was dying. He looked around, but ironically, considering his social commentary art project, there was no sign of his charger. "My battery's dying, so I'd better go."

Thora yawned. "Okay. We'll talk more about it tomorrow."

"Tomorrow." Brady liked the sound of that.

▶ ▶▶

MIRI

No word from Fatima about the arrests?

[scrolls through phone] No. [sighs] I just hope she gets some sense of relief from it. She must feel completely alone these days.

She just hit the New York Times bestseller list.

[puts phone down] The *New York Times* bestseller list? What are you saying? Do you think that serves as a consolation for her? Fatima left her home! Wherever she is now, she has no friends. Zero. This woman who lives and breathes to make authentic human connections has *nobody.* What do you think she'll do— prop the *New York Times* beside her on the sofa and converse with it?

No, I'm not suggesting that. But the list must mean something to her.

I know what it means to her: nothing. She won Author of Promise and didn't even tell us. I heard it from Soleil. Don't you get it? Fatima didn't want to be the Author of Promise for a book about her dead mother any more than she wants to be on the bestseller list because Jonah is hooked up to machines.

How do you know this list isn't exactly what she was hoping for when she set out to write this book?

Because over the months that we spent with her, Fatima confided in us about a million things: when she was sixteen she lied and told her doctor she had irregular periods so that he would give her a prescription for the pill, and that her first boyfriend was so boring he turned her off to boys her age for the rest of her life. But do you know what? Of the million things she confided to us, she never once mentioned wanting to hit some list in the paper. I am confident that she didn't give two shits about that list.

What did she care about?

Us.

Stranger Than Fiction

The True Story Behind the Controversial Novel

The Absolution of Brady Stevenson

SOLEIL JOHNSTON'S STORY, PART 3 (continued)

FATIMA

Are you back yet? I'm at a snoozer

publishing event, so can't talk but

OMG I'm dying to know how the

date went!

SOLEIL

I MET CLETUS!!!!

That's so special! What

else? Tell. Me. EVERYTHING.

We took him to Sands Point beach.

Perfect spot. Walked up the trail to . . .

drumroll . . . Fall Medieval Fair! Very

cool. Horses, jousting, tents, costumes,

fortuneteller (long story), stone castle!!!

Last time I was there was 2nd grade

nature walk. Didn't remember it was so
beautiful.

How was Jonah? Suave? Fun?
Awkward? Cute? Sexy? WWJ???

ALL OF THE ABOVE

Awww . . . Ok, shit, gotta go.
I'm getting an award right now for
Undertow. It's nonsense. Have to give
an acceptance speech blaaahhh.

WOW! No, that's awesome.
Congrats! Go get your award!
I'll tell you (hottt) deets about the
castle later! ☺<3

Huzzah!!! Happy for you bye!!!

Soleil and Jonah went to a fortune-teller.

They did?

When he took her to a Renaissance fair.

Oh.

Jonah told me. He didn't want his fortune read. He was, like, dead set against it. But Soleil kept telling him it'd be fun, you know, like spooky Halloween kind of fun. She's always down for anything. That's just Soleil; she convinces you that everything's gonna be a blast. So Jonah went along with it. But it turned out to be a bad idea.

Why was that?

The fortune-teller said that Jonah's fortune was incomplete.

Okay, that's . . . creepy.

I know. She said Jonah had a "dark cloud following him." She also told him there was a very wise woman in his life, and if Jonah followed her guidance, he could escape the darkness. Then she charged Soleil five dollars for the reading.

Huh.

Do you believe in that stuff? That people can predict the future?

I believe that some people can, but most who say they can are probably fakes.

That's what I think, too. [sighs] I hope that one was a fake. [pauses]

What are you thinking about?

Do you think all the guys that beat Jonah will be tried as adults, even the minors?

That's a good question. There's a chance they will. There may be a lot of pressure and backlash from the last time.

[shakes head] It just keeps going and going.

What does?

If these guys get off, is someone gonna beat them up afterward?

Let's hope they don't get off.

[phone buzzes] [reads text] It's my father from the home office.

I made him promise not to come downstairs anymore. He just saw Fatima on the *New York Times* bestseller list. He's saying she's profiting off of Jonah and some other stuff I can't say on camera. [looks up] He's really mad.

Well, I can understand his anger. But Fatima might've hit the list with or without the scandal. Her reviews were good. There was a lot of pre-release buzz. The advance sales were strong. It seemed to be headed in that direction on its own.

Okay. [texts]

What do you think about it—the bestseller list?

I think it's so gross, for real. This *just* happened to Jonah. It's still happening right now, and she's getting on lists. She must be making a lot of money.

Some.

It's not like it's a book about the *Titanic* or something. That boat sank, like, a hundred years ago. Fatima wrote about us today, while we're still in the world walking around. Well . . . not Jonah. But you know what I mean.

The Absolution
of Brady Stevenson

BY FATIMA RO

(excerpt)

The fortune-teller was a bad idea. Brady paced outside Madame Lola's tent, texting Thora in a hurry. "The fortune-teller said I have a black cloud following me." What else could Madame Lola see in those tarot cards? He had rushed out, afraid of what the old woman might say in front of Sunny.

"Why the hell did you go to a fortune-teller in the first place? Brush it off! You make your own destiny. You carve your own path. Stop texting me and show Sunny a good time. Get thee to the castle!" Thora, the "wise woman in his life," replied. Brady stuffed his phone in his pocket. He was determined to take her advice and say "Screw you!" to his black cloud.

Sunny stepped out of the tent with one hand over her heart. "I'm so sorry. She shouldn't be allowed to say stuff like that. Isn't there a fortune-teller's code of conduct? What a batty old crow. I shouldn't have made you go in there. She charged me five dollars. Such a rip-off." She felt awful. She'd thought it would be fun. Sunny wanted so badly to text Thora and ask how to rebound, but she didn't want to text in front of Brady.

"No, it's fine." Brady shrugged. "Cletus had to go out, that's all. I think he was getting claustrophobic."

"Oh." Sunny looked down at the dog. Cletus seemed

perfectly content scratching his ear. Thora would say, "Keep calm and girlfriend on. Do what comes naturally." Sunny decided to do that the rest of the day.

"Come on." Brady took Sunny's hand. He led her and Cletus past a face-painting tent, a puppet theater, a tent peddling handmade jewelry, and a tent for henna and body art. Little kids ran in front of them, chasing one another with plastic swords. "No more tents. We're going in there." Brady pointed to Hempstead Castle, where visitors were streaming in and out. He was going to turn this date around.

They hurried to the side of the building and snuck in through the delivery door with Cletus. "It's never locked. We came through here last week," Brady said as they wove their way through the maids' kitchen. "I also came here this morning." Brady opened a cabinet beside the sink. "To hide this for us." He pulled out a blue cooler.

"This is ours?" Sunny pulled the cooler toward her and rose onto her tiptoes. "What did you do?"

"Packed us a lunch and some iced tea." He opened the lid to show her the deli sandwiches, plastic containers, Arizona iced teas, and a beach towel inside.

Sunny spun to face him. "Are you kidding me?"

"What's the matter? You've never seen a picnic in a castle before?" Brady asked proudly.

"Sure I have. On *The Bachelor*!" She laughed and then kissed him on the cheek.

Brady carried the cooler. They passed through a formal dining room with an intricately carved table and heavy satin drapery. In the classic wood-paneled library, faded books stood between copper acorns and stone busts. "Beautiful room," Sunny said. "I love the woodwork."

Cletus's nails clicked across the floor into the sunroom. There he lay, exposing his belly under a patch of sunlight. Earlier, Brady and Sunny had taken turns holding Cletus's leash while he scampered along the shore, picked up sticks, and teased the waves.

The couple joined the dog on the hand-painted tile and took in the view through the French doors. Brady unpacked BLT sandwiches. Potato salad, fruit, and drinks rounded out the lunch. Voices and footsteps traveled down from the staircase. Sunny and Brady looked over their shoulders at a group tour getting ushered into the foyer. The visitors took a few final pictures before exiting through the front door.

Sunny stretched her legs and relaxed back on her hands. "I still can't believe you did this. Thank you." She couldn't wait to tell Thora how romantic and thoughtful Brady was.

"You're welcome," Brady said. He couldn't wait to thank Thora for planning all of it.

"It's nice and warm right here. The sun feels so good," Sunny said as she took her jacket off. "It was getting chilly out." She opened her iced tea. Cletus's ears perked when the cap popped.

"Cletus always finds the sunny spots," Brady said, giving his dog a pat.

Sunny admired the expansive lawn and the glassy surface of the Long Island Sound. Children with painted faces were cartwheeling on the grass. "I think there's a *Great Gatsby* party here in the summer. We should come back for that. I could wear a long string of pearls, and you can wear a bow tie," Sunny said, smiling. A Gatsby party sounded pretty classy and was unlikely to have a fortune-teller. "It's such a great castle. The diamond shapes in the windowpanes are so pretty." She looked behind her at the fountain in the middle of the front room. "This reminds me of the Irish castles in *The Drowning*, only much warmer," Sunny said. "In the book, Jules and her mother go from one castle to another; each one is colder and damper than the next. There's this one character they keep bumping into, a British guy who wears a dressing gown and slippers to each castle because he likes to pretend that he lives in them."

Sheridan Thompson. Brady knew the character, but at this point couldn't admit to knowing the novel so well. It'd be embarrassing. It was fun, anyway, hearing the girls talk candidly about the book. It was like eavesdropping on foreigners who don't know you understand their language.

"How does Thora think up this stuff?" Brady asked, as Cletus began to snore lightly beside him.

"No idea. She thinks of crazy things, crazy but realistic; that's why it's so good."

"Like what else?" Brady asked, thinking of the racy chapters he had annotated with comments such as *Is this porn?*

"Like . . . kissing," Sunny said, anxious to take this date to the next level. "She writes some very realistic kissing." She tilted her head.

"Oh, really?" Brady glanced at Sunny's bottom lip.

"Yes. And other stuff," Sunny teased.

Brady looked down at Sunny's cleavage. "Other stuff?"

Sunny's low-cut sweater had been a good idea. She was happy to distract Brady from his incomplete fortune. "A little of this and that."

He kissed her then, brushing his lips lightly over her cold mouth. She tasted of tea. Sunny leaned closer, adding pressure and opening her mouth. She rubbed her knee against his and pulled at his shirt as their kiss intensified. How far could they go in the castle? She dragged her hand down Brady's chest and stomach to find out, but Brady caught her hand and broke away. He clearly wasn't ready to go further than this. She would have to be patient.

Brady exhaled deeply. All this off-the-page real-life kissing was torturing him. "I want to do 'other stuff' and 'this and that' so bad right now. A lot of it," Brady whispered.

"Really? Then why don't you?" Sunny's big eyes begged.

"We can't." He leaned back and pointed to a dark globe in the ceiling. "There are cameras in here."

"Oh, thank god!" Sunny burst out laughing. "I thought it was because you didn't want to!"

"I want to! Believe me!" Brady squeezed her hand.

Sunny threw her head back and waved at the camera. It was such a relief to know that Brady wanted her as much as she wanted him. He didn't need more time to heal from his dark cloud. He was perfectly fine.

▶ ▶▶| 1:50:20 / 3:04:23   🔊 ━━   [ ]

MIRI

[camera settles] How's your week going, Miri? We're filming.

[fixes hair] Oh, I don't know. [sighs] You've seen the internet. *Miri Tan: Loyal Fan.* Very clever. Why is it so hard for people to understand why I defend her? Hear me when I say this: Fatima showed up for us. And when I say that she showed up, she literally showed up—to *Graham*. She walked right into our cafeteria just as natural as could be.

Wow.

I had no idea she was coming. I was just sitting there after school one day, eating leftover cupcakes from the student council elections, when in walks Fatima Ro. I kid you not. By then everyone knew her from our photos, and Ms. Grauss bought a class set of *Undertow* that very week. It was as if Fatima had leapt off the book jacket and into the cafeteria. It was the stuff of life.

[laughs] Wait. Did you run for student council?

God, no. My plate was full. It was Natalie Singh versus this prick Hugh Lambert, a cocky Graham Seven, who thought he had it in the bag. Natalie deserved to be student council president.

Did she win?

She did. I was happy to campaign for her. That's how I am. When I believe in someone, I will support her to the nth degree.

Like with Fatima.

Especially with Fatima. [takes a breath] Picture this. I'm sitting at a table with ten, maybe fifteen *Undertow* fans. I'm holding a VOTE NAT cupcake and my copy of *Undertow* when in walks the author herself, in vintage suede and cat's-eye sunglasses. Hello!

Nice.

She walks straight up to me and gives me a hug, so now I'm hugging Fatima Ro, holding a cupcake behind her back.

[laughs]

And then what does she do?

I can't even guess.

She grabs my wrist and licks the icing off my cupcake.

[laughs]

That put an end to the doubters. Not to the haters by any means, but it was the end of the doubters. I smiled and thought, "Don't you ever question my friendship with Fatima Ro again, negative bitches."

Stranger Than Fiction

The True Story Behind the Controversial Novel

The Absolution of Brady Stevenson

SOLEIL JOHNSTON'S STORY, PART 3 (continued)

PENNY

Hi! Where are you?

> SOLEIL
>
> Art room working on
> #DoorsAsAMetaphor. I'm learning how
> to use a jigsaw to cut openings behind
> the doors. I feel like a lumberjack. Let's
> shop for flannel shirts. Not joking.
> Urban Outfitters run!

Come to the cafeteria!

> Why?

Fatima is here!

> What!!!! I'll be right there!

PENNY

Did you know that Fatima came to Graham?

I heard. That was a big deal, wasn't it?

It was crazy. Travis Foley hit on her. Teachers were worse than the students—asking for selfies and wanting her to sign books for them. Ms. Grauss, my English teacher, asked her how to do a topknot. It felt like . . . [pauses]

Like what?

It felt like the end to me. The beginning of the end.

Of your quiet little group?

Uh-huh. And another thing was weird.

What?

I got this feeling like there was something going on between Fatima and Jonah. First I saw them talking all secret-like in the courtyard. She didn't even want to come inside, like she was there just to talk to Jonah. And then while Fatima was talking to the group, she kept looking over at him, and he kept looking over at her, and I just got a vibe.

That doesn't sound like Fatima to be interested in him that way.

I know—what would she want with him? He must've been a kid to her. She dates older guys. Men, actually. And she is Fatima Ro, right? But who knows why artsy people do what they do? Celebrities on TV are always, like, cheating with the nanny or whatever. Anyways, you don't have to be a brain on student council or on the debate team to have a gut sense. I know a vibe when I feel it. I couldn't just stand there with Soleil and not say something, so I asked her flat out, "WWJ and F?" and I pointed out their knowing glances.

How'd she react?

She said, "I'm sure it's nothing." She brushed it off. Maybe it really was nothing, or maybe Soleil didn't want to know, so I left it alone.

The Absolution
of Brady Stevenson

BY FATIMA RO

(excerpt)

October 26, 2016
Thora Temple in the Morley Cafeteria!
3:21 p.m.

Gaaah! I can't believe I missed half the convo. Thank god
Paloma texted me to come down. Will try to catch the rest
here:

Q: Where'd you get your jacket? I love it.
A: Thank you! I found it in a vintage shop in the Hamptons,
   but I can't remember the name of the store, and now I've
   lost the receipt. It's killing me that I can't remember. I can't
   even find the place online.
Q: Can I touch it? I love suede.
A: Sure. Soft, huh?
Q: Where did you go to high school?
A: A private school in Massachusetts. It's a little bit like here,
   except much smaller. And it's definitely a lot more hippie.
   We didn't get letter grades, just narratives. And the faculty
   let us call them by their first names. Our teachers were

more like friends to us. It was the kind of environment where it was acceptable to have emotions. I felt free there to express my point of view.

Q: Were you writing back then?

A: Yes. I wasn't writing novels yet, but I wrote short stories and poetry for *Vent*—that was our literary magazine. My writing was horrible, horrible! But it was my outlet, my forum. It gave me confidence and visibility. It was an important time for me.

Q: How much of *The Drowning* was based on your life?

A: The heart of *The Drowning* is real. The heart of my characters is always real.

Q: Do you have a boyfriend?

[laughter all around]

A: No.

Q: Don't mind him. Trevor's the class player.

Q: Do you *want* a boyfriend?

[more laughs]

A: It depends on who's asking.

Q: I'm asking!

[hooting and hollering]

A: You're too young for me.

Q: I'm mature for my age.

A: And I'm mature for mine. But nice try.

[various expressions of Trevor Foy getting owned]

Q: Are they going to make *The Drowning* into a movie?

A: I doubt it. I love movies—these guys know that. [She gestured to us!!!] I'd love to see that happen. But *The Drowning*'s been out for a little while now, and there hasn't been interest in that, so, probably not. It's a little too quiet of a book for a film. So much of the conflict is internal rather than external. Maybe the next one.

Q: What's your next book about?

A: I can't really talk about it yet.

Q: But I thought you practiced the theory of human connections by disclosing your precious truths.

A: Oh, I do. That's very important to me. Please know that. But I'm still in the early stages of the manuscript, so I don't know what its precious truth is yet. When I'm writing something new it takes a while for me to recognize the soul of the story. And when it comes to the theory of human connections, you have to understand the truth for yourself first before you can share it with others.

Q: Can I quote you on that for the paper? I write for *Echo*, the Morley newspaper.

A: Of course.

Q: I'm going to be senior editor next year. And for *The Drowning*, Marni put me in charge of school outreach. I'm doing everything I can to spread the word here about the theory and the novel.

A: That's incredible. I appreciate that. And congratulations on being senior editor. That's a big deal.

Q: Oh my gosh, thank you so much!

Q: What were your favorite scenes to write in *The Drowning*?

A: My favorite scenes to write . . . I guess I have to say the sex
   scenes!

[laughter]

   Only because I was going through a rough time when I
   wrote that manuscript, so those scenes just allowed me to
   forget my life and focus on something fun temporarily. The
   rest of the book was cathartic, but not in a fun way what-
   soever.

Q: Why are you *here*?

A: [glances at Brady] [???] I just wanted to say hi.

▶ ▶▶

MIRI

According to The Absolution of Brady Stevenson *and* New York City *magazine, Fatima went to the school to visit Jonah.*

I know that.

Does that bother you? To learn that Fatima went to Graham to see Jonah, not you?

I never said I was her favorite. I said that Fatima considered me the leader, which she did. But I wasn't her favorite. Neither was Soleil. Jonah—*he* was her favorite. She swooped into the cafeteria and hugged me because she didn't want anyone to know that she was there for Jonah. I know that. It's fine. She was trying to protect him, didn't want anyone to know they were tight. She never meant to expose him. Can't you see? She loved that kid like a brother. She committed herself to him, wanted him to have the North Shore private school; the girl; the big, bright future; the confidence; the dog; all of it. People can go ahead and slam Fatima left and right for blasting Jonah's secret, but can't you at least see the precious fucking truth? Jonah Nicholls . . . Broke. Her. Heart.

Stranger Than Fiction

The True Story Behind the Controversial Novel

The Absolution of Brady Stevenson

SOLEIL JOHNSTON'S STORY, PART 3 (continued)

> SOLEIL
>
> Jonah just told me the reason you
> came to Graham was to see him &
> you've been talking on the phone.
> He asked me if I'm okay with that.

FATIMA
Are you? There's nothing else
happening, cross my heart.

> I know. I trust you. Of course I'm okay
> with it. He hasn't been opening up to me
> any more than when we first got
> together. At least he's talking to you.

I hope it's not a problem for you and me.
I want to be a friend to each of you.

> It's not a problem. I understand why

he's comfortable with you. And I'm glad
I don't have to handle his issues alone. I
don't mean "his issues" as in a burden.

I know what you mean.

He's a good guy to ask me how I
feel about it.

That he is.

But Penny thinks you're having a
thing with him behind my back.

Bahahahhahaaa!!! No offense.
He's adorable. But my last boyfriend
was 38.

Fatima said she was only in the beginning stages of her book, so she wasn't sure what it was about yet.

Yes.

It's weird to think about that now.

Why?

She was in the beginning stages of us.

The Absolution
of Brady Stevenson

BY FATIMA RO
(excerpt)

This tour of Morley Academy, through the quad, past the library, and out to the athletic field, is what Thora called a "walk and talk"—questions and answers accompanied by a stroll around the natural habitat. Brady felt that Thora had this backward; he should be asking her questions. She was the interesting one.

"I think there are eight playing fields," Brady said dryly, as he watched the boys' soccer team running practice drills to the sound of the coach's whistle. The athletic grounds held no significance for Brady.

"Beautiful property. Last time I was here it was pitch dark," Thora said.

"There are stables down at the other end, supposedly." Brady pointed past the fields. "You can bring your own horse for a stall fee, if you can believe that shit." Brady shook his head.

"Not exactly like public school?"

"No," Brady scoffed. "I haven't seen any horses, though. I only read that on the website. Once in a while I see a girl walking around carrying her riding helmet. She's probably a model Morley hired."

Thora laughed. They walked on toward the courtyard they knew well, passing students and teachers who looked curiously at Thora. "Do you miss sports at all? Or do you just feel like, to hell with that?" After their many phone calls, she felt comfortable enough with Brady to ask.

"I miss, like, the physicality of it." Brady watched the soccer players running suicide drills back and forth at the other end of the field. "I still work out at home. If I don't do something active I feel like a slug. Plus, you should always keep in shape in case there's a zombie apocalypse. You don't want to be the slow, heavy guy."

"No, you wouldn't want that," Thora said.

"So, I do miss sports, yeah," Brady said. "I just don't miss . . . being on a team."

"I get that. It's understandable." They reached the courtyard gate. Thora took a deep breath. "What is it about being on a team that makes people behave violently?" she asked.

Just then, Paloma burst through the courtyard calling Thora's name. Brady didn't have a chance to answer the author's question. They would both have to think about it good and hard.

MIRI

[checks her phone]

Have you heard back from Fatima?

No. But it's fine. She's doing what she needs to do for her own welfare. Ms. Halpin, my AP Psych teacher, said that people with high emotional intelligence identify their feelings, evaluate their options, and move forward with positive action. What Fatima does is, she eliminates obstacles to her own mental health. I've seen her do it—the way she dropped her dead-weight college friends and the way she spoke to her father. She knows what's healthy for her. When she comes back, it'll be because she's ready and strong.

Stranger Than Fiction

The True Story Behind the Controversial Novel

The Absolution of Brady Stevenson

SOLEIL JOHNSTON'S STORY, PART 3 (continued)

SOLEIL

Can I ask you one thing, though?

FATIMA

Always.

Why didn't you tell me you've been
talking to Jonah?

He asked me not to. He wanted to
tell you himself when he was ready.
I hope you can understand that.

I do.

And maybe it shows that when he's
ready to tell you something he will.

▶ ▶▶

PENNY

Is there anyone else you think I should interview at Graham?

Ms. Grauss was in the cafeteria that day. Dr. Beals was there, too, my history teacher.

All right.

You know, after Fatima showed up, Ms. Grauss started being nicer to me. She has her favorites; every teacher at Graham has favorites even though they go around saying "one heart and one mind" all the time.

I take it you weren't one of Ms. Grauss's favorites.

No way. She caught me copying homework in the hallway once, so she kind of hated me. But after she saw that I was friends with Fatima, I was smart all of a sudden.

[laughs]

That's what it was like knowing Fatima Ro. My English grade went up, like, ten points.

Not bad.

Uh-huh. My parents missed seeing me around the house, but they were happy about my grade. For real.

NAKED TRUTH TV

Nelson Anthony interviews Nan Grauss, Dr. Jim Beals,
DeeDee Halpin, Martin "T-Bone" Henry
May 15, 2018

© Push Channel 21, Bellmore, NY, 2018

▶ ▶▶| 0:00:04 / 0:04:55 ◀)) — [ ]

NAN GRAUSS,
GRAHAM ACADEMY ENGLISH TEACHER

I remember Fatima at Graham. What a breath of fresh air. I was
surprised at how personable she was, because *Undertow* felt very
dark to me. I could see why my students were drawn to her.
She made you feel like you were the most important person in
the room. She shook my hand and held on to it and told me
that her English teachers were always her favorite people when
she was in school. Such a kind thing for her to say. We made a
human connection; I felt it. My best students, Miri and Soleil,
created a fandom in my class. The other kids look up to them,
they're real trendsetters here. A couple years ago they and their
friend Penny started wearing adorable silk neckerchiefs with
Chanel brooches, and then everyone started wearing them. It's
hard to make fashion statements with the uniform, but these
girls? They can. [pauses] I thought their love of *Undertow* would

be a positive interest for me to encourage, so I ordered sets for my classes. I didn't even assign it. I just opened the boxes on my desk. The next thing I knew the books were gone. At Monday assembly, I talked about Fatima's visit, about how proud we should be that Graham is the kind of high-performing institution that attracts people like Fatima Ro. Miri was kind enough to share photos from the visit, even a photo of Fatima and me. Fatima had us all talking about her for days. [pauses] I can't help but feel somewhat responsible for the trouble that's occurred. [tightens topknot] That poor, poor girl. I really feel for Fatima with everything that's happened to Jonah.

JIM BEALS, PhD,
GRAHAM ACADEMY HISTORY TEACHER

These kids. [sigh] When they don't care about something they *really* don't care. But when they do care, they go overboard. [shakes head] I see it with everything, with their grades, music, sports, drama club, their relationships. It's either "*Whatever*, Dr. Beals" or "Ohmigod, Dr. Beals! This song is my *life*!" There's no in between. [pauses] If I could say one thing to that damn writer, what would I say? [grumbles] I'd say, if you knew these kids the way you claim to have known them, then you should've realized that when they admire you there's a responsibility in that. [straight into the camera] Look in the mirror and know that you did this to Jonah, you selfish, opportunistic egomaniac.

DEEDEE HALPIN,
GRAHAM ACADEMY AP PSYCHOLOGY TEACHER

Miri, Soleil, Emma, and Quinn were my top students; enthusiastic, analytical, very serious students. After Fatima's visit, Soleil demonstrated a marked interest in my class. She had always been interested in the material, but as soon as we hit the unit on social psychology, she really took to it. She was intent on learning and so full of questions, always offering examples. Now I know why. Reading Fatima's new book has been a bit shocking, to say the least. To see my class notes used in the story? [shakes head] It's disconcerting. I wish Soleil had come to me; I wasn't aware that she was struggling with such heavy issues in her personal life. And Jonah, well, I didn't have him as a student, but the support team in our building is the absolute best. Our counselors could have helped him. I don't know if he ever visited the Graham website, but it highlights our dedicated staff members and their credentials, as well as the many top-notch services readily available in terms of student mental health and wellness. I wish he'd taken advantage of what we have to offer.

MARTIN "T-BONE" HENRY,
GRAHAM ACADEMY SECURITY GUARD

Is that what they were doin' in that courtyard? Talkin' about a book and that crazy writer? Are you serious? I thought they were out there smokin' pot.

The Absolution of Brady Stevenson

BY FATIMA RO

(excerpt)

As Brady walked into Dr. Nihati's office, a girl around eleven years old walked out. Brady smiled at her; she smiled back, sort of. Not really. She'd already been smiling. She must've had a good session. Brady was happy for her. He watched the girl meet her mother in the waiting room—watched them greet each other with a side hug. Brady wanted so badly to ask the girl if she was the one who'd made the K'NEX crane. It had to have been her. He wanted to tell her how impressive it was; she should be an engineer or an architect. But he stopped himself. There was probably a confidentiality clause: toys made in Dr. Nihati's office stayed in Dr. Nihati's office. On top of that, Brady didn't want to come off as some creep who knew all about her therapy sessions.

"Thora Temple came to school to see me," Brady said, once he was settled into the familiar leather chair.

"She did?" Dr. Nihati leaned forward. A dog-eared copy of *The Drowning* sat on her desk along with Brady's file folder.

"Yup." Brady lifted his chin. "She wanted to talk to me in my natural habitat. 'Walk and talk like Barbara Walters,' that's what she said. She gets these weird ideas. She didn't want to come inside; she didn't think it was a good idea, but I knew Sunny would be happy to see her."

Dr. Nihati scribbled on her memo pad. "But what brought this visit about initially?"

"Oh, I didn't tell you?" Brady's eyes lit up. "We've been talking on the phone a lot. We're pretty close now."

"Is that so?"

"Yeah. She's real cool. I like talking to her, probably because she's older so she doesn't judge me. She's also not part of Morley, where people talk shit all the time. It doesn't matter how fancy a school is, people still talk shit. Sorry. I shouldn't curse, I know. I'm trying to break that."

"That's okay." Dr. Nihati jotted down another note. "What have you discussed with Thora?"

"Lots of things. My dog, me and Sunny, that kind of stuff. I even mentioned church to her. I wouldn't talk about that with anyone else—not that I'm embarrassed to be Catholic. I'm not. It's just not something I usually have conversations about."

"What did you say about church?"

"Just that I've been going with my parents since I was a kid."

"I see."

"I always thought that if I had the choice I wouldn't bother going to church, but even when I was away from home, I went and sat in the chapel."

"Why do you think that is?"

"I guess because it was comforting—the stained glass and

the candle smell. They had a different Bible than I was used to, but the messages were the same. I liked going. It felt familiar."

"I'm sure it did."

"I talk about nothing special with Thora, too. Like, uh, when she called Morley my natural habitat it was kind of funny, you know?"

"Why?"

"Morley didn't feel like my natural habitat until recently. My house—my old house, I mean. The gym back at South Carlisle, those places were my habitat."

"Your old town."

"Right."

"What changed for you recently?"

"Well, it used to be that when I put the school blazer on, it wasn't me, it was more like a costume. No, not a costume—a disguise—like the goofy glasses and mustache, do you know the thing I'm talking about?"

"Yes. Groucho Marx glasses."

"Who?"

"He was a comedian. Those glasses were fashioned after him."

"Oh. Well, when Sunny gave me a chance, I started to feel differently, because she saw me as that clean-cut, all-American guy, so then I got to thinking that, hey, I could be that."

"And now when you put the school jacket on, how do you feel?"

"Better. Great, actually. Anyway, it's nice to talk to Thora and to have someone who's genuinely interested in me, you know?"

"Of course."

"No offense to you. I know you're interested in me, but it's also your job."

"No offense taken. I understand what you mean. But what about Sunny? Do you think she's genuinely interested in you?"

"Oh, yeah, yeah. She's interested in me. She's a sweet girl, real sensitive. She cares about important stuff, sure. But I don't want to get into anything complicated with her. We both want to have a good time together, right? We're in high school."

"What does that mean to you—being in high school?"

"Well, it's supposed to be fun, isn't it? Like in books and movies. Well, maybe not books so much; Thora's book is pretty depressing. But in general, high school is supposed to be the best years of your life or something. I'm not expecting that. Really, who would even want that? I mean, I don't want to be thirty-five thinking my best years were back in high school. That'd be sad. You see, Sunny's upbeat. She likes TV shows and pop music—Bruno Mars and Beyoncé, that stuff. She's a Belieber. I don't know why I said that, I'm actually not sure if she likes him or not. My point is, I don't want to bring her down. She wants me to 'turn that frown upside down' and that kinda thing. She deserves that. What I mean is, high school's not supposed to be tragic and shit."

Dr. Nihati leaned forward and clasped her hands together. She was getting to something serious. "But sometimes tragedies do occur. Then we have to deal with them." Dr. Nihati spoke slowly, the way she did when she wanted her message to sink in.

The best thing for Brady to do was be agreeable. The less he resisted, the easier Dr. Nihati would be on him. "Oh, I know. That's true. Bad things happen to good people all the time. It's terrible. Awful."

"Brady." Dr. Nihati squinted. "Have you told Sunny or Thora anything about your past?"

Brady looked at the mini refrigerator against the wall and wondered what was inside. He could go for a sandwich and chips right about now.

"Brady?"

"I told them I used to wrestle."

"You did?"

"Yes, and that I used to go to S.C."

"Well, that's a big step." Dr. Nihati nodded. "Did you say anything else?"

Brady was getting a headache. "No."

"Okay. How did you feel when you told them you used to wrestle and that you used to go to South Carlisle?"

"I don't know. Weird."

"Weird in what way?"

"In the way that I didn't want to talk more."

Dr. Nihati sat back. "That's all right. You made very good progress. Quite good. These relationships must mean a lot to you."

"They do."

"That's why it's particularly important for you to continue to talk more openly. I understand why you want to keep the incident to yourself, but it's never fair to withhold this kind of information from those with whom you're engaging in physical intimacy or speaking to on an emotional level and making genuine human connections."

Brady looked up when he heard the familiar phrase.

"When we first discussed why you were transferring to a new school, you and your parents decided that the priority was academic success, so that you could have a promising future despite S.C. I mentioned that you might make new friends and that you needed to be prepared to disclose your past. However, you insisted very adamantly that you would not socialize; your focus would be schoolwork and getting into college, so I respected your intentions. But now you are talking about friends and even a girlfriend." Dr. Nihati spoke slowly again. "You must realize that if you're to pursue intimate relationships, you will need to revise your plan to include how you'll tell them what occurred at South Carlisle."

Somewhere after "talking about friends and even a girlfriend," Brady tuned Dr. Nihati out. She wasn't helping him anymore. She wanted him to move backward, not forward. That's not progress. Thora was getting to know the *new* Brady and helping him forget the past. That's what it means to move on.

"Brady?"

The boy nodded at whatever it was she had said and then remembered that Dr. Nihati preferred that he answer aloud. "Yes."

"It is your choice whether or not to share anything or everything about your past. But there are serious issues here that will affect your relationships. If Sunny and Thora find out in another way, that could be difficult for them and for you. There will be consequences."

Dr. Nihati was out of touch. She didn't understand signs from God or the concept of tabula rasa. Brady was done with her and her old-fashioned therapy. He was looking at a clean slate and a future. Just as the girl who made the K'NEX crane would be an engineer, Brady would be a surgeon. He would have Thora Temple and fun and a girlfriend, too, no matter what Dr. Nihati thought.

"Do you understand?" she asked.

"Yes," Brady answered, although he didn't agree with a word.

▶ ▶▶

MIRI

Earlier you mentioned Fatima's father.

Yes.

I didn't realize her dad was in the picture.

He is. Fatima's parents divorced when she was young, just like
my parents. I always felt close to her because of that. We had
a lot in common, honestly. She told me that divorced kids like
us have resilience. It's because we learn to count on ourselves
for stability when other kids depend so much on their parents.

I can see that. Did you meet Fatima's father?

No. But he called Fatima one day when we were at her place.
She had him on speaker. The conversation got heated. We
could hear him barking on the other end. Dr. Ro is not a subtle
man. I cannot emphasize that enough.

What did he say?

He was expecting Fatima to have a new book already, reminding
her of her deadline and her two-book contract. If she was serious about making a career of writing, she had to buckle down.

We heard him calling her a hack, a one-hit wonder. He couldn't understand what could possibly be taking her so long. She said she didn't expect him to understand. As a doctor, patients come to him, they tell him what hurts, and he fixes them using the list of cures he learned in med school. It's not the same as conceptualizing an entire world out of thin air. Nobody comes to a writer's office and tells her what needs writing. He yelled that she had a mortgage now. "Grow up! You've nearly exhausted all of your mother's trust money on that ridiculous house; it's not going to last forever. I don't want to support you again!"

Yikes.

She was curled up in her armchair with her hands on her head, yelling, "I am not lazy! I *am* working on it! That's why I came here—to write this thing. No, I'm not sleeping all day and clubbing at night. And nobody says 'clubbing.'" She said, "Don't call me a teenybopper idol! I help my readers in ways you couldn't possibly understand. I change people's lives. Just because I'm not a cardiologist doesn't mean I don't help people. You have no idea of the good I can do."

Whoa.

I know. Her father is an arrogant prick. Fatima told him that being called a hack and a one-hit wonder wasn't helping her to write any faster, so if he wanted to call her and check in and be supportive, he was welcome to. But if he couldn't do that, then he shouldn't call her at all.

Is that strange for you now, to know that the manuscript she was struggling with was about you?

No! [sighs] It wasn't about me. Good lord. Let's all stop saying that it was about me and my friends, because the book is about Jonah. And Jonah *wanted* her to write it! Can't you understand that? He was desperate to be rewritten. She was helping him.

Stranger Than Fiction

The True Story Behind the Controversial Novel

The Absolution of Brady Stevenson

SOLEIL JOHNSTON'S STORY, PART 3 (continued)

Journal Entry

November 5, 2016

Fatima's house

4:23 p.m.

Fatima's on the phone with her father. Her dad is a doctor. My mom is a doctor. We share this thing in common that only kids of doctors understand—our parents hold a standard of excellence that we can't live up to unless we become doctors, too. Even if you're successful in a different way, even if you're Fatima Ro, in their eyes you still haven't done anything as difficult or as important as going to med school. For Fatima and me, this is another thing that we *get* about each other. Seeing Fatima cry is a shock, but for me, not surprising. I understand more than the others what she's up against. Fatima being a writer is a rebellion—the opposite of doctor. She's standing up to her dad by doing it. And she's far from a hack. She's no one-hit wonder. She's going to prove him wrong. I know she will.

▶ ▶▶

PENNY

Fatima was crying on the phone with her dad.

That must've been awful.

It really was, yeah. But it also kinda made me feel like we were real friends, you know? 'Cause she could be so inside/out with us.

I can see that. She was comfortable around you.

Uh-huh. She said that when she wrote *Undertow*, it was about her, so the only person she had to please was herself. Since nobody knew she was writing the first book, it didn't matter if she finished it or not. It was a "flash of grief, a purging," she called it. She said she was struggling with the new manuscript 'cause the book was about someone else this time. She had to do it right.

That's a lot of pressure.

Yeah. I didn't really get it, though. I thought that if you were talented, that stuff just sort of poured out automatically. And why did she *have* to write a second book? She should've just agreed to write one. Isn't it cool just to say you did it once?

It would be for me.

That's what I thought. Her dad called her a one-hit wonder. But what's so bad about that? One hit is, like, a *goal* for most people. Do you remember Carly Rae Jepsen?

Sure. "Call Me Maybe."

See? She only had one big song, but you know her. Everyone and their grandmother remembers that song.

[laughs] I know what you're saying. Now I'll have it in my head for the rest of the day.

Sorry. Me too. But that's the point.

It's a damn catchy song.

I know! I got bangs cut because of her when I was a kid.

[laughs]

They were terrible. I looked like a Lego man.

[laughs]

It was the worst. [laughs] But anyways, Fatima said that people expected more of her after *Undertow*. It wasn't just her dad either. Publishers and editors and her agent were waiting because her second book had to come out by a certain date. There was a lot on her shoulders. I thought Fatima was, like, super chill. I didn't know she was so stressed out until that night.

I can't imagine working under those kinds of expectations.

Me neither. No one expects anything from me.

THE ABSOLUTION
OF BRADY STEVENSON

BY FATIMA RO

(excerpt)

"I need you guys to leave," Thora said, wiping her tears. "I have to work on this manuscript, and I need to do it now."

"Thora, don't let your dad upset you," Marni said. "He's not creative like you. He doesn't get it."

"He's talking like a doctor, that's all. My mom gets like that all the time," Sunny said.

"This isn't about my dad." Thora rubbed her forehead. "It's me. I've hardly written anything, and I have to get it right."

Brady carried his plate to the sink. He was flattered by how much trouble Thora was going through to write a character based on him.

"How about we help you?" Sunny said. "Do you know the premise yet? We can brainstorm with you. Or we can come up with characters. I'm good with names."

"Yes!" Marni said. "This is perfect. After all, we are your target audience."

Thora snatched the remote from Marni's hand and turned the television off. "This isn't high school homework, Marni. This is my career. I'm the goddamn Author of Promise!" She picked her laptop off the table, pulling its plug from the wall.

"All I have are notes! Can you comprehend that? And none of them make any sense. I don't know where they're going or what they mean! But by some miracle I have to pull a novel out of my ass in three months!" she yelled as she threw their backpacks and coats at the front door. "So go home, will you? There is nothing interesting happening here! Just leave so that I can concentrate for once." Thora disappeared into the hallway and slammed her bedroom door.

Her laptop was open on the table. She left it out when her dad called. I didn't mean to read her email, but it was right there. I couldn't *not* see it.

So, what did it say?

It was from her literary agent, asking to see her first draft.

Pressure.

Believe it. And Soleil and Penny had the balls to be shocked when Fatima asked us to leave. I told them to get over themselves. It was her job to write, not to babysit us. At least Jonah understood. He didn't want to be in Fatima's way. But then again, he knew she was working on something important, didn't he?

I suppose he did.

Stranger Than Fiction

The True Story Behind the Controversial Novel

The Absolution of Brady Stevenson

SOLEIL JOHNSTON'S STORY, PART 3 (continued)

FATIMA

Sorry I kicked you out.

SOLEIL

No prob. I understand. How'd your
writing go?

It's shit. I need something to
distract me. Anything good happen
after you guys left?

Um. Sort of.

Tell.

Went to Penny's house to play pool
and listen to music. Jonah & I went
into the pantry to get snacks . . .

"Get snacks" means????

Omg are you really going to make me text this?!!!!!

Now that you've said that?
YOU BETTER!!!

PENNY

Fatima was mad at us.

What do you mean?

When she said, "Nothing interesting is happening here," she wasn't asking us to leave because she couldn't concentrate. She was asking us to leave because we weren't doing or saying anything interesting enough for her to write about.

Huh.

It makes sense now. She got frustrated with us when we were boring because we weren't adding to her plot, but she would keep checking in just in case anything exciting happened later.

You seem to be coming to a lot of new conclusions lately.

That's 'cause it's all I do—think about the stuff that happened and worry about Jonah.

Don't let it drive you crazy.

At least I found something I'm good at. [pauses]

What else is on your mind?

Uh. . . . [shakes head] Nothing. Never mind. I wasn't going to talk about it.

Well, you can't drop it now. I'm intrigued.

I don't know. It's kinda . . . embarrassing. [pauses]

Embarrassing for whom?

For all of us—me and Soleil and Miri. [takes a deep breath] Because we thought that Fatima was so wise with her writing and her, like, life-changing philosophy. We followed her around like her baby ducklings. But— [pauses]

But what?

Well, I used to read Fatima's magazines. Sometimes I'd borrow them 'cause I don't buy magazines; I look at fashion and celebrity news online, you know?

Right. Same.

Well, I found this. [pulls out *Us Weekly* magazine] [slides it across the table] It's about *The Bachelor*, from Chris Soules's season, season nineteen.

Okay . . .

It starts on page twelve.

"How to fall in love on The Bachelor. *1. Look each other in the eyes like Sean and Catherine in the fantasy suite. 2. Use your partner's name. It'll make her feel like the only woman in your life, even if you're on a group date with five other women, as seen here with Jake and his remaining hopefuls. 3. Mirror body language like Ben and Courtney. Notice how they walk perfectly in sync on the beach under the moonlight."*

Wait. What the hell is this?

Keep reading. There's more.

"4. Share intimate truths, like when Brad told Emily he was ready to be a father; seen here on her hometown date to Charlotte, NC. 5. Ask open-ended questions like Chris and Whitney discussing the pros and cons of life in a small (very small) Iowa town. 6. Share an intense experience that will raise your feel-good endorphins, like Jason and Molly bungee jumping."

Did Fatima circle these numbers or did you?

Fatima did.

Holy shit. So, you're telling me that Fatima Ro got her theory of human connections from . . .

The Bachelor. We worshipped her. Soleil had a relationship with Jonah, and Miri ran an entire student movement based on a theory Fatima Ro stole from *The Bachelor.*

Oh my god.

The Absolution
of Brady Stevenson

BY FATIMA RO

(excerpt)

One of the many attractions at Paloma's house was the pantry. The big draw was that it was always fully stocked, thanks to a smart-home system the family called "Mr. Belvedere," after a long-defunct TV sitcom about a butler. In Paloma's pantry, family members simply say, "Mr. Belvedere? We need tortilla chips," and the system automatically adds tortilla chips to the grocery list.

"Hello." Mr. Belvedere turned the light on and greeted Sunny and Brady when they slid the door open.

"What the hell is that?" Brady asked.

"It's Mr. Belvedere, the smart-home butler."

"Are you kidding me?" Brady squinted at the touch pad on the wall.

"No one kids about Mr. Belvedere. He organizes the pantry. Listen to this," Sunny said. "Mr. Belvedere? Do we have chocolate-covered pretzels?"

"There are four bags of Snyder's Pretzel Dips on shelf number two," the robotic voice answered in a British accent.

"Whaaaat!" Brady said.

Sunny grabbed a bag of Snyder's Pretzel Dips from shelf

number two. "Impressive, huh?"

"Yeah." Brady took the pretzels from Sunny and looked at the bar code on the bag. "So when you finish a bag, what do you do, scan the bar code?"

"Yup. Mr. Belvedere subtracts it from the system. When they run out he adds it to the grocery list, which is linked to the delivery service Home Grocer."

"This is some Bill Gates shit," Brady said.

Sunny laughed. "What other snacks do we want?" She glanced up at the shelves. "Take anything. If you finish a bag you can scan it. Good times."

"Hang on a second." Brady leaned against the counter and faced Sunny. She looked so cute in her tight little yoga pants and slouchy sweatshirt. "We don't have to get back yet."

"What's wrong?" Sunny asked.

"Nothing's wrong." Brady set the pretzels down and gave a mischievous smile. Things had been feeling good between them lately. The awkwardness had faded. He could tell Sunny wasn't thinking so much about South Carlisle anymore. "I'm just not very hungry."

"Shut up," Sunny teased. "You're always hungry." She was right. Brady could eat anytime, anywhere, any food. When Thora wanted to clean out her refrigerator, she asked him over to finish her leftovers, and he did.

"Not right now." Brady shut the door with his foot. "Mr. Belvedere?" Brady said. "Turn the pantry light off." The pantry went dark.

"The pantry light is off," Mr. Belvedere said. Brady reached for Sunny and pulled her toward him.

Sunny giggled in the darkness as she raised her arms over Brady's shoulders. "I'm not hungry either," she said. Brady was right: she wasn't thinking about South Carlisle. "Mr. Belvedere? We're going to make out now."

They found each other's mouths on the first try and kissed hurriedly, excited to continue where they'd left off at the castle.

The smart-home butler responded, "I did not catch that command. Please repeat."

"You heard him," Brady said. "Please repeat." He leaned back and spread his legs apart. Sunny kissed him again and felt Brady's hands slide down her back, around her waist, and even lower still. Sunny felt as if she were living inside a fantasy. Specifically, she felt as if she were in *The Drowning*, chapter eight, in which Sam leans against his bedroom wall and rubs Jules "hard and fast against his body until they were both sweaty and panting."

Brady had read chapter eight at least ten times and thought about it even more often. Lost in the sensation inside his jeans and the memory of Thora's words, Brady gripped Sunny again and again and thought, *Here, Sunny, here's the fiction we both want to live, here and here and here* . . .

Fatima ended up writing a whole scene that night.

Did she?

Yes. That's what she told me. I knew she'd be productive once
we left. We just had to respect her space and give her time to be
creative. She's very centered.

*I don't doubt it. [pauses] Look, Miri, I wanted to show you something
that Penny found. It might be of interest to you.*

All right.

[A copy of Us Weekly *magazine slides across the table to Miri] Penny
found this in Fatima's house. Fatima marked up page twelve.*

[flips pages] "How to Fall in Love on *The Bachelor.*" So?

Just take a look.

[reads] [her face reddens] What are you trying to prove here?
[closes the magazine]

*I'm not trying to prove anything. I just want to know what you think
of this.*

I think you're trying to make a fool out of me, and I think you should shut your camera off.

What do you make of—

Shut the camera off. *Now.*

Stranger Than Fiction

The True Story Behind the Controversial Novel

The Absolution of Brady Stevenson

SOLEIL JOHNSTON'S STORY, PART 3 (continued)

> SOLEIL
> Jonah makes out like Wes
> in UNDERTOW.

FATIMA
WHAAAAT.

> He chapter eight-ed me!

Gasp! In the pantry???

> Hahaha! Yes. And it was
> goooooooood.

PENNY

She was a fraud, wasn't she?

Because of the magazine?

Yes. Don't you think she was a fraud?

I don't know. The magazine looks bad, no question about that. It looks ridiculous, actually. You saw my initial reaction. But does it make her a fraud? Not necessarily.

What about her story about the old lady at the Amtrak station and the Conway Twitty song?

Could've still happened. It might've solidified all of the concepts together in her head.

[pauses]

What's the matter, Penny?

I just wish I knew . . .

Knew what?

Whether or not I should hate her.

[pauses] Do you miss her?

[shrugs]

I know you're angry. But that doesn't mean you can't miss her and the time you spent with her.

I do sometimes. I miss movie night.

I was wondering about movie night. She devoted a lot of scenes to it in the book. I wasn't sure how much of that was true.

Oh, it was all true. [pauses] [smiles] Movie night was the stuff of life. We watched *Pleasantville*, *Whiplash*, *Rocky*, and a few others.

Rocky? Really?

Yeah. The first one. I know there's a bunch of 'em. Did you know that Rocky wrote the first draft in three days? Sylvester Stallone wrote it, I mean.

No, I didn't know that. That's amazing.

For real. He had $106 in the bank, and his wife was pregnant. So he wrote the screenplay and convinced producers to make the movie.

Wow.

His success story really motivated Fatima. She called him unassuming, 'cause, like, you'd never guess him being so intelligent with his looks and how he talks.

I see that. I always forget that he wrote it.

She also said you shouldn't underestimate people when they're hungry.

Huh. That's definitely true.

And she told us to be proud of the things we like—our music, our designer clothes, our TV shows or movies—even if other people think they're unintelligent or lame or frivolous. For creative people, you never know where inspiration will come from.

Like The Bachelor.

What? [pauses] . . . Oh.

The Absolution
of Brady Stevenson

BY FATIMA RO

(excerpt)

"So, tell me how it's been going between you and Brady." Thora hopped onto her bed and crossed her legs. "I'm dying to get the full report."

Sunny sat on the edge of the bed. "Things are getting better," she said. "We've been meeting in the art room during lunch so that I can work on my project. I'm desperate to finish it by Christmas break. I can't think of what else to add, but Brady gave me a photo of his front door."

"Cute. It's important to be with someone who supports your creative endeavors. It's not easy to find a guy like that. Believe me. Too many men are all about themselves and their money. Me. Me. Me. So, what else?" Thora asked, patting Sunny on the leg.

"Well . . ." Sunny bit her lip. "We've been heavy-duty making out behind the shelf of unclaimed pottery."

"Aha! I knew it! You two are oozing with sexual tension," Thora said. "So, what's the problem? You look like you're about to throw up."

"I'm just not sure that it's healthy," Sunny said. "I mean, after the nightmare he's been through? It's like we're avoiding his problems every time we fool around. Maybe he needs to emotionally heal. Do you think that we're displaying a classic case of denial? Because if we're just avoiding some deep-seated traumatic—"

"Stop." Thora grabbed Sunny's hand. "If you don't stop psychoanalyzing this with Psychology 101, I will disown you. Seriously, it's good that you're learning about that, but you have to stop thinking so technically and start trusting your feelings."

"Okay." Sunny dropped her head into her hands. "Ugh, I have zero self-control around him. I'm just so embarrassed."

"Don't be embarrassed! Are you forgetting who you're talking to? The author of a semiautobiographical novel about a girl who uses sex to avoid the reality of her mother's illness." Thora shook Sunny by the shoulders. "Helloooo!"

"Oh my god," Sunny said. "I'm an idiot."

"Not at all. But I do know what you're feeling! You and I are so much alike," Thora said. "You know, that relationship I wrote about in *The Drowning* was a learning lesson in real life. I grew and matured from it." Thora leaned back against her pillows. "You keep searching for a guidebook for right and wrong to guarantee that no one will get hurt. But that doesn't exist. You either connect with him on an authentic level—which is the only way to truly live a meaningful life—or you don't."

Sunny bit her lip. "How do I know if it's authentic or not?"

"Well, how does it feel to hook up with him?"

Sunny smiled. "Earth-shattering."

Thora laughed. "Really? Well, well, you've found his hidden talent. Then why are you even questioning it? Let yourself go! Be happy. I'm happy for you!"

"Are you positive?" Sunny asked.

"Yes!" Thora insisted. "So, tell me, what exactly goes on behind that pottery shelf?"

"He chapter ten-ed me," Sunny blurted, referring to the steamy scene where Jules sits on Sam's lap and he rolls her tights down "slowly and torturously, inch by inch."

"Well, shit!" Thora gave Sunny a playful shove. "No wonder you can't finish that damn art project!"

▶ ▶▶

MIRI

Are you all right?

[sits down] I'm fine. [slides *Us Weekly* back across the table]

Do you want to address this at all?

Yes. [clears throat] As a matter of fact, I do.

Great.

Penny thinks this discredits Fatima, but it doesn't.

How do you figure that?

Well, let's say Fatima did get the idea for the theory of human connections from *The Bachelor*. She took something trivial and developed it into something deeper that can be applied to strengthening real relationships.

That's fair.

This magazine doesn't take away the fact that she wrote two novels and encourages people to live fuller lives. Penny needs to get a grip, honestly. She does this. She blows things out of proportion.

Did you say you were the captain of the debate team at Graham?

Yes.

Stranger Than Fiction

The True Story Behind the Controversial Novel
The Absolution of Brady Stevenson
SOLEIL JOHNSTON'S STORY, PART 3 (continued)

Journal Entry
November 26, 2016
Fatima's house
Movie night
9:42 p.m.

Chinese takeout from Pearl East. Penny newly infatuated with Kate Hudson, Googling her outfits, trying to find her stylist. Miri in her element hanging on Fatima's every word. Jonah looking cute in track pants and sweatshirt, reading over my shoulder as I type this, so I had to say that, haha. SOLEIL LOOKING HOT IN JEANS AND #TheTheory TANK TOP!!!! <<< Okay, that was Jonah. Very charming. Don't you know that it's rude to type in caps??? Give me back my laptop!!!

Analysis of *Almost Famous* as discussed by Fatima Ro begins now:

GOOD LUCK PAYING ATTENTION BECAUSE WE ARE UNDER A BLANKET AND I CANNOT BE HELD RESPONSIBLE FOR WHAT HAPPENS UNDER HERE. <<< So funny. And I *will* pay attention because this is Fatima's favorite movie. I've always wanted to see it, and we are not going to disrespect her.

SHUT DOWNNNNN!!!

Seriously this time, let me try this again. Movie notes begin *now*:

Theme of authenticity in storytelling:
William Miller, 15, journalist, wanted to write the truth about the band Stillwater (including stupid things said on tour, how often they fought, how badly they treated their groupies). But the band members didn't want William to write about that. They only wanted William to "make them look cool." But William felt that wouldn't be honest, interesting, or authentic. So, against the band's wishes, he wrote the *truth*.

In the end, the band members couldn't deny the story. William's profile was real, whether they liked it or not.

Rolling Stone wanted William's article because it revealed ugly details about what it was truly like to be a band on tour. The magazine appreciated William's raw portrayal, which did not make the band "look cool" all the time.

Artists are most successful when they reveal the *precious truth*, no matter how painful or embarrassing.

- William's article made the band Stillwater famous because his article was honest.
- Because he was associated with Stillwater, William became somewhat famous, too.
- *Almost Famous*

SLICK FILM. JONAH GIVES IT 5 STARS! HOW DO YOU MAKE STARS ON THIS KEYBOARD? AHHH: ★★★★★!

Almost Famous was my favorite of all the movies she showed us.

Oh, that's a great movie.

Yeah. I love Kate Hudson. Doesn't she seem like a really happy person?

She does. She's always smiling.

I know, right? It's like nothing ever bothers her. I wish I could be like that. Even just a little. [pauses] Did you see Miri's Instagram from movie night? She posted pictures of the screen and quoted Fatima, like, "'The only story worth telling is the truth.' #FatimaWasHere #AlmostFamous."

I saw them, yes. Did those posts bother you?

Yeah. Why did she have to advertise everything we did? Our time with Fatima was, like, nobody's business.

Did it bother Fatima?

No. But it bothered me. And you know what? Sometimes it matters what I feel. Maybe not to Miri, but sometimes it does.

THE ABSOLUTION
OF BRADY STEVENSON

BY FATIMA RO

(excerpt)

Down in Paloma's basement theater, movie watching was a pastime. At Thora Temple's house, it was an education. Brady was never more content than when he was at the author's house analyzing a filmmaker's cinematic intent and charging Chinese takeout on Thora's credit card.

"This is one of the movies that made me want to be a writer." Thora pulled the movie from her DVD collection and held it to her heart. "Understand this." Marni, Paloma, Sunny, and Brady waited for her next word. "I love *Almost Famous* the way I love a person. That is passion in its truest form. A thing can cause the same chemical reaction in your brain as a person: oxytocin and vasopressin. Did you know that?" Sunny typed that factoid into her phone while Marni took a picture of the DVD and posted it on Instagram: #ThoraWasHere #MovieNight #AlmostFamous #TheDrowning. "Love is simply your brain releasing those chemicals, these feel-good endorphins, and causing you to feel euphoric," Thora said. Brady elbowed Sunny. She elbowed him back. They had familiarized themselves with euphoria these past couple of weeks by sharing frequent bursts of oxytocin and vasopressin in the art room behind the shelf of unclaimed pottery.

Mulder the cat jumped off the sofa to roll over and scratch his back on the carpet. "So, even the question of whether animals can love us back has been answered by science." Thora gestured to the cat. "Of course they can." Brady thought about how Cletus would sit and wait for him in the front window after school. "When our pets see us, their brains release those same chemicals." Thora placed the DVD in the player. "Do you know what I'm feeling right now as I'm about to press Play?" She lifted the remote.

Brady watched her intently. "What?"

"Euphoria." Thora clasped her hands together. "Who needs a chaotic house party when we have movies like this?" The group nodded. They would have thrown a party this weekend over Thanksgiving break. Their priorities were different with Thora. "And besides," she continued, "there is one thing cooler than owning the scene."

"What's that?" Marni asked.

"Disowning the scene."

The doorbell rang: Chinese takeout from Pearl East, Thora's usual restaurant of choice. Pearl East wasn't a takeout counter, but an upscale, five-star restaurant on Northern Boulevard. "Marni, can you sign for me? And give him a tip, will you, please?"

"Sure!" Marni hurried toward the door with her head high. Brady followed to help with the bags. Beaming, Marni opened the door. She signed the bill in large, looping letters: *Thora Temple.*

"Thanks," Brady said, taking the bags from the deliveryman.

Marni tipped with her own five-dollar bill. "A pleasure seeing you again," she said as the man turned away. "Always lovely to see a fan."

▶ ▶▶

MIRI

After the movie, Fatima got a call from a guy, and she said that she was going out. Correction. I should say the call was from a "*man*." [uses air quotes] A phone call, by the way, is the proper way to ask a woman out, according to Fatima Ro. Never accept a date from a text. It sets the stage for the entire relationship. Men treat you the way you allow them to treat you. That's an important takeaway. And I have to tell you that Fatima's going-out process was something for all women to aspire to.

Why is that?

She didn't even change her clothes. Same pair of jeans and black tank top she wore the whole day. She popped into the bathroom, did her topknot, and put on red lipstick. Then she threw on a pair of heels on her way out the door, and that was it. In five minutes? [snaps] Date-ready.

Impressive.

It takes some people longer to take the garbage out. I wish I'd taken video, but I was too mystified to even think of it. It would've gotten a zillion hits by now.

Stranger Than Fiction

The True Story Behind the Controversial Novel

The Absolution of Brady Stevenson

SOLEIL JOHNSTON'S STORY, PART 3 (continued)

Journal Entry

Fatima's bedroom

10:12 p.m.

The secrets to the perfect topknot (either all up or half up/half down) according to Fatima Ro:

1. With your head upside down, spray dry shampoo on your roots.
2. Secure a high ponytail with an elastic band.
3. Pull hair slightly, especially at the top of the head, so that it's not flat. Pull a few hairs loose around the face and at the nape for a more casual look.
4. Tease the ponytail from the base to the ends of the hair. Teasing is key! Spray with hair spray.
5. Wind the ponytail around the base, securing with bobby pins as you go.
6. Tuck the end underneath and pin.
7. Set with hair spray.
8. The perfect topknot!!!

Secrets to the perfect matte red lips according to Fatima Ro:

1. Apply lip conditioner (matte lipstick tends to be dry).
2. Use lip liner that matches the lipstick. Outline lips first. Then fill them in. Don't forget the corners of your mouth.
3. Apply lipstick.
4. Trace lightly outside the lip line with concealer using a small brush.

Secrets to dating according to Fatima Ro:

1. If a man texts you for a date, he's a coward and you don't want to date a coward anyway. "If a man can't step to you in person or call you up and formulate full sentences, he's obviously lousy in bed." (Hahhahahaa!!!!)
2. Never put too much effort into getting ready for the date. It sets your expectations too high, and you look better the less you try anyway.
3. If the date's going badly, LEAVE!!!

▶ ▶▶

PENNY

I don't think that Fatima really had a date. I think she left so that Soleil and Jonah could be alone.

Wait a minute. You think the date was a sham?

Uh-huh, so that something could happen between the two of them. Soleil would tell Fatima all about it, and then Fatima would have a hot sex scene to write about.

That is some accusation.

[shrugs] Well, Fatima's personality changed after her dad called. She was always thinking and worrying. She didn't have enough to write yet because of how dullsville we were, and so she was desperate for something major to happen. And her so-called date? [sighs] I bet you she sat in the café by herself all night. I mean, she didn't shower before she left. She didn't even change her outfit. Why would she go out like that? She had her mother's vintage Chanel and Dior in her closet! And Halston! [shakes head] She even owned a Balmain double-breasted blazer; it's literally the mother of all blazers.

Well, some might find it admirable that she didn't get all dressed up. It shows confidence. Or maybe it was just a casual date.

It's easy to think those things when you're around her 'cause she's so glamorous and so sure of herself. We were, like, mesmerized watching her get ready. I wanted to *be* her—getting a call from an older guy and going out late—Fatima seemed, like, super mature. But later, when you're alone, your best friend is crying, and your other friend is in a coma, you don't see things the same anymore, and Fatima doesn't seem so perfect.

The Absolution of Brady Stevenson

BY FATIMA RO

(excerpt)

Brady and Sunny were alone.

"I guess it's just you and me," Sunny said.

"Yup." Brady smiled. "I guess so."

They kissed their way into the hallway. There, they pawed each other against the wall and kicked their shoes off.

"What are you thinking?" Brady raised his eyebrows. "Bedroom?"

Sunny nodded. She wanted to "grow and mature" and live a "meaningful life" by getting naked with Brady. They groped each other as they passed the bathroom and the hall closet, and then pushed the bedroom door open with their bodies. At the foot of Thora's bed, Brady pulled his sweatshirt and T-shirt off in one motion. Sunny shouldn't have been surprised at how fit he was beneath those layers. He was an athlete. Sunny pulled her tank top over her head. She ran her hand down his stomach and then backed herself onto the bed.

Weeks of torturous behind-the-pottery-shelf action had left Brady aching to have Sunny stretched out beneath him and to feel her, skin against skin. He lowered his pants, too impatient to take them off, and crawled on top of her.

"Did you know Thora had a date?" Brady asked.

Sunny adjusted the pillow under her head. "If I'd known I would've worn matching bra and underwear."

"What underwear?" Brady said, pulling the elastic down.

"Hey, do you have something?" Sunny asked. She hadn't expected a sexy time tonight.

"No. Damn." Brady paused. He hadn't expected this either. "I bet Thora does."

Sunny rolled over to open the nightstand. Condoms in a purple box. "Score." She took one from the pack and handed it to Brady.

Talk of Thora added another dimension of excitement for Brady. Lying in Thora's bed, with her T-shirt shoved under the covers and holding one of her condoms in his palm, Brady felt almost as if he were with both girls at the same time. Sunny had her hair up like Thora, she even smelled like her—like vanilla and coconut—and it was driving him out of his mind. He moaned into Sunny's neck.

"Do you know how to put that thing on?" Sunny asked.

"I'll figure the shit out of it," Brady said, determined to catch up after a year of falling behind when it came to girls.

Sunny felt sexy and fearless in Thora's bed, like the author herself. She knew this was right. It felt natural. Sunny laced her fingers between Brady's just as Jules had done with Sam in *The Drowning*, chapter thirteen. Fiction and real life intertwined as Brady kissed her slowly at first and then with more urgency. It felt as if she and Brady were reading each other's minds.

Sunny teased, "Look into my eyes, and tell me what you want from this life."

"Oh, I think you can feel exactly what I want," Brady answered. Sunny laughed, arching her back. This turned Brady on even more. "Get ready," he said, "because I'm about to give you my precious truth." Sunny laughed again. "How much time do you think we have?" Brady asked.

"Depends how her date goes," Sunny answered, eager to continue. "Either thirteen minutes or thirteen hours. Let's not think about it."

Brady stopped with his hand holding Sunny's panties halfway down her thighs. "Why did you say that?" Wrestling camp flooded back to Brady's mind. Thirteen minutes of yelling, begging, crying, laughing, the smell of beer in the air. Those thirteen minutes torched his life.

"What?" Sunny asked, confused.

"Why did you say thirteen minutes?" Brady asked louder. What had Sunny read? How much did she know? Was she thinking about South Carlisle right before they were about to do it? Sunny would never sleep with him if she knew the full story. Brady knew that beyond question. Sunny didn't know who she was with.

"It was just a random number," Sunny said. "What's wrong?" Suddenly it hit her: thirteen minutes. That's how long the attack was at wrestling camp. She'd read it in an article. The victim's attorney reprimanded the attackers for being unable to make the right choice for thirteen minutes. Sunny covered her face. *Shit, shit, shit.*

Brady stood and hiked his pants up.

"Are you okay?" Sunny asked, pulling at her own clothes.

"Yeah, yeah, uh," he stammered, crumpling the condom into his pocket. "It's just weird doing this here, isn't it? In her bed?"

"I guess it is a little," Sunny lied. It wasn't weird for her, not at all.

"It's like she's watching us or something," Brady said, putting his T-shirt and sweatshirt back on.

Sunny sat up. "Oh, I know. I was just going to say . . . it's a little too much universe sharing. Awkward."

"We should get on the road. It's supposed to get icy." Brady waited in the doorway. He didn't want to stay here too long and regret it later. A good boyfriend always thinks about things like dark roads and black ice and regret.

MIRI

[checks phone]

Any news?

No. It's just that I've been trying to get in touch with Emma Irving since the arrests. I haven't been able to catch her around school either; it's so strange. We're supposed to plan an Undertow meeting.

You've still been meeting?

No reason to stop. We made major headway with the theory. Our last two meetings at the Witches Brew we included kids from other private schools—Harbor Academy and Porter Ridge. The plan is to expand our network for professional as well as personal benefits. We've been accepted to universities all over the country. We can help each other down the line. It's all about who you know. It sounds elitist, but that's just how things are.

I'm impressed with your plans.

Well, I've decided to go to law school. Some of the parents and siblings of Undertow members are in law. These people are important connections for me. We intend to share a bigger universe together. You see, that's what it means to take an idea and expand upon it in your own way. Fatima would be . . . well, if she were here, Fatima would be proud. [laughs]

What's funny?

I wish I knew where "hashtag Fatima was." [uses air quotes]

Stranger Than Fiction

The True Story Behind the Controversial Novel

The Absolution of Brady Stevenson

SOLEIL JOHNSTON'S STORY, PART 3 (continued)

> SOLEIL
>
> I'm really sorry to bother you on your
> date.

FATIMA

It's okay! Is everything all right?

> This is what happens when I live
> in denial and pretend everything's
> normal.

What happened?

> He wasn't ready for a girlfriend. He
> definitely wasn't ready for sex. He
> freaked out. He didn't say a word to me
> in the car home. I'm humiliated.

Shit.

I'm so stupid—playing King and Queen
of the prom in my head, thinking a walk
on the beach could heal the South
Carmine sophomore.

I totally pushed you into it.

No, no. I'm selfish. It was me. I'm a
screw-up.

I'm so sorry . . .

I have to go. I'm sorry I ruined your
date.

You didn't. Call or text me later
if you want.

Thx. Bye.

PENNY

Soleil didn't want to talk about what happened that night. All she wanted to do was work on *#DoorsAsAMetaphor* in the art room. I went in there to see her. She was, like, fixated on it. She had to finish by holiday break.

What was she doing with it?

You can see the pictures on Instagram: #LargosStudioArt. She cut openings behind every door. She had to use this serious blade tool thingy and wear safety goggles. It was hardcore DIY; I don't even know how she learned to use that machine. The project turned out kinda interesting, though. She clamped it onto another piece of wood, and then she sliced all the door photos with a razor so that they each opened up. The whole thing reminded me of one of those Christmas calendars that people put chocolate in.

Advent calendars?

Yeah! It was like one of those, except giant. And then she cut strips of black velvet—she let me help her—we lined the insides like jewelry boxes.

What'd she put inside the boxes?

Nothing yet.

The Absolution of Brady Stevenson

BY FATIMA RO

(excerpt)

The *Drowning* remained on Dr. Nihati's desk beside Brady's file folder week after week. Brady wondered if she took it out specifically for his meetings or if it was on her desk all the time. What would Dr. Nihati think of Thora writing a character about him? She was bound to read the new book and recognize him. Dr. Nihati might be jealous of Thora's impact on his life compared to the therapy sessions.

Brady picked up a Matchbox car from the coffee table. This metallic blue car with a white racing stripe looked and felt very familiar. He must've had the same one as a kid, or maybe one of his friends did. "I wasn't going to come back here," Brady said to Dr. Nihati. "I got tired of coming, to be honest."

"I was getting that impression." Dr. Nihati picked up her memo pad. "What made you come back?"

"You know that I *have* to come." Brady ran the Matchbox car back and forth against his palm. "Then I thought . . . I should just go and say yes to everything but do whatever I want anyway." Brady pushed the car along the edge of his chair.

"I see. Why are you telling me this?"

"Because then I changed my mind again and thought that I

should come for real and get help."

"I'm glad you decided to return, and not just because you *have* to." Dr. Nihati relaxed her shoulders. "What is it you want help with?"

"I guess I just want to know about talking to people more— how I would go about doing that—if I decide to." Brady had already blown it with Sunny. He might as well be inside/out with her now.

"Recognizing that you need help is excellent progress for you." Dr. Nihati's words were optimistic, but her voice was monotone. Brady didn't blame her for mistrusting him; usually he was full of crap. "Let's talk about what you want to disclose at this point and the different ways you can possibly go about doing it."

If Brady was going to do this, he'd have to tell all of it. Everything. What more could he lose?

MIRI

I hate to be the one to tell you this, but Emma Irving called herself a sucker for trusting Fatima Ro. She also called Fatima a whack job.

[laughs] She did not.

She did. And just this morning she tweeted that Fatima Ro was a sick, manipulative phony. She posted it with a selfie with Fatima from Book Revue. It's all over the internet today.

Bull. Shit.

Go ahead. Look it up.

[checks her phone] What the *fuck*!? We were a team. How could she do this?

I'm sorry.

[texts furiously] Emma! You traitorous bitch!

Stranger Than Fiction

The True Story Behind the Controversial Novel

The Absolution of Brady Stevenson

SOLEIL JOHNSTON'S STORY, PART 4

DATE: November 30, 2016

TO: fatima.ro.author@gmail.com

FROM: soleil410@gmail.com

SUBJECT: AP Psych continued

Jonah hasn't spoken to me since that night. It should've gone differently.

I wanted to.

He wanted to.

We were ready.

We were laughing right up to the moment it went wrong. I can't stop thinking about that—that he can laugh one second and then be completely fucked up over South Carmine the next. I hate the assholes who messed him up this badly.

I'm in AP Psych right now studying Gustave Le Bon on the "psychological crowd." Did you know that in a group people feel and act differently than they would on their own?

Individuals feel less responsible for their actions. Ms. Halpin said this can lead to excitement and violence. Sometimes this can lead to acts of heroism. When in doubt, people follow what the crowd is doing in order to avoid embarrassment. Even imagined intoxication can contribute to an individual's participation in group violence.

"Sometimes this can lead to acts of heroism." HEROISM? Does this mean that wrestling camp could have gone either way? Why didn't anyone do the right thing? It's eating me up inside.

One article mentioned that the South Carmine boys got camp T-shirts, which they wore the night of the attack. Imagine the team all dressed alike. When people hide behind a costume they tend to behave less like individuals and more like a single-minded mob. It's like warriors painting their faces before battle.

The camp T-shirts were army green. Army green! That very color encourages conformity and falling into line with the group! This kills me. There must've been one or two or three who knew it was wrong to hurt Jonah. But because they didn't want to be *embarrassed*, they joined in? I want to throw up just thinking about this. What happened to the possibility of heroism? What would've made the difference? What turned the boys into monsters rather than heroes?

TO: soleil410@gmail.com
FROM: fatima.ro.author@gmail.com
SUBJECT: RE: AP Psych continued

Imagined intoxication!?? THIS! THIS! THIS! I have
been wondering about this for weeks: How could a team
of athletes drink and then show up at training camp in
the morning and perform at a championship level? The
answer is they didn't get drunk. They were hardly even
drinking.

I knew it, I knew it. It wasn't the alcohol that made them
violent. It was the group dynamic. They assaulted Jonah
under *imagined intoxication*, which made them feel less
responsible for their behavior. What a sick excuse for
behaving like beasts.

I missed having Jonah around. He stopped hanging out with us after he broke up with Soleil.

That's too bad.

He did come by my house once, though.

He did?

Uh-huh, to help me with something.

What?

He brought me a piece of poster board from the scrap pile in the art room. He said that I should make a design board for Fatima like the ones on the home makeover shows on HGTV, you know, like with a color scheme, materials samples, that kinda stuff. He said Fatima was probably just having trouble visualizing my ideas 'cause I was bringing examples piece by piece. Jonah thought if I had a better presentation she could appreciate it more.

Jonah did that?

Yeah. It surprised me, too. His mom watches the home channels all the time; that's why he thought of it. He was bored, I guess, so he asked if he could stay and work on it with me.

Oh! He actually helped you make it?

[laughs] It was kinda fun. Do you want to see it?

Sure!

Okay. You can follow me up. [walks inside and up the stairs to the bedroom]

[opens closet] [takes out poster board of colors/fabrics/magazine clippings] This is it. [sets board on desk] Up here in the corner is a digital layout we did on the computer. We found a design planner online that we downloaded free. [points] If Fatima knocked the wall down between the kitchen and the living area, it would've looked like this. See?

That looks great.

It would've opened up the space a lot. [points] And over here I realized that her bedroom closet was back-to-back with the linen closet in the hallway, so I broke that wall down, too, in order to make a bigger master closet. I know she'd lose space for the linens, but it would've been worth the loss of space, I think. Who doesn't want a bigger master closet?

Nobody.

And you could get a shelving thingy for towels and use a drawer in the bedroom for sheets. In any case, a designer is supposed to customize for the individual client. That's what they say on the show *Fixer Upper*. Fatima loved clothes as much as I do, maybe more, if that's possible. So that's why the master closet made sense.

Makes sense to me.

I did a white-on-white backdrop with teal and orange punches of color. And I put pictures of upholstery and drapery and carpets from magazines and catalogs.

I like it.

I tried. I wanted to keep the feel of the time period. See, I did chrome fixtures with touches of gold to go with the pendant lights from the sixties. Metals don't always have to match, you know? Mixing and matching metals adds, like, more depth to the space.

I see that. Very elegant.

Thank you. It was fun putting it together with Jonah. We got into it. This carpeting was his idea. [points to a picture]

Did you show this to Fatima?

I brought it to her house one night and left it on her kitchen table.

What'd she say?

It took her two days to text me.

Ouch.

And she said, "Thanks for the poster! Can you pick up some oatmeal if you have the chance?"

Double ouch.

THE ABSOLUTION OF BRADY STEVENSON

BY FATIMA RO

(excerpt)

THORA

Turn on Channel 4—there's a thing
happening in Queens called "flash
mob robberies."

Groups of guys bursting
into convenience stores and taking
anything they want!

SUNNY

YOU CAN SEE THEM on the
surveillance! Are they idiots?!!!

The "psychological crowd" mentality!
They don't even realize that we can see
their individual faces on camera.

Awful . . . I never should've pretended
that Brady was okay.

We both wanted to believe it. I'm sorry
things went so badly. I'm more sorry it
happened at my house.

                                     Not your fault.

I still feel like shit about it. Are you
guys still together?

                                  We barely talked at all, so I don't
                                  think so. ☹

So sorry. ☹☹☹

▶ ▶▶

MIRI

What happens next with the guys who jumped Jonah?

Well, they're in police custody now for questioning. There will be an arraignment where the prosecutor will present the case and the charges. The boys have all secured attorneys, so depending on what they negotiate, they may or may not go to trial. The charges will depend on . . . well, I'll just say that these kids better hope and pray that Jonah makes it.

Stranger Than Fiction

The True Story Behind the Controversial Novel

The Absolution of Brady Stevenson

SOLEIL JOHNSTON'S STORY, PART 4 (continued)

> SOLEIL
>
> I just read that it only takes 5% of the
> group to influence the whole crowd.
> Everyone else just follows along.

FATIMA

FIVE PERCENT overpowers the entire

crowd? How weak can people be?

> At wrestling camp, 3 guys took the lead,
> 5 others went along. Humans are
> spineless, weak-minded followers.

Getting angrier and angrier by the

second. What the actual fuuuuuuuck.

UNEDITED VIDEO FOOTAGE

NAKED TRUTH TV

Nelson Anthony interviews Miri Tan and Penny Panzarella

May 3–17, 2018 (cont'd)

© Push Channel 21, Bellmore, NY, 2018

▶ ▶▶I   2:18:20 / 3:04:23   🔊 ▬▬   ⌜ ⌟

PENNY

What would you like to talk about today, Penny?

Well, I've been thinking about the designs since the last time you were here. I was too boring for Fatima. I wasn't main character material. I didn't have any drama for her to—

[phone buzzes] Excuse me, Penny. I should get this.

Sure.

Hello? Yes. Tell me. Shit. Fuck. Shit. [hangs up]

What? Is Jonah—

He's brain-dead, Penny.

[breaks down in tears] Oh my god.

I'm sorry, Penny. I'm so sorry. [hands her a tissue]

[Penny's phone buzzes and buzzes]

Do you want to answer that? It's probably Soleil's mom at the hospital.

No. [covers her face] I don't want to hear it. I don't want to!

Okay, okay. You don't have to.

[cries] It's my fault!

Don't say that. It isn't your fault.

Yes it is. You know what I did. Everybody knows what I did. None of this would've happened if I'd kept my mouth shut.

No, Penny. Listen to me. Fatima made the decision to write it. That was on her.

But it came from *me* and everything I said was true. It is my fault! I was at Fatima's house watching television. I felt something buzzing under the sofa cushion; it was Fatima's phone. I guess she couldn't find it and so she went out without it.

I looked, and it was Jonah calling her. It was ten o'clock at night.

Okay . . .

I *knew* something was going on! Since the day she came to visit Graham, I knew it. Fatima and Jonah were always looking at each other funny, and sometimes they stopped talking when I walked in the room. I was staring at her phone, and texts started coming in: "Are you out? I thought we were talking again tonight. I'm used to falling asleep hearing your voice . . ." They were *all* from Jonah. [sniffles]

Shit. Go on.

[wipes tears] I didn't tell anyone because Soleil wouldn't listen to me last time. So, that whole night I was tossing and turning about it. I didn't want to think they were messing around. I thought, maybe Fatima was talking to Jonah about the breakup. I wanted to give him the benefit of the doubt. The next day I said to Jonah, "You haven't been hanging out with us lately. We miss you. You should come to movie night. You don't have to date Soleil to still be friends with us. Have you talked to Fatima at all?" and he said no. Why wouldn't he just tell me they were talking? It bothered me the whole day that he lied, so I . . . [cries] I never meant for this to happen. [breaks down]

I know, Penny. This must be so overwhelming. I'm sorry. But it's good that you're telling your side. It's not fair that we only get Fatima's version.

[sniffles] After school I followed him to his house. [covers face] Oh my god! I can't believe he's brain-dead. [wipes tears] [pauses]

Go on, Penny. It's okay.

[blows nose] [takes a deep breath] I waited outside his house for a few minutes. The door opened. He came outside with his dog. They walked up the block. He didn't lock the door behind him, so when he turned the corner, I got out of my car and went into his house. I knew I didn't have a lot of time, so I went upstairs right away to find his room. I don't know what I was looking for, anything to prove I wasn't crazy, that there was something going on besides phone calls.

And you found something.

Yes. [sobs]

THE ABSOLUTION
OF BRADY STEVENSON

BY FATIMA RO

(excerpt)

The first bedroom Paloma opened belonged to Brady's parents. She found a made bed, folded clothes in a laundry basket, a vacuum plugged into the wall. Paloma stepped inside. There were over a dozen photographs on the dresser, each in a gold or silver frame. One photo was of Brady and his father at a ball game—Citi Field, Paloma guessed, by all the blue and orange in the crowd. Brady was in a red-and-white school letterman jacket. Paloma squinted to make out the patch on his shoulder: SOUTH CARLISLE. Paloma had only asked him about his old school once. All Brady said was "Public school. It sucked." Her question put him in a bad mood, so she never asked again.

Down the hall, Brady's room was stuffy, cluttered with video games and clothes on the floor. Paloma ran her fingers along the books on his shelf. *19: The Boys of the Vietnam War, Unsung Heroes, The Greatest Generation, Medical Marvels, Guinness World Records 2010, Guinness World Records 2011, Guinness World Records 2012, The Drowning.*

Paloma pulled *The Drowning* off the shelf. Its spine had never been cracked. She opened to the title page:

For Brady—
What is your precious truth?
Thora Temple

The night of the signing had been a great time. Paloma remembered how awkward Brady was. "Thank you," he'd said when Thora handed him the book. "Writers are, uh, like, our most important artists." Marni swatted him on the shoulder. "What? I'm being serious," Brady insisted. "Writers say things that other people are afraid of saying. And if you think about it, the written word is, like, the cheapest, most convenient, most fulfilling kind of entertainment."

Paloma laughed to herself and slid the book back into its place. There was probably nothing to find here. Brady was just Brady. The phone calls between him and Thora could be innocent. He was probably getting advice on how to win Sunny back and was too embarrassed to admit it. Paloma turned to leave. But something on the night table caught her attention. Half buried beneath gaming magazines was *The Drowning*. A different copy. A second copy. Why would Brady have two books? Paloma picked it up and opened it. It was underlined and highlighted, starred and circled and riddled with exclamation points, checks and question marks, and it was annotated, page after page, with Brady's notes:

Girls sure like floppy-haired new boys in town. I empathize.

Obviously this guy is some kind of major asshole

This imagery blows my mind!

WTF this metaphor???

This is what girls read? Oh, shit!

Holy fuck. Is this porn?

"Sexy times" are no joke

Nice move here, man.

Better sex tips than Maxim mag.

I need a girlfriend.

This language right here making me an emotional
   wuss

Pregnancy tests. How do these things work?

Forgiveness from all unrighteousness

Forgiveness, forgiveness, forgiveness . . .

There was an inventory receipt from Amazon tucked into back, dated September 9. That was at least a week before the book signing. On the inside cover, Brady had written two questions:

Do you believe in absolution, the cleansing of the body, mind, and soul? Is that why you wrote THE DROWNING?

MIRI

Brain-dead. What a total fucking nightmare. [picks up phone] I'm texting Fatima. She's going to be devastated. [pauses] I don't even want to think of her reaction. [texts] Don't ask me if she's contacted me yet because you know I would've told you if she did.

I wasn't going to ask.

Yes, you were.

You're right. I was.

Stranger Than Fiction

The True Story Behind the Controversial Novel

The Absolution of Brady Stevenson

SOLEIL JOHNSTON'S STORY, PART 4 (continued)

> SOLEIL
>
> Penny, where are you?
>
> Are you coming to movie night? It's late.
>
> Fatima said it's your turn to choose.
>
> Are you on the way? The choices
>
> are book-to-film adaptations:
>
> Atonement, Whip It, Willy Wonka
>
> & the Chocolate Factory.
>
> Jonah showed up!!! Fatima asked him
>
> to come. I need you to be the buffer.
>
> Where are you? Hurry over!

> PENNY
>
> I'm gonna be late. I'm sorry.
>
> You choose the movie.

Is everything OK?

Yeah, just gotta do something first.

I'll get there as soon as I can.

PENNY

I didn't know what to do after I found the book. I drove away. Then I sat in my car for a while. I remembered South Carmine being in the news, so I searched #SouthCarmine, and I saw there was a party that night.

Oh, man.

Somebody posted the address, so I punched it into my GPS, and I went. [tears up]

Okay.

My navigation sucked. I hate that thing; it kept taking me in circles. I'd never driven to the South Shore before, and I'd only been driving local roads. I had to take the Southern State Parkway. I didn't know any of the exits off the Southern State. Some of the exists are, like, north-south, some are only north or only south. It was so confusing. I don't know how I got finally got there, but I did. [takes deep breath] I watched people going in and out. It was weird, you know, watching them. I missed hosting parties. I don't care if they weren't intellectual or whatever. I was better at being shallow. [sighs]

Go on.

On #SCParty there were pictures from inside—just the regular stuff, like drinking and dancing, and couples making out. I wasn't sure about going in, 'cause I didn't know anybody. I was used to being the host and all that. But then I saw a picture of some guys in South Carmine baseball jackets posing with pool sticks and Solo cups. I figured, maybe they knew Jonah, right?

Logical guess.

I got out of my car and I went in the house. I saw the baseball guys from the picture—one was Jon and another one was Harry and the other was Matt—I read their names off their jackets. I went into the kitchen and got a soda, and I looked at some of the pictures around the house. It sucked not knowing anybody. But then after a few minutes, I just got angry. If I were Soleil I bet a bunch of guys would've spoken to me. And when Jonah was new everyone was all, "Hey, who's the new guy?" It pissed me off, kind of.

I can totally understand that.

I thought about Fatima and how she would act at a party, 'cause she can talk to anybody pretty much anywhere, so that's how I got my nerve up.

Okay . . .

So I went into the living room and started talking to the baseball players and the girls they were with.

What did you say?

When they asked me who I was with I didn't know what to say.
I just said "Mike," 'cause usually there's a Mike.

That was smart.

And then I asked them if they knew Jonah Nicholls.

[silence]

It felt like time stopped. The baseball guys and everyone around,
they all stared at me like I was out of a horror show or something. One girl said, "Are you talking about Nicholas Jonna?"

Oh my god.

I just stood there while it sunk in that Jonah changed his name.
I didn't know why he did, but he changed it. Soleil looked up
the wrong name when she met him.

Holy . . .

I just played it off in front of them, like, "Oh, yeah. That's what I mean, Nicholas Jonna." Then Matt said, "Hey. I'm gonna be courteous to you because you're a girl. But we're sick and tired of strangers who come here to ask questions about our private business because they saw some shit about us on the news. And for your information, we don't talk about that perverted fuck around here."

Oh, man.

Harry said, "That perverted fuck was down the hall from us at wrestling camp. He fucked up our boy, Daniel. He stood on the dresser and called himself the master of ceremonies and got everyone chanting and jumping on Dan, and he got our wrestling program cut. Nine months in juvie was a joke." The other guy, Jon, said, "Shut *all* your mouths. We don't talk about that shit. EVER. Especially with people who aren't from here."

What did you do?

I ran out. I got into my car and I . . . I went straight to Fatima's. [covers face] I didn't mean to cause this. I swear. I never meant to hurt him. [sobs]

THE ABSOLUTION OF BRADY STEVENSON

BY FATIMA RO

(excerpt)

Brady and Thora had been speaking on the phone, but he hadn't spent time with the group since *Almost Famous*. When he was new at Morley he'd told himself that these girls were nothing more than company to pass the time with until he graduated, but he actually missed their energy and their banter, which had filled the quiet holes in his life.

The smell of sweet-and-sour sauce, ginger, and sesame made Brady's stomach rumble. Marni set the takeout bag on the living room table. Brady brought paper plates from the kitchen. He missed General Tso's chicken from Pearl East almost as much as he missed the girls. He hadn't been able to say no when Thora had insisted he come over.

"Did they give us enough chopsticks this time?" Brady twisted the cap off his ginger ale.

Marni pulled the chopsticks out of the bag and counted six sets. "A bunch."

"Here's your fortune cookie." Sunny handed Brady a cookie. She knew he always ate them first.

"Thanks." Of course, Brady missed Sunny most of all. It was terrible avoiding her at school. Once you've pulled a girl's underwear down it's hard to pretend it never happened. "Is it okay with you that I'm here?" he asked.

"Of course." Sunny touched Brady's hand. She felt bad that he'd been keeping his distance and blamed herself for the breakup. She shouldn't have gone so far with him. "We're still friends. All of us."

"Do you think we can talk later tonight—just you and me?" Brady asked.

Sunny smiled. "Okay, sure."

At that moment, the lock on the sliding door unclicked. Red-faced and panting, Paloma pulled the door open and stepped inside.

"Hey, P! I ordered for you. Shrimp lo mein, right?" Marni asked, as she took containers out of the bag.

Paloma stared Brady down.

"What's wrong?" Sunny asked.

Thora clutched a container of white rice. "What is it?"

"Let's ask Stephan," Paloma said, squeezing her keys so hard that they dug into her palm.

"What are you talking about?" Sunny asked. "Why are you calling him Stephan?"

"What's going on?" Marni asked.

"I was just at a party at South Carlisle," Paloma said. "I asked if they knew Brady, and they had a lot to say about that."

Sunny stood beside Brady. "Paloma, stop. Don't say it. I already know."

"You *know* that he attacked that kid at wrestling camp and you still went out with him?" Paloma said.

Brady took a step back. He didn't want it to happen this way. He was going to tell Sunny tonight; he had every intention to. Dr. Nihati had warned him that this would happen. Instantly, Brady realized that it was Dr. Nihati, not Thora, who was the wise woman in his life. He should have listened to her.

"What are you talking about?" Sunny asked.

"Do you want to know WWB?" Paloma held her chin high. "Well, his name isn't Brady Stevenson. It's Stephan Brady. He was one of the ringleaders at the wrestling training camp that was on the news. He called himself the master of ceremonies and started the chants."

Brady pulled his hoodie over his head as he backed away toward the front door. He heard Dr. Nihati's voice in his head. *"If Sunny and Thora find out another way, that could be difficult for them and for you."*

"He was in a juvenile detention center for nine months before he came to Morley," Paloma added. "Ask him. Go ahead."

Sunny remembered the way Brady had avoided her eyes the day they met, and her dead-end online searches for BRADY STEVENSON. "Brady? Tell me she's wrong, tell me that it was the other way around." Sunny's voice shook. "Wasn't it?"

Brady looked from Paloma to Marni to Thora.

"Don't look at them," Sunny yelled. "Look at *me*, and tell me it's not true." When Brady's stricken gray eyes met hers, Sunny knew that Brady was a liar. He wasn't the South Carlisle sopho-more. He was someone far worse: a ringleader. "Five percent. It only takes five percent of the group to influence the crowd," Sunny murmured to herself.

"And this is his." Paloma reached into her bag and held out Brady's copy of *The Drowning*. "He's been lying about every-thing. He read this before we even met Thora. He scribbled comments all over it." Paloma held her shoulders back and quoted Thora. "Your authentic self will always surface. You can't hide your true self. Not in this house."

Brady had read it? He'd kept that from her this whole time? Sunny grabbed *The Drowning* from Paloma's hands. She flipped it open. There was Brady's handwriting in the margins, page after page after page. She turned deliberately to chapter eight. Chapter ten. Chapter twelve. Chapter thirteen.

> Holy fuck. Is this porn?
> "Sexy times" are no joke.
> Nice move here, man.
> Better sex tips than Maxim mag.
> Ugggghhh I need a girlfriend.
> I need a girlfriend as horny as this.

Sunny's chest tightened. The thought of Brady's hands on her skin, his mouth on her mouth, and his body against her body made her feel filthy, as if she were coated in his crimes and lies.

"Give me that!" Thora grabbed the book. She pored over it for herself. Her hands trembled as she read.

> This imagery blows my mind!
> WTF this metaphor???
> This is what girls read? Oh, shit!
> This language right here—making me an emotional wuss
> Pregnancy tests. How do these things work?
> Forgiveness from all unrighteousness
> Forgiveness, forgiveness, forgiveness . . .

Thora checked the title page.

Blank.

She must've autographed a different copy for him at Book Revue. She'd written, "For Brady—What is your precious truth?" He'd been lying to her ever since.

Brady knew there was no defending himself. Deep down, he'd known this months ago when he drove away from his South Carlisle house. His mother and father had been ready to send him to military school. Even they didn't think nine months was enough punishment. His grandparents had insisted they give him a second chance at Morley. But no North Shore private school, no grandparents' prayers or perfect girlfriend, could change the facts for him: there is no forgiveness or tabula rasa. The weight of his past was too great to lift. It was heavier than his hope and his religion. It was heavier than his soul. Quietly, swiftly, without slamming the door or dramatic parting words, Brady slipped out of Thora's house.

Sunny felt for the sofa behind her and sat on its arm. "Are you okay? Sunny? Sunny? Are you all right?" Marni asked.

"I can't breathe. I can't . . ." Sunny clutched her chest.

Marni turned to Paloma. "Get her some water."

"No, no," Sunny said. "I just, I need—" she said, and then broke into tears.

Thora threw Brady's book across the room. "Take her home."

"What?" Paloma said with one hand on Sunny's back.

"I said take her home." Thora opened the front door.

Marni shook her head. "But Thora—"

Thora stared at the unopened fortune cookie on her coffee table. "Just go. Please."

▶ ▶▶

MIRI

We were all in shock. Shock. [looks into the camera] If you missed that, the word was *shocked*. Positively effing *shocked*. [sits back] Hear me when I say this: Jonah was the quietest, mousiest kid I ever met. So, to think of him calling himself the Master of Sexually Deviant Ceremonies or whatever the hell he called himself, ordering his teammates to rip a kid's clothes off and fuck a mannequin, was near freaking impossible.

Soleil asked Penny to pull the car over so that she could throw up. Imagine how dirty she must've felt. Jonah had his tongue down her throat and who-knows-what-else where. I will never forget how white he turned when Penny called him out that night. "It was the look of a sinner caught in a web he had spun himself." That's from *Undertow*, chapter nineteen.

[Pauses] Miri, I took a drive out to South Carmine and spoke to a few of the students.

[leans forward] Seriously? What did you ask them? What did they say? Do they know the guys who did this? Did they defend them? What?

They have a young adult book club over there.

Oh.

Absolution was at the top of their list because of the "former high school wrestler" plotline. I spoke to a few of the girls who read it. They were pretty surprised to read all the other similarities.

Jesus.

And then they did a little digging on #FatimaWasHere.

They didn't.

Yes. They showed their boyfriends. Then their boyfriends found Jonah.

Shit.

Their friend, the sophomore who was attacked, he's not doing well at all—homeschooling, depression, he's a wreck and getting worse. And the guys who hurt Jonah, they're convinced that colleges rejected them because of the scandal.

[exhales deeply]

South Carmine kids all thought Jonah was sent to military school. When they read about "Brady" living it up in a North Shore prep school with a new name and applying to Cornell and MIT, that was it. They snapped.

[drops head in hands]

In the book found at the crime scene, the South Carmine boys scrawled FUCK NO! on the last page.

[shakes head] [pauses] It's ironic, huh? [looks up] The one person who swore he'd never read Fatima's work ended up with three copies of her books.

It's pretty messed up. [pauses] Fatima's novel really pissed them off. It really did lead them to him.

[sighs] Don't say that to Penny, okay? She'll lose it.

Stranger Than Fiction

The True Story Behind the Controversial Novel

The Absolution of Brady Stevenson

SOLEIL JOHNSTON'S STORY, PART 4 (continued)

PENNY

You're probably awake. I'm still in shock.

I know you are too. I'm sorry, Soleil.

I just had to tell you. I didn't want to hurt you.

You're my best friend.

MIRI

Are you okay, Soleil? Have you heard from Fatima?

She's probably in shock. We all are.

I'm sure she'll call you soon.

▶ ▶▶

PENNY

[crying] I didn't know any of this would happen.

It's not your fault . . .

I did it for Soleil.

Of course you did.

She deserved to know.

You did what you thought was right.

[blubbering] No. That's not true. [crying]

What do you mean, Penny? What's not true?

I didn't do it for Soleil. I did it for *me*. I wanted to impress Fatima. I wanted her to pay attention to me. She didn't think I had anything important to say. I just wanted to walk into her house and say something that would make her interested in *me* for once.

Oh, Penny.

I shouldn't have told her. I should've talked to Jonah and left it up to him. It was *his* past. [cries] Fatima told us to share our precious truths. But that wasn't my precious truth to tell! [cries] I didn't know she would write about it! I ruined Jonah's life just to impress some author whose book I never even read. [sobs]

[pauses] Wait. What?

[cries]

What did you say? You never read Undertow?

No! No! I never read it, okay! I can't even keep up with books for class. I went along with the book club the way I go along with everything. [cries] And now Jonah's brain-dead 'cause of me. [covers the camera with her hand] Turn it off! Don't let them find out that I never read it. Please, just turn it off and edit it out! Please! I want to talk about something else now. Can I talk about something else?

The Absolution
of Brady Stevenson

BY FATIMA RO

(excerpt)

I f Brady were a character in one of Thora's favorite movies, he would've driven full speed down the highway into
the night. But in real life, he only drove two blocks away. He
stopped the car randomly in front of the security call box outside a two-story modern home. Brady pressed his head against
the steering wheel and cried. *Do you want me to start over? Is that
what you want? Do I deserve another chance?* Brady had asked God
these questions countless times—in the chapel at the juvenile
detention center where he'd prayed every day without fail, in
his old bedroom as he'd stared at the ceiling, each morning as
he'd pulled on his Morley Academy blazer, and the very instant
he'd kissed Sunny on the mouth. He thought he had received
an answer, but he was wrong. God was only answering now:
No. There was no way to start over. Brady deserved nothing.

Brady heard a crackling from the security call box. He lifted
his head. There was a beep followed by the voice of a woman
with a European accent. "Hello? Hello? You there! Who's
there, please? I see you on the camera. Who's there?"

*If we confess our sins, He is faithful and just to forgive us our
sins, and to cleanse us from all unrighteousness.* Brady opened his

window. He clutched the call box with his left hand and pressed the red button with his right. "I'm *Stephan*. My name is *Stephan Brady*." He cried into the speaker and shivered at the sound of his own name. "And I'm sorry . . . I'm sorry . . . I'm sorry . . ." he sputtered. "They pulled me out of bed, stood me up in front of everyone. I was so scared that they'd picked me, I was shaking. . . . But then they said, 'Tell us, Stephan. Who's tonight's MVP?' So I pointed . . . I pointed to the bed next to me, and I told them, 'Donny' . . . because he was smaller and weaker. I was so scared that it was me." Stephan was a coward. He knew this without a doubt, because he had thought about it long and hard. Fear makes guys on teams do what they do. "But I'm *good*," he insisted. "I'm a good person who did something bad. . . . I'm sorry," he sobbed. "I'm so fucking sorry. . . ."

Jonah, I mean Nicholas—or whatever the hell his name is—was still at Graham after that, can you believe it?

That's ballsy.

No, it wasn't. He hid from us like the coward he was. He switched out of art class, ate lunch in his car. But he was still around, taking up oxygen at our elite private school, which he had no right to attend. He probably didn't have a choice but to stay, because what would he tell his parents? He already transferred once, right?

You're right. Graham was already his second chance. I'm sure his parents were counting on him to fly under the radar, get on a straight and narrow path, and then move on after graduation. I doubt they planned at all for what he would say to his classmates at Graham, whether or not he would tell the truth about South Carmine. That must've been a tough line for him to navigate.

Oh, no, don't do that. Don't sympathize with that pervert con artist.

I'm not. I'm just acknowledging that it was a rough situation, having to decide how much of his past to reveal to new people.

Okay. You can stop right there before I ask you to leave my house.

What?

A bowl haircut and buckteeth—that's a past. Having your period leak through your pants in middle school—that is a past. Doing time for being a sick fuck is grounds for mandatory disclosure. It's grounds for not being admitted to one of the most prestigious schools on the East Coast in the first place. We should sue Graham for letting him within a hundred feet of us. How did he get into our school anyway? We should've had him expelled. But we weren't thinking straight. We were waiting for advice from Fatima. If Nicholas lied to get in, he would've been kicked right out of—

He didn't lie to get in. As a minor, he wasn't required to give Graham that information.

That's insanity.

That's how the system works. As a society, we have to believe that our young people can be reformed.

Do you believe that?

In some cases, yes, I think so.

What about in this case?

I don't know what I think about it yet. But it was probably for the best that you kept it quiet. Nothing good would've come out of it if you'd exposed Nicholas at Graham.

You mean like him ending up brain-dead in a coma?

Stranger Than Fiction

The True Story Behind the Controversial Novel

The Absolution of Brady Stevenson

SOLEIL JOHNSTON'S STORY, PART 4 (continued)

SOLEIL

Fatima? Are you there???

I've been skipping school. I can't go
back with him there.

Can't stop crying. I feel disgusting.
How could he do this to me?

Why aren't you answering
my texts?

Calling you now . . .

Is there something wrong
with your phone?

I need to talk to you. Please
answer if you get this.

Sending you an email.

PENNY

It's all right, Penny. We don't have to talk about Undertow. *That's over with now. We can talk about what happened afterward, okay? [passes her more tissues] After you told Fatima and everything died down. You can tell me about that.*

[sniffles] Okay. [blows nose]

What happened after?

[wipes face] I, uh, I waited for Fatima to call me. I waited and waited.

Why? What did you expect?

I thought that . . . [sniffling] I thought she'd be thankful that I found out Jonah's secret—*me*, the one she ignored all year. [takes a deep breath] And we all needed her. I mean, we didn't know if we should tell people about Jonah. Or should we ask him why he lied to us? We wanted Fatima to help us figure out what to do.

But Fatima didn't call you, did she?

[cries] . . . No.

I was devastated for Soleil. What a sad, sad situation.

She must've been distraught.

She missed days of school. The poor thing couldn't even hold out until Christmas break. She was literally sick over Nicholas. She only came in later to take her midterm exams and finish that art project. I knew that no one but Fatima could help her deal with everything, so Penny and I went to Soleil's house. When we got there . . .

What?

We went up to her room. [pauses] She was sitting in front of her full-length mirror, cutting her hair with a pair of purple kindergarten scissors and reciting the steps to making the perfect topknot.

Christ.

"With your hair upside down, spray your roots with dry shampoo. Then secure a high ponytail. Then tease. Teasing the ponytail is key."

Poor kid.

We couldn't stop her; she'd already cut part of her hair off—right above her shoulders. She was just so angry at Fatima, and at herself, I guess, for being so trusting.

We forced Soleil into the shower; she was not smelling like roses, I can tell you that much. She refused to put anything on besides sweats, but at least she got out of her ratty pajamas. Then Penny and I took her to Fatima's house.

It was good of you to do that.

Soleil was my best friend. I wanted her to get the help she needed. Nicholas's head games shredded her into pieces.

What happened at Fatima's house?

We rang the bell. Fatima came to the door, but she wouldn't open it all the way. She left the chain on.

That wasn't like her.

No. [sighs] It wasn't like her at all. I could see her through the four-inch crack in the door, and she looked even worse than Soleil.

I'm not surprised.

Soleil said she needed to talk to her. But all Fatima could say was that she wanted to be left alone. Soleil started getting loud. "You can't leave me alone in this," she kept saying. "You're the only one who understands. I need you, Fatima."

That's so sad.

It was. But then Soleil started saying some stuff that was completely out of line, like, "You *made* me go out with him! You *pushed* me into it! I almost slept with him because of you! This is your fault!"

Wow. That's rough.

She was out of her mind at that point, honestly. I mean, no one can force you to go out with someone. She was grasping for somebody to blame for her pain. I told her that, but it only made her angrier.

So, then what happened?

Fatima shut the door.

That's it? She didn't even respond to Soleil?

No. That was the last time any of us spoke to her.

I don't even know what to say about that.

Have a little bit of perspective. Soleil wasn't the only one who was hurt. As far as Fatima knew, Nicholas was a kid who needed help. He took advantage of her goodness by expecting her to rewrite him. That's what happened. *He* manipulated *Fatima*. Get it straight.

But why would Fatima shut Soleil out like that?

Fatima was heartsick, I'm sure. Her own theory led to this disaster. That's humiliating. How could she face us?

You won't consider that maybe she was ashamed because she was betraying you with her manuscript?

No. [sighs] Fatima wasn't betraying us. She was being loyal to Nicholas and to her writing. And she retreats when she's hurt; you know that. I tried to remind Soleil and Penny, but they were only thinking about themselves. They're *still* thinking about themselves.

Stranger Than Fiction

The True Story Behind the Controversial Novel

The Absolution of Brady Stevenson

SOLEIL JOHNSTON'S STORY, PART 4 (continued)

DATE: December 17, 2016

TO: fatima.ro.author@gmail.com

FROM: soleil410@gmail.com

SUBJECT: THE PRECIOUS TRUTH

I've texted you. I showed up at your door. I've emailed.
You wanted me to tell you everything, but now that *I* need
to talk—WHERE ARE YOU? You only cared about Jonah,
didn't you? You chose him over me—his happiness and
his well-being over mine. He was your pet because he
seemed to need you and love you more. You wanted
to give him food, shelter, compassion. You wanted to
give him *me*. "Be calm and girlfriend on!" "Do what feels
natural." "You've found his hidden talent!" "Let yourself
go!" But now that he's lied to you, you have no use for
me anymore. Who cares that he lied to me, too? All that
matters is that he hurt YOU. It's always been about You,
Yourself, and Fatima Ro. WHAT ABOUT ME???

This is the last time I'm going to write, because I cannot give you any more of myself! You pried every word out of me! "WWJ???" "What exactly goes on behind the pottery shelf?" "I'm dying to know how the date went." "Tell. Me. EVERYTHING." You made me feel that I owed you. You squeezed my guts out—my energy, my time, my thoughts, my emotions, my experiences. And for what? To see how much I was willing to give you, because your old friends couldn't care less about *Undertow*! Waah, waah, you poor, underappreciated author. You bled on those pages, but your old friends did nothing in return but throw your deck chairs in the pool! But Miri, Penny, and I—we really were "your people." We were your adoring fans who raised you up when you felt like a disappointment of a doctor's daughter.

And my psych notes! You couldn't get enough of them to help you understand *my* boyfriend and get closer to him. "Helpful and insightful. Necessary." You want my class notes, Fatima? You want to know what I've been learning? You want to see my research? You want to hear the precious truth? Well, here it is:

Dear Fatima,

I read something I think you'll find particularly interesting: an article in *Psychology Today* called "The Communal Narcissist: Another Wolf Wearing a Sheep

Outfit." As I read it, I felt as if St. Peter opened heaven's gate and showered me with enlightenment. (Thought you'd appreciate that imagery. Doesn't the use of a religious reference make me sound deep? I've learned so much about writing from *Undertow*, the most brilliant piece of fiction possibly ever written. I find myself writing like you, speaking like you, thinking like you. I'm even smelling like you, thanks to Cake Batter Whipped Body Cream.)

Do you know what a communal narcissist is? No? You weren't paying attention in class that year because you were having the kind of sex that made you "grow and mature"? Well, sit back, relax, and enjoy the education, as I did time and again with your films that inspired you to be a writer, your vintage Chanel and Halston that I could try on, your favorite Chinese takeout, your dating advice, your instructions on the perfect messy topknot and the perfect matte red lips.

A communal narcissist is someone who appears to do helpful things for others. They appear empathetic, nurturing, understanding. But in actuality, they perform their so-called "good deeds" in order to receive praise and show themselves off as noteworthy and above the rest of their social circle.

Ms. Halpin would ask me to give an example of a communal narcissist. Let me see . . .

How about an author who wrote a novel about her

deepest shame and claims to have done so in order to help readers forgive themselves for their own failures, but in reallty she's only seeking admiration? Or how about an author who invites a bunch of teenagers to her home in the name of "human connections" when all the while she's just using them to feed her ego?

Isn't this simply fascinating? I'd never heard of such a thing as a communal narcissist before. I'd like to thank you for encouraging my studies in psychology. Thanks, Fatima, for all of your "good deeds," which I'm sure weren't meant to validate your own self-worth. What an engrossing study. Honestly, these findings are truly the stuff of life.

Good luck with your new novel. I'm sure it'll be as successful and as self-serving as *Undertow*.

By the way, you'll be proud to know that I completed my art project just in time. I decided what to put inside the doors: plastic army men, all frozen in position, all wearing green, waiting to follow the 5%. Inside Jonah's door: a trophy cracked in half. Behind your door, I placed the final piece: a figurine of a wolf that I wrapped in sheepskin. Feel free to take a look at the photos at #LargosStudioArt #DoorsAsAMetaphor #WolfInSheepsClothing. Thanks for your advice on adding a layer of depth to my project. Once again, you know everything. You're always right. I got an A.

The precious truth,

Soleil

P.S. Yes, this is a "Dear Fatima" email because FUCK YOU.

P.P.S. If you should ever decide to get back in touch, follow me on Facebook, where you'll find:

Soleil Johnston

ABOUT SOLEIL: Reformed Fatima Ro fan, future psychologist

RELATIONSHIP STATUS: single

▶ ▸▸

PENNY

Soleil kept yelling, "Don't shut me out! Open the door! You did this to me!" It was awful seeing her that way.

It sounds terrible. What happened then?

I picked her up off her feet and pulled her away from the door. I kept looking back at the house because I wanted Fatima to see how much she was hurting Soleil. But Fatima wasn't watching. She didn't care about her at all.

It must've been hard for you girls to understand.

It hurt to go from eating from her fridge and trying on her Louboutins to getting turned away—I didn't think it was really happening. Miri said, "It's not Fatima's fault. She's hurt too. Just give her time." I kinda knew then that Miri would side with Fatima. I just knew it. Way before Fatima or Jonah came along, it was me, Miri, and Soleil. Miri should've sided with *us*.

Graham Sevens.

[whispers] Trendsetters.

What was that, Penny?

Nothing. [pauses] I ended up going back to Fatima's house on my own about a week later.

You did?

Yes. To see if she was ready to see us. Plus, I was used to seeing Mulder. That week felt so long. I barely knew what to do with myself. I was, like, in withdrawal or something.

I understand. So you went over there?

Uh-huh. [pauses] I really thought she'd answer the door and invite me in, and we'd talk about everything and call Miri and Soleil and we'd all sit in shock together.

That's not what happened, is it?

[shakes head] No. She wasn't home. I could see through the garage window that her car wasn't in. So I went around back and used my key.

That's right, you still had a key.

She never asked me for it. I thought things were going to go back to normal. [sighs] So, I opened the sliding door, same as I did a dozen times. I went in, and everything was gone.

What do you mean everything?

I mean that ratty sofa and her DVDs, the toaster oven, her mother's Bee Gees and Police records. The *Undertow* box. I ran to check the closet. All of her gorgeous clothes were gone.

And Mulder?

Gone. Even his gross chewed fur toy was gone. Everything. Except some wire hangers and dry cleaning bags, and empty shampoo bottles. And the horseshoe that Soleil gave her; it was still nailed over the front door.

That's so sad. I'm sorry.

[sighs]

What did you do then?

I took a picture of the living room with nothing in it but the indents in the carpet from where the sofa used to be. I sent it to Soleil and Miri. Jonah, too, but that was an accident, it was out of habit. And then I . . .

You what?

I went into the bathroom . . . and I did my hair half down, half up in a topknot the way Fatima showed Soleil.

Why?

I don't know.

Come on. Tell me.

Because I wished that was me, okay? I was jealous of Soleil since the housewarming for being closer to her. Even after Fatima abandoned her, I still . . . I wanted to feel like a main character.

THE ABSOLUTION
OF BRADY STEVENSON

BY FATIMA RO

(excerpt)

The three girls stood on Thora's doorstep with their arms around each other. Marni knocked quietly at first and then louder the second time. The door opened. Thora Temple, with bloodshot eyes, fell into the girls' embrace. "I was afraid you'd never come back here," she said. "I thought you hated me. I'm so sorry, Sunny. I'm so ashamed that I pushed you to be with him. I wanted him to be happy. I didn't know who he was."

Over Chinese food and vinyl records, the girls came together just like on Orientation Day when they'd climbed the spiral stairs to the roof to win the Morley scavenger hunt as a team. They talked with Thora into the night about a kid who had them fooled. Sunny spoke in spurts and starts. She had fallen for him, she said, because he was "quiet and brave and didn't want or need attention." She agonized over his copy of *The Drowning*, in which he'd scribbled dates and places where he and Sunny reenacted heated scenes between Sam and Jules. Marni and Paloma were occupied with the details, trying to connect the dots from South Carlisle to juvenile detention to Morley Academy.

As for Thora, she sat cross-legged on her living room floor. From a box labeled "Book Two," she handed out copies of a working manuscript. She'd been agonizing over it since September but had recently unearthed the novel's precious truth. It was about a boy, who, given Thora's profession and experience, she should have recognized from the start: the Bad Boy, the dark, brooding new guy who comes to town to escape a shameful history and to win the love of everyone who looks into his deep, sad, soulful eyes.

MIRI

After Soleil heard Fatima's interview on the radio in California, we knew the book was coming in April. You won't believe this, but the release date was April tenth, Soleil's eighteenth birthday.

Oh, man. That's brutal.

Happy birthday. [toasts with a Starbucks cup] The months leading up to it, we saw the synopsis, and then we saw the cover of the cracked trophy, and then we read the industry reviews calling it "riveting" and "thought-provoking," "a tale of desperation and betrayal." Fatima's book revealed itself to us little by little by little; it felt like it was coming to get us. The anxiety working up to that moment . . . I can't even explain.

It must've been stressful.

I can't. [shakes her head] I could hardly think about anything else.

I can imagine.

I hoped to god that I was right, that Fatima wouldn't screw us over. I knew I'd never hear the end of it otherwise. [sighs] And then when the book finally came out, that was it for me. Do you know what I felt?

What?

Relief. I read it front to back in twenty-four hours, and that's honestly all I felt. Relief. It was indescribably . . . beautiful. Fatima liked to joke that every teen novel has the line, "She let out a breath she didn't know she was holding." [laughs] Well, that's how it was when I read the last word. I literally let out a breath I didn't know I was holding. [pauses]

If I had to critique it, my one complaint would be that it's too generous. Nicholas didn't deserve it. That's why I'm so surprised that Soleil and Penny are still outraged. But let's face it: they were outraged by Fatima's first radio interview, and never gave the book a chance after that. They made up their minds to feel manipulated and betrayed, and so they've remained manipulated and betrayed. There is nothing I or you or anyone can say to change their minds.

Penny, Soleil, the reason I asked you to meet me at the Witches Brew
today is because—

MIRI

[enters] What the fuck is this?

An ambush?

SOLEIL

You didn't tell us *she* was going to be here.

MIRI

You set me up, Nelson?

Forget this. I'm out of here.

[puts jacket on]

PENNY

He set *us* up. We don't want to see

you any more than you
want to see us.

MIRI

Shut up, Penelope.

Please, girls. Miri, I'd really appreciate it if you'd sit down.

MIRI

Fine. [sits] But only because
I have my end of the interview
to finish. [looks at Soleil]
I'm surprised *you're* here, Soleil.
Will you be taking notes for
New York City magazine?
A journal entry about an
interview about a novel about
your journal entries? How meta.

SOLEIL

[rolls eyes]

Just give me a second here. I spoke to Fatima's publicist.

MIRI

You did? Is Fatima okay?

SOLEIL

What'd she say?

Fatima canceled her own book tour. Twenty-one appearances. She's getting hounded for interviews but refuses to take any. She won't talk to anyone right now. No one.

MIRI

Why would she give interviews
when the media is berating her?
And how can she go on tour
when she's grieving?

SOLEIL

[laughs]

PENNY

Fatima's not grieving.
She's being mysterious.

MIRI

What are you talking about?

PENNY

She said it herself, remember?
What's cooler than owning
the scene?

SOLEIL

Disowning the scene.

PENNY

Now she's more popular
than ever.

MIRI

[pauses]

That's . . . that's ludicrous.

You have zero clue.

And don't try to use

her words against her!

SOLEIL

Fatima used her words against Jonah!

She blew up our lives!

*All right. Listen. This is why I brought you together. I realize how
confusing this situation is without being able to ask Fatima about her
intentions. You shouldn't have to deal with this alone. As her friends,
it's difficult for you to understand—*

PENNY

Fatima wasn't our friend.

We were just characters to her.

MIRI

Just because she wrote about
us doesn't mean she wasn't our
friend. How many times do I
have to say that?

SOLEIL

She used us all for her own selfish
reasons because she wasn't talented
enough to create something original.
She wrote intimate things that I told
her in confidence. She betrayed me.
Friends don't use each other, Miri.

MIRI

Bullshit! You're a published
writer now because of your
friendship with Fatima! [laughs]
Everybody uses everybody.
Sure, Fatima used us for
inspiration. We used Fatima
to hang out with a celebrity,
so she could save us from our
vapid lives. Nicholas used us
to hide from himself. We used
Penny for seats in the skybox

and her tricked-out party house.
Everyone takes what they can
get. So what?

SOLEIL

So what? Jonah is brain-dead because
of what Fatima wrote.

PENNY

And because of what I told her.

MIRI

No. He's brain-dead because of
what *he did*. He brought this on
himself. He had it coming.

PENNY

How can you be so cold?

MIRI

You really think that he was
your friend but Fatima wasn't?

PENNY

I was Fatima's cat sitter.
But I had a connection with
Jonah. We *were* friends.

MIRI

His name was Nicholas, for
Christ's sake! How could he
be your friend when you don't
even know his name! The only
reason he hung out in your
dark basement and came over
to make your little poster was
because he was escaping his
conscience. Your house was the
farthest corner of Long Island
from South Carmine. That's not
a friend. That's a fugitive.

SOLEIL

He's in a coma. Don't talk about him like that.

MIRI

Why are you defending him?
You hooked up! He used you
the most!

SOLEIL

That doesn't mean he should suffer
this way. It's no use being mad at
him now that he's hurt.

MIRI

He was a fucked-up pervert
who ruined some poor guy's life
forever. Nicholas Jonna deserves
to be a vegetable!

PENNY

Don't say that!

SOLEIL

He's *not* a vegetable.

MIRI

What the hell do you think
brain-dead means?

PENNY

He's young, and he's strong.
That means he can recover and be
rehabilitated. He's an athlete.

MIRI

He's an *eggplant*, Penny!

SOLEIL

You heartless bitch. You and Fatima
deserve each other.

You guys, fighting isn't going to
make him better.

MIRI

Better? Nicholas isn't going to
get better. He's going to die.

PENNY

No, he's not! He's only eighteen,
he's—

MIRI

He will die, Penny. I'm not
telling you this to hurt you, I
swear it, I wouldn't do that. I'm
telling you this to prepare you.
The next time all our phones
ring, it'll be because he's dead.

SOLEIL

Miri!

PENNY

[shakes head] You just don't want
him to get better, Miri. But he
will. You'll see.

MIRI

[sighs] Even if he could, why *should* he get better? So that he can graduate from Graham, go to Cornell, and live a charmed life like the rest of us who were never convicted of a sex crime? Why should he have the same future?

SOLEIL

Because he was sorry. People change.

MIRI

Evil doesn't change. "You can't hide your true self." You believed that when Fatima said it. "Your authentic self will always surface." Evil only lurks until the next victim. Nicholas Jonna ordered his team to sexually assault someone. That's not something that can change; that's his character. That's who he is.

SOLEIL

No. He was a good person
who did something bad.

MIRI

You're wrong, Soleil. Fatima
only wrote him that way to
redeem him. The character
Brady Stevenson was a good
person who did something bad.
That's who you feel sorry for.
You have no idea who Nicholas
was.

SOLEIL

Yes, I do. He was decent. I know it for a fact.

MIRI

Because he didn't have sex
with you?

SOLEIL

Yes.

MIRI

He shouldn't have dated you

to begin with! Don't be a fool,
Soleil—not again.

SOLEIL

It's not foolish to forgive someone
who learned a lesson. It's not foolish
to let your anger go so that you can
live your life again. You have no idea
how much anger weighs! [bursts into
tears] I should've forgiven him.
I should've talked to him when
I had the chance.

MIRI

This is exactly why Fatima
wrote this book. Soleil, can't you
see that Fatima did this because
she cared about you?

SOLEIL

No. She cared about herself. You saw
how desperate she was. She needed
to turn in a story on time, any story,
no matter who she hurt. As soon as
Penny gave her the rest of the plot
she abandoned me.

MIRI

Wait. You didn't finish
reading it, did you?

SOLEIL

[cries]

PENNY

Why would she? She's had
enough of Fatima's garbage.

MIRI

No wonder you're still angry.
Fatima didn't abandon you,
Soleil. She did the very opposite.
You need to read the book.
Finish it. Then you'll understand
what Fatima did, not just for
Nicholas, but for *you*. You'll see.
I promise you that once you read
it, everything will be—

[Soleil's phone buzzes]

[Miri's phone rings]

[Penny's phone buzzes]

[Nelson's phone rings off camera]

MIRI

[gasps]

PENNY

No! [cries] Oh my god!

SOLEIL

[stares, eyes wide, at buzzing phone]

[Nelson steps into frame] Hello?

The Absolution
of Brady Stevenson

BY FATIMA RO

(excerpt)

It was a rough winter for Sands Point Preserve. The beach took a beating from several late-winter storms that eroded miles of the rocky shore. Finally, the first week of April, it seemed that the harsh weather was gone for good. Warmth and sunshine brought the regulars back to the shore, the married couples hand in hand, North Shore runners wearing Fitbits and Lululemon, and a remorseful former championship wrestler with his dog.

Cletus spotted Sunny Vaughn before Stephan did—from at least twenty yards away. Tail wagging and tongue hanging out the side of his mouth, Cletus bounded toward her, expressing all the joy that Stephan held back. He followed behind, lengthening the leash as Cletus picked up distance.

"Hey," Stephan said when he caught up to Sunny.

"Hey." She knelt down and hugged Cletus. Her heart warmed as she nuzzled the dog's neck. "Hi, Clee! You remember me, don't you? How are you, pup?"

"He's surprised to see you," Stephan said, giving Cletus a pat.

Sunny stood. "And what about you?"

"I'm surprised too," Stephan said. Sunny hadn't spoken to him since his final movie night. Dr. Nihati was right—there were consequences. Stephan had transferred out of studio art class. He'd been eating lunch in his car, or when it was too cold outside, he ate in the stairwell.

"It sucks that there's so much erosion." Sunny looked up at the newly exposed roots on the cliffside. "It looks so different here now."

"It was a shitty winter," Stephan said, referring to much more than the weather. There'd been no Snow Ball for them.

Sunny nodded. She'd spent the winter angrily recounting every minute she had with Stephan Brady, whom she'd believed was Brady Stevenson. Although he had two names, Sunny and the girls referred to him mostly as "that bastard," "that sicko pervert," or "that lying fuck." At home every night, she continued to email articles to Thora about the South Carlisle hazing scandal, research on the psychology of betrayal, the psychology of deception, the psychology of manipulation.

The ex-couple walked while Cletus barked at waves and sniffed seaweed. Stephan wanted to tell Sunny how much Cletus missed her, but he didn't have the right to express affection, even from his dog.

"Why are you here?" Stephan asked. He couldn't take another second of silence.

Sunny took a deep breath before answering. "Thora thought I should talk to you."

"Oh." Stephan braced himself.

"I've been emailing Thora ever since we met her—about us, being inside/out, sharing details," Sunny said.

Stephan had suspected as much. He knew they were close, almost as close as he was with Thora. He nodded and kicked a rock into the water.

"The other day she showed up at my house. She had printed out all my texts and emails since . . . since I found out about you. It was a stack of papers this thick." Sunny held up her fingers, measuring three inches. "Sometimes I sent her three emails a day. She handed me the papers and asked me where my scale was, so I brought her upstairs to my parents' bathroom, and she made me put the pages on the scale." Sunny stopped to face him. "They were almost three pounds."

Stephan looked away.

"She said, 'If you keep obsessing about him it'll be too heavy to carry.' Then she started reading the emails aloud, just kept reading louder and louder about how much I hated you and how sick I felt for getting into bed with you." Sunny shuddered.

Clearly, Stephan disgusted her. He wanted to walk away, but Sunny was in the right to tell him off.

"All I did was curse you; page after page and week after week." Sunny slapped her hand repeatedly into her palm. "But then, after seeing and hearing my words in that form like my own emotional timeline, I didn't hate you anymore. I only hated how bitter I sounded. I used to be a happy person. I didn't recognize myself in those emails. I was just . . . angry. I don't want to be angry. That's not who I am. That's why I'm here."

Stephan peered at Sunny and saw the kindness and compassion he recognized in her the day they met. He was almost friends with this girl; he could hardly believe it. He'd almost been her boyfriend. Almost. He swore that with the next girl he would do better. He'd start from someplace authentic.

Sunny crossed her arms. "I came to ask you . . ."

"Anything," Stephan said. He owed her.

"Why did you lie to me?" she asked, fighting back her emotions.

Stephan had prayed every night for this chance. He'd thought of a dozen ways to explain himself, but all it came down to was his precious truth. "I was scared . . . I was afraid that if I told you what I'd done, you wouldn't see anything good in me. I wanted to be good again. I thought that . . . if I could be with you, I would be." He looked Sunny in the eyes. "I'm sorry."

Sunny had wanted to hear those two words for a long time but hadn't known how she would feel if she heard them. Right now, she believed him. She was wrong about who he had been at South Carlisle, but when he could have crossed the line with her, he hadn't. If that meant he was a fraction of a decent person, she had to let her anger go.

"I have something of yours." Sunny opened her bag and returned his first copy of *The Drowning*. "Thora wanted you to have this back. She said there's something for you inside."

Stephan tucked the book under his arm. "Thank you."

As she glanced up the hill, Sunny remembered the Gatsby party they wouldn't attend in July and Madame Lola's prediction of Stephan's incomplete fortune. "I hope you become the person you want to be," Sunny said.

"Me too," Stephan said softly. He looked up at the castle where they had kissed—Thora's castle that symbolized God's house. *Thou preparest a table before me in the presence of mine enemies: thou anointest my head with oil; my cup runneth over. Surely goodness and mercy shall follow me all the days of my life: and I will dwell in the house of the Lord forever.*

Sunny leaned forward to rub the top of Cletus's head. "Bye, pup. Be a good boy." She straightened and looked into Stephan's eyes. "I didn't know you before you came to Morley. I can't speak for what you did back then. But when I met you, I saw something good. I know you're sorry for hurting me. And . . . I forgive you." Sunny stepped back. "See you around, Brady Stevenson."

Stephan watched her turn and walk away. "Thank you, Sunshine Vaughn," he said, but she was too far away to hear. When Sunny disappeared up the trail, Stephan felt a tug at Cletus's leash. "You wanna run, Clee? You wanna run?" Stephan asked. The dog leapt and spun and pulled. Stephan ran with him then. "Come on, boy! Come on!" They raced along the edge of the water. Waves rolled up to meet them. Embraced by the first warmth of spring, the dog chased his boy; the boy chased his dog. Stephan caught Cletus by the collar and unclipped the lead.

"Let's run free! Let's run free!" Stephan called. His eyes welled with tears. Cletus sprinted fast as a blur, cutting through the thin sheet of water, barely touching the sand. Stephan ran and cheered behind him. With each stride, Stephan's weight lifted. Lighter and lighter and lighter he felt. *I'm lighter than that bird, lighter than that branch, lighter than that pebble, that reed, that leaf!* Stephan waved his dog's leash high over his head as if to wave every last cloud away. With his other hand, he clutched a familiar book. Inside was the answer he'd been waiting for, clear and simple, handwritten by the author herself:

Do you believe in absolution, the cleansing of the mind, body, and soul? Is that why you wrote THE DROWNING?

Yes.

ACKNOWLEDGMENTS

Can you tell us about the publication journey for All of This Is True?

Well, [clears throat] I started writing this book for myself alone. It was a secret. I didn't intend to publish it, I swear. But my agent, Molly Ker Hawn, read the opening pages and told me to keep writing. She basically pushed me into it. And then editor Andrew Eliopulos got ahold of it. He went and shared it with his team at HarperTeen. They thought it'd be a grand idea to publish it, so if you want to point fingers, this is mostly Andrew's fault. And Erin Fitzsimmons—she made the cover that's making everyone buy it. Bria Ragin played a part, too, you know. [shakes head] When Ellen Holgate at Bloomsbury UK read it, she just had to publish it on an entirely different continent, so that happened. I can't even express how much Ellen contributed. And you wouldn't believe the Sweet Sixteens, my friends, my family, and my husband—they encouraged me to finish the book when they didn't even know what it was about. That only proves that people will blindly follow a crowd. But if you want to get psychological about it, I should really blame my parents for never pressuring me to be a doctor, because that's probably how I got here in the first place. [pauses] Anyway, apparently lots of people are enjoying this novel now in a bunch of different languages, so I guess things work out sometimes—even if you don't intend them to. [sighs]